Southern Loss

A MAX PORTER PARANORMAL MYSTERY

Stuart Jaffe

Copyright © 2026 by Stuart Jaffe
Cover art by Mari Morgan

ISBN 13: 978-1-963517-23-1

First Hardcover Edition: February 2026

For Audrey, Kylie, and Caitlyn,

without you all keeping me healthy,
I'd never be able to write.

Also by Stuart Jaffe

Max Porter Paranormal Mysteries
Southern Bound
Southern Charm
Southern Belle
Southern Gothic
Southern Haunts
Southern Curses
Southern Rites
Southern Craft
Southern Spirit
Southern Flames
Southern Fury
Southern Souls
Southern Blood
Southern Graves
Southern Dead
Southern Hexes
Southern Hart
Southern Kin
Southern Lies
Southern Loss

Nathan K Thrillers
Immortal Killers
Killing Machine
The Cardinal
Yukon Massacre
The First Battle
Immortal Darkness
A Spy for Eternity
Prisoner
Desert Takedown
Lone Star Standoff
The Puppeteer
Blowback
Prime

The Pathway Ring
    Pioneers of the Pathway
    Lions of the Pathway

The Ridnight Mysteries
    The Water Blade
    The Waters of Taladoro
    Waterfire

The Parallel Society
    The Infinity Caverns
    Book on the Isle
    Rift Angel
    Lost Time
    Pages of Glass
    The Bold Warrior
    City of Infinity

The Malja Chronicles
    The Way of the Black Beast
    The Way of the Sword and Gun
    The Way of the Brother Gods
    The Way of the Blade
    The Way of the Power
    The Way of the Soul

Gillian Boone novels
    A Glimpse of Her Soul
    Pathway to Spirit

Stand Alone Novels
    After The Crash
    Real Magic
    Founders

Short Story Collection
    10 Bits of My Brain
    10 More Bits of My Brain
    The Bluesman
    The Marshall Drummond Case Files: Cabinet 1-4
    The Illustrated Marshall Drummond Case Files

Non-Fiction
    How to Write Magical Words: A Writer's Companion

Southern Loss

Chapter 1

SITUATED ON THE OUTSKIRTS of western Winston-Salem, the forgotten barn had been swallowed by forest. Not too far to the south, construction workers cleared away trees for a new housing development that, little by little, would change the rural into the suburban. If the city grew enough, maybe even into the urban. Eventually, the forest and the barn would be razed, but the Porters had years until that happened. At least, a couple.

For now, Max, Sandra, and Drummond had to focus on the headless witch tied to a chair and decorated like an offering to a pagan god of the harvest. She had straw poking out of her open neck and old heads of corn stuffed into her pockets. The chair had been placed in the center of the barn, and a casting circle had been dug into the dirt. A dark, thick liquid followed the trench of the circle. Max guessed it was blood.

He wanted to feel something, empathy for the torture this woman had endured, but Max had been stuck in sporadic numbness for months. Ever since his mother had passed away.

She had suffered too long with MS, and in many ways, her death had been a mercy. Her agonizing mornings had ended. Her tortuous days had ceased. And the unbearable pain that kept her awake throughout the night had finally come to its conclusion. She deserved to rest.

Still, no matter what he told himself, he couldn't shake the feeling that her ghost hung over him. Max's wife, Sandra, could see all ghosts, and she promised that his mother had moved on. Drummond, an actual ghost, also insisted that there was no sign of Mrs. Porter. Yet Max often felt the cold in the air that accompanied a spectral presence.

"This is ancient magic," Sandra said as she inspected the

corpse. "That corn means it's probably tied in with a harvest ritual. This is the kind of thing that predates organized witchcraft."

Drummond tipped back his Fedora as his shoved open his long coat. "We've been seeing a lot of that lately."

"With Madame Ti running her witch war, I suspect many covens are exploring the older ways. They've got to defend themselves, and Madame Ti's Coven of Ti is leaning hard into these ancient magics, too."

"I can't believe I'm thinking this, but it was nicer when the Hulls were in charge." Drummond clicked his tongue. "At least back then, there were rules. Nobody would dare mess with this old stuff."

"It's dangerous. Too unstable."

"Kind of like your husband."

Max heard the jibe, heard the silence that followed as both Sandra and Drummond awaited a snarky reply, yet he stayed quiet. His dead partner often had snapped him out of his funk with a sharp comment, but not today. Not while Max squatted before a dead witch and reached for her purse. From a small wallet inside, he removed her driver's license. "Pauline Georgia-Ringo Lennon."

Sandra chuckled. "Guess her parents were Beatles fans."

Drummond said, "Guess her parents wanted a boy."

Max lifted his gaze toward Drummond. "Is she in here?"

"Pauline?" The ghost quickly scanned the barn, then shook his head. "It took a lot out of her just to talk with me in the Other. She's probably resting there, trying to build up her strength."

The Porter Agency had been hired by ghosts before, but not like this — not by a headless one. Drummond had been patrolling the Porter's neighborhood late at night, making sure nothing human or otherwise aimed to harm his favorite mortals. Max added that last detail, and as a smirk rose on his lips, he thought maybe this recent wave of malaise was lifting. While on his patrol, at the two o'clock witching hour, a call came from the Other. That was the word Drummond had used. *A call.* Max didn't press for an explanation of how ghosts residing in that plane of existence contacted those outside the Other, but he did file the question for another time.

"Now, the Other tends to be a changing place," Drummond had said when he woke the Porters before the sun rose with this news. "It's full of strange things, too. Mainly because the world keeps changing and because people die in all sorts of strange ways. So, I wasn't too concerned when a headless woman drifted over to me."

From her clothes, Drummond guessed she was a modern woman, and from her wrinkleless skin, he put her around her early-twenties. He had no clue how she knew where to go when she couldn't see, but then, there were many mysteries about being a ghost that he expected to go unanswered. How did he feel pain? How did he run out of breath? How could he smell things? The list was endless. So, a headless ghost behaving as if it could see didn't bother him.

"Hey, there, doll," he said as the woman approached. "You called for me?"

The headless ghost tilted forward. A nod, Drummond guessed. Apparently, she couldn't speak without a mouth.

"I don't mean to be unkind, but how is it you think we're going to have a conversation? I don't see a pencil and paper, and I'm sorry, but I don't know sign language."

She swirled her hands in a prescribed motion that meant only one thing to the old detective — witchcraft. He told Max and Sandra, "That was the moment I first started to worry. I deal with too many witches in the flesh. Ghost-witches in the Other? No, thank you."

From the headless witch's hands, clouds of smoke streamed into the air. The swirling mist solidified into a flat square hovering in front of Drummond like a canvas. When the witch moved her finger through the smoke, she left an open trail behind. In this way, she wrote words and drew pictures. If the canvas got too full, she swiped her hand across, and the smoke rushed in, filled the gaps, and created a fresh cloud slate to write upon.

"It wasn't the best way to communicate," Drummond had said, "a bit unclear at times, and it exhausted her, but it worked enough."

The story required little to relate. She had been murdered, and she wanted The Porter Agency to help put her to rest. She knew next to nothing about her attackers. There had been more than one. They jumped her from behind. She never saw them.

But she did know where her body could be found. So, as the sunrise warmed the dew-covered ground, Max and Sandra followed their partner to this old barn and this young corpse.

"Driver's license has an address we can check out," Max said. "Maybe Osorio —"

"No, no," Drummond swished over. "You've got to believe me on this one. Leave Detective Osorio alone. He'll come to us when he needs our help. If we keep going to him to use the police for our work, we'll end up losing him. We also might cost him his job."

"It was just a thought."

"Not a good one." Drummond floated higher and gazed down at the crime scene. "Besides, eventually, somebody will find this mess and call it in. Once the police get involved, and if it comes across Osorio's desk, then maybe he will come to us."

Sandra used her phone to take photos of the barn. "I guess I'm researching ancient magic again. I'm really starting to hate those books. They're written in old, old languages that take a long time to translate, and the spells — if you can call them that — take even longer to decipher. When can we get back to modern witchcraft with spellbooks that actually make sense?"

With a slim smile, Max said, "It's the curse of being the best. We get all the hard cases."

"Then we're definitely taking this on?" Drummond said.

"I guess."

"Why the hesitation?"

"It's not like ghosts pay us. I'm happy to help them out, but we do need income now and then."

"Then are we helping Pauline or not?"

Sandra gave a firm nod. "Absolutely. If for no other reason,

Max needs this."

"I do?"

"You can't spend another week moping around. I know it takes time to go through grieving, but a little work will help you. Get your mind back to the present."

He shrugged. "Maybe."

Tapping on her phone, Sandra said, "No doubt about it." Then she put the phone to her ear. "Brenda? We've got a bunch of witchcraft research to do. The Porter Agency's got a case."

Chapter 2

As Max drove down Peters Creek Parkway toward the southern end of Winston-Salem, Drummond floated in the passenger seat. The two had spent hours in this car over the years, and Max thought of it like a favorite blanket. But the most loved objects, no matter how special, eventually reached the end of their powers — a blanket or a car or whatever drew the initial connection.

The city had changed around them, too. Pointing to a development under construction, Max said, "That's been fields as long as I've lived here."

"It's a shame to see it go, but it's nothing new."

"What are you talking about? When Sandra and I moved down here, so much of Winston was farmland. The city keeps growing. In the last few years, it's been building up so fast."

"I got news for you, partner. It's always been like that. When I was alive, the city took up half the blocks it does now. That's life. We keep growing. Things keep changing."

Max lifted an eyebrow at his partner. On a longer drive, these comments might have opened the door to more important discussions, but the maps app on the phone chimed that they had reached their destination — Pauline Lennon's house. Max pulled to the curb.

The area looked like many planned communities in America. Each house had been chosen from a selection of three basic models, and while some flourishes of individuality had been allowed, modern uniformity was the goal. The will of the HOA lorded over the owners. Max had always thought that odd. In a country that prided itself on self-reliance and individual spirit, people willingly gave up the right to distinguish their home from others to be part of the group.

"Take this one with kid gloves," Drummond said as they approached the house. "Assume the parents don't know their little girl went off to college to become a witch."

"College? How do you know that?"

"She's the right age. Hands looked soft, so no manual labor. Plus, her ghost told me."

Max pressed the doorbell. "Which school?"

"Forsyth Tech. Got her Associates Degree in business. Accounting and finance. Planned to go to a four-year college next."

A woman with straight, auburn hair and a curious brow opened the door. "Yes?"

Realizing he had forgotten to prep a good story, Max fell upon ol' reliable. "Good morning. I'm writing an article about the unusual families in Winston-Salem and wondered if you'd be interested in an interview."

"An interview? That's sweet of you, but there's nothing unusual about us."

This woman looked too young to be the mother, so Max took a stab. "I met with your sister, Pauline, and her name alone makes her interesting."

"I'll bet." The woman snickered as she opened the door wider. "Come on in. I'm Bennie."

"And the Jets?"

"That's the one."

"Your parents are really into music."

"Of a certain era." She walked him into a living room and gestured to the couch.

With two words, Drummond expressed everything Max thought. "Holy crap."

The inside of the house had been ripped from the pages of *Good Housekeeping 1952 — Grandma's Edition*. Doilies decorated the arms of the couch. Heavy curtains darkened the room. Porcelain statuettes lined the mantel of a fireplace and several shelves. A larger figurine depicting a rickshaw, driver, and a kimono-clad girl as the passenger dominated the dark wood coffee table. A small glass dish held wrapped butterscotch candies. The room smelled musty, and as Bennie settled in a high-backed reading chair, Max caught a puff of dust billowing out the side.

From a swinging door in the back, another young woman entered. She had reddish curls that framed her freckled cheeks. "Oh, I didn't realize we had guests. Should I put on some tea?"

"No, thank you," Max said.

Bennie gestured to the woman. "This is my other sister, Layla."

While Bennie dressed in a casual, modern manner, Layla could have been plucked from that same ancient magazine. She had a frilly apron covering an overly-conservative blouse and skirt, and black, horn-rimmed glasses. If she added a feather-duster, Max thought she'd have perfected the part.

"Is it just the three of you living here?" Max asked.

Layla's lips turned up but not into anything Max could call a smile. She said, "We come from a large family. There are always more here."

Sharing a nod with her sister, Bennie said, "Watch what you say, Sis. This man is a reporter. He's doing an article on strange families."

"About us?"

"Pauline sent him."

"He's got the wrong family. Why, we're about as bland and boring as you can get."

"Except our names, apparently."

"What would anybody care that we're named after music and musicians? I can't see an article like that be worth reading." To Max: "You might want to find something else to write about, mister. This dog ain't got no bark."

The longer Max sat in that room, the more it closed in on him. Everything about these sisters screamed caution, yet he couldn't point to any sign of witchcraft. The old style was odd and stuffy, but not a guaranteed witch thing. Lots of people preferred older décor. And while most witches cluttered their homes with collections of oddities, they behaved more like hoarders than these ladies. There was an unsettling collection of figurines, yet the statuettes were carefully displayed rather than the chaos found in most witch homes. These women acted more like hobbyists.

Drummond clearly felt the same. "Keep them talking. I'll check out the house. And stay alert. I don't know what's going on here, but something's off about this place."

Forcing a relaxed crossing of the legs, Max watched Drummond disappear. "Perhaps you could tell me about your family, or how you ended up in North Carolina. You never know what might spark a truly fascinating story. For instance, Pauline had mentioned that she had an interest in the occult. Now, I would never have guessed that by looking at her. She seemed more like the cheerleader type."

"Cheerleader?" Layla said. "She would rather've been thrown in a crocodile pit with fresh meat strapped to her sides."

Bennie chuckled. "She has always been the feisty one of us. But you know what's strange about her?"

Though Max sat back with a nonchalant gesture, his nerves jazzed up in anticipation. "Please, tell me."

"That she would ever tell anybody about the occult."

Drummond dropped from the ceiling. "Get out. This is a coven."

Jolting to his feet, Max said, "You got me. I was fishing. She didn't say anything like that. I got a feeling about her, that's all."

Both sisters rose in unison, and Max finally understood that they were not sisters by blood. Bennie moved toward the doorway leading outside while Layla blocked the back door.

"You are certainly not a reporter," Bennie said. "Who are you and why are you interested in Pauline?"

"Partner," Drummond said, poking his head through the ceiling and then returning. "There are five more witches upstairs."

Max moved toward the exit and tried to look charming but meek. "Clearly there's been a mistake. I apologize. I meant no harm. I only wanted to learn a little about you, that's all."

"For what?"

Layla said, "Ain't it obvious? He's a witch hunter. He come to check for sure if we're witches or not, and then he's fixing to kill us."

"No, I'm not. I don't want to hurt anybody. When I found Pauline, she looked like she was a nice woman and —"

"What do you mean *was?*" Bennie said. "Has something happened to her?"

From behind, Layla whimpered. "Is Pauline dead?"

"Um," Max said, his eyes darting for an alternate exit.

Bennie scowled. "Then you're going to join her."

"Time to get you out of here." Drummond swooped forward and slashed his icy hand across Bennie's head.

Chapter 3

BENNIE STIFFENED AT THE SUDDEN SHOCK OF COLD, but either Drummond moved too fast or she had dealt with the touch of a ghost before. She recovered quickly. Max never had a chance to bolt for the door.

"In here," Layla yelled, wrenching open the back door.

Two more witches entered the room — an eager one with a '70s afro, and a mean-looking one with the crooked nose of a boxer. Both women held a ghost ward. Bennie indicated the general area she thought Drummond was in, and she was right. Freezing her had given away his position for an instant, and she clearly had enough experience to take an educated guess from there.

As the two warded witches tried to corner Drummond, tried to shove him out of the room, Layla and Bennie pressed towards Max.

"Don't worry." Drummond had floated to one corner of the ceiling. He ground his teeth, enduring spurts of pain from the wards. "I won't leave you."

Max stumbled back against the couch but managed to stay standing. "Ladies, this doesn't have to be a fight."

"You killed Pauline," Layla said as tears rivered down her cheeks.

"Not me. No."

"Liar!" She rushed at him, swinging her hands wildly. Not the attack of a spell but with aggrieved fury.

Max batted away her attacks, but he couldn't inch any further back. He fell onto the couch. Layla's wild motions tumbled her to the floor at his side.

He peeked at Bennie. She watched without reaction — at

least, no reaction he noticed. If she was an accomplished witch, she might be trying to cast a spell without a casting circle. Whatever she did, it wasn't hurting him for the moment. He grabbed the back of the couch and hoisted himself over. The distance between the couch and the wall offered little room, but his body pushed it forward enough to slip through. Mostly. His toes reached the floor, at least.

Drummond yelled as he smashed downward at the witches cornering him. They stumbled back as the force hit their ward field. Max caught the worried glance between them. It gave him a taste of satisfaction, but nothing more. He had seen Drummond crack a ward before — it could take a long time, a lot of hits, and the ghost took a hellish beating in the process. Max had a better idea.

He picked up one of the couch pillows and flung it at the mean-looking witch. As he snatched the next pillow, he saw the witch stagger aside. Not that a pillow hit hard, but she had not been expecting it. The surprise factor broke her concentration. While it wouldn't work a second time, it gave Drummond an opening.

He bashed down on the other ward, forcing afro-witch to the side. He then swept across the room, and since they couldn't see him, they no longer had a read on where he was. Max made sure to avoid eye contact with his partner, in case the witches got the idea to follow his eyeline.

Layla had returned to her feet, but Max flung the second pillow at her. She flinched, covering her face on instinct. Max shoved the couch forward a few inches, its old feet scrapping on the floor, and caused Layla to crash into the coffee table.

Scooting sideways, he slipped out. The two ward-witches ignored him, waving their wards in the air, hoping to make contact with the ghost.

"Give up, now," Bennie said, as her hands started to glow, "and we won't make you suffer."

As Max negotiated around an end table with a lovely figurine of a little boy holding a kite, he stopped long enough to wonder why he was being so careful. That gave him the second his brain needed to both recognize that he had a great weapon in front of him and to admonish him for being an utter idiot.

He seized the figurine and hurled it at Bennie.

The kite-boy bounced off her shoulder. Max had thought being struck by the figurine would have broken Bennie's concentration, but she held fast. What stopped her spell-casting was the sound of kite-boy shattering on the floor. Max winced, expecting an explosion of magic from the porcelain shards and wishing he had jumped out of the way. But nothing happened. In fact, as he widened his focus to get a read on the room, all the witches had frozen in stunned silence at the destroyed figurine.

Drummond reacted first. "That's the ticket." The ghost winced as he touched the nearest figurine — a woman with a parasol — and knocked it to the floor.

"Stop it," Bennie said, all her collected magic dissipating as her eyes widened over trembling lips.

Max picked up a porcelain dog sniffing a fire hydrant. Holding it like a weapon, he said, "I did not kill your sister."

"Fine, fine," Layla said, one hand covering her mouth as tears dribbled over her fingers. "Whatever you gonna say, we're gonna believe. Just, please, put that down."

The back door opened again. This time an elderly woman, thin and tall, stark white hair, and wearing a few distinguished wrinkles, entered the room. In a voice that filled every space around them, she said, "This stops now." She looked straight into Max. "Mr. Porter, kindly set that down. It is expensive and sentimental."

As if scolded by his mother — her dying eyes looking at him, begging him, shivered across his skin — he gently returned the figurine to the nearest shelf. Clearing his throat, he said, "I assume you're Madame Lennon."

"I am. Your ghost can come off the ceiling. It's Mr. Drummond, correct?"

As Drummond lowered, Max said, "That's right. I'm sure he'd appreciate it if your sisters would put away their ghost wards."

Madame Lennon twitched a finger, and the two ward-witches

left the room. She then motioned her head at Layla and Bennie. They hurriedly pushed the couch back into place and reset the pillows. The ward-witches returned with a broom and dustpan. As all four sisters cleaned the mess of the fight, Madame Lennon stood statue still.

Max opened his mouth, but Drummond raised a warning hand. They waited.

At length, when the sisters had restored order to the room — taking particular care to place the figurines in exact locations — Madame Lennon crossed her arms and leveled her stern glower upon Max. "All covens know of The Porter Agency, though clearly not all witches know what you look like. I apologize that my daughters failed to recognize you. But then you lied to them about who you were, didn't you?"

"We didn't know this was a coven when we got here," Max said.

"You knew Pauline was a witch."

"Being a witch doesn't mean being in a coven. I had assumed this was where her family lived."

"It is."

"Her birth family. We only had Pauline's driver's license to go on."

Layla cried out, "And you killed her."

"I didn't. I swear. She's been the victim of a witch attack." Max explained how Pauline's ghost found Drummond and essentially hired The Porter Agency. "We're just trying to find out who did this to her and why. Hopefully, that'll be enough to help Pauline move on."

Madame Lennon said, "Those are easy questions to answer. I'm surprised you can't figure it out."

Standing at the witch-mother's side, Bennie said, "Obviously, it was Madame Ti and her pathetic coven of misfits. They started this witch war, and they've been brutal in their ways of doing things."

"I agree. Decapitating a witch to send a message to our coven bears all of Madame Ti's crude lack of subtlety."

Drummond said, "She's got a point."

"Probably," Max said. "But the Coven of Ti isn't the only one out there trying to win this thing. And clearly, since we didn't even know about the Lennon coven, there are more of you than we realized."

"The number of covens doesn't matter," Madame Lennon said. "Madame Ti is an enemy to us all. If she is stopped, then this witch war ends."

Drummond said, "Maybe that was true at the start, but now—"

"We don't think that's true anymore," Max said.

"Your opinion isn't important. My coven knows better. That's why we have decided you will stop her."

"Stop who? Madame Ti?"

"Of course."

"No, thank you. I like my head on top of my shoulders."

Madame Lennon stepped forward, and it felt as if the entire house moved with her, ready to crash down upon Max if he challenged her further. "You will do what I say. If any coven defeats Madame Ti, that coven will become the head of magic in this area. We've seen how that power corrupts the minds of a witch. But if you defeat her, then no coven gains power. We can all go on as we have for centuries in the past. Free from anybody's rule."

Though his right leg started to shake, Max kept his voice steady. "Sorry, but The Porter Agency isn't a charity. We already have a *pro bono* case with Pauline. She's not asking for vengeance or the end of this witch war. She wants to know who killed her and why. Help us get her to move on, and maybe when that's done, we can consider your situation. For a fee, of course."

"You want to help Pauline? Then help her sisters." Her body tensed. "This war has taken too much already."

"I'll follow the evidence where it leads. If it turns out Madame Ti is behind this, then I'll do what I can. But stopping her takeover of the witch community is not something I can do alone."

"You have your team."

"If it were that simple, we'd have done it already."

Madame Lennon lowered her head to look down at Max. "You keep speaking as if I'm offering you a choice. Let me be clear. Stop Madame Ti. Fail, and I'll curse you with spells your wife has never heard of. Spells she'll never be able to break. A curse so vile, you'll spend the rest of your life weeping in agony and regret."

Max held back the whine crawling up his throat. He inched toward the door. "Well, thank you for your hospitality. I'm afraid I have to go now."

As Drummond slipped through the wall to the outside, Madame Lennon said, "This is not an idle threat."

"I didn't think it was," Max said. "I promise we'll fix things for Pauline."

"And Madame Ti?"

With a shivering grin, he said, "We'll do our best."

He felt the door at his back, fumbled the knob, and sprinted for his car.

Chapter 4

SOME DAYS, Max wished he had never taken that job for the Hulls, never came down to North Carolina, never moved his desk to release Drummond, never met a witch. With Sandra at his side, they could have worked through their financial troubles in Michigan, they could have found other jobs, they could have survived. Maybe they wouldn't have thrived, but they wouldn't have had to worry about risking their lives with each new case. Between the threats, the curses, and the brushes with death, he had to wonder if this was worth the effort. The answer came as fast as the thoughts — *of course*. The Porter Agency helped people, helped ghosts, even helped witches on occasion. And if they didn't do the work, who would?

Those thoughts proved harder to swallow as Max drove home. Drummond had returned to the Other to give Pauline an update and possibly glean some information about her coven.

"If we're lucky," Drummond said, "we'll find out Madame Lennon is more bark than bite."

"This isn't the first time I've been threatened with a curse. Heck, I've been cursed before." Max rubbed at the bruise forming on his hip. "That coven had plenty of bite, though."

He parked in the driveway and entered their small home. He cut through the kitchen, ignored the closed door to his mother's bedroom, took a few steps down the hall, and entered the master bedroom. He wanted to inspect his injuries and grab a change of clothes.

Not bad, it turned out. A few angry black-and-blue marks from banging into furniture. He had undergone far worse over the years. Still, he never took lightly the act of facing off against witches.

Putting on fresh clothes helped soothe his fried nerves. He no longer stank of sweat or magic. What he really wanted was a long, hot shower. That would have to wait. He knew the day was far from over.

When he left the bedroom, he froze. His mother's closed door faced him, and though he had walked by it numerous times since her passing, he found his legs would go no further. Sandra had told him that he needed to deal with this and accept that his mother had died. She didn't understand. Or perhaps she did, but her perspective was skewed by her tumultuous relationship with his mother. Or maybe some other factor caused her to sound callous towards him.

She wasn't, of course. He knew that. Sandra loved him and only wanted to help him through this tough time. In fact, he knew the real reason she couldn't understand, and every time he gazed upon that closed door, that reason hit hard. Sandra had not been in the hospital room with him when his mother died. She never heard what his mother had said.

Mrs. Porter had been admitted one night after a terrible MS attack that clenched her muscles causing excruciating pain. Her body locked up like an abstract sculpture of twisted limbs. They rushed her to the Emergency Room afraid that either the strain might cause a heart attack or that the constricting muscles might break some of her bones. Thankfully, neither of those nightmares occurred. The doctors, however, wanted her to hold her a few days for observation.

Max had stayed by her side the entire time. The hospital even provided a cot so that he could sleep in the room with her. That small courtesy filled him with gratefulness — and alarm. He wanted to be thankful that the staff recognized his need to be close to his mother and simply desired to help him despite the hospital rules for visitor times. He wished he could stop his thoughts there. But he saw only one main reason for them to risk liability by bending their rules — they didn't think she had much time left.

The Porter Agency had been involved in a minor case, and he sluffed his work off to Brenda. Or maybe Sandra had picked up the slack. Maybe even Drummond. Max didn't know, and at the time, he didn't care. His entire focus had been on his mother.

"You've been a good son," she said, reaching for his hand.

She had been saying such things since their arrival, as if she might die at any moment. The first few times, Max told her she would be fine, that they would soon return to the house, and that she could then go back to complaining about him. That got a weak chuckle.

But this time, though the words were the same, he heard a difference. Her voice had altered as if the sterile, mechanical hospital room had managed to extract the last bit of warmth, of hope, from her heart. She clenched his hand tight.

Turning her head towards him, she opened her eyes wide — he could not recall them ever being so open — and he glimpsed a little, terrified girl. "I know the kinds of things you deal with. I've never believed in it, but I'm not blind to what you and Sandra do."

Clinging to old arguments as if that might negate what he heard creeping in her tone, he said, "We believe in what we do, and so do our clients."

That little girl's eyes glistened. "Is ... is it real? Am I going to be a horrible specter floating through the walls?"

"When your time comes, you just have to let go. That time is far away, but if it happens in a hospital, you might see a lot of pale-looking people. Ignore them. Look for a light — there really is one — and you follow it so that you can move on."

"To what?"

Tears shivered out of him. "Nobody knows. But don't fight it, and don't let yourself stick to old grudges or bad memories. Things like that will keep you here. That's how you'll end up stuck. Just allow yourself to move on."

She closed her eyes, and Max feared she had done as he said — let go and moved on. Instead, she looked straight at him. Into him. "I don't regret anything in my life. I don't hold a grudge. But I do need to tell you something to lift a burden I've carried too long."

He had no desire to hear a deathbed confession, but he knew

better than to stop her. Besides, she wasn't dying. Not yet. He needed more time with her.

"Sure." He caressed the back of her hand.

Time passed in silence. Max thought maybe she had changed her mind. Maybe she had realized she would be fine and had no need to relieve any guilt over some imagined wrongs — at least for a few more months — but her brow wrinkled and flattened as she thought over her words. Unless her MS had attacked again. That expression might be physical pain. Max reached for the button to call the nurse, but his mother patted him back in his seat.

"When I was five, maybe six, I would play in my room or the backyard, and I acted like any other child. If I was alone, I'd talk with my imaginary friends — that's how my mom referred to it — or I'd throw a tea party for them or play hide-and-seek. When I got older, I put those days to rest. Like everybody else.

"But when I had you, and I saw the way you talked to your imaginary friends, it didn't sound like with me. You never paused long enough to listen. You would say your part, wait a second or two, and talk on as if your friend had said an entire speech. I talked to the other mothers, and I watched their children play. They said their children acted mostly like you. That scared me.

"When I was that age, I never would have jumped in to interrupt my imaginary friends. Before I would say whatever I wanted to say, I always waited until my friends stopped speaking. You understand?" She lifted her head, her thin hair sticking to the pillow as if the hospital clung to her, her body quivering as she relived her memory. "Those friends, those imaginary friends — they were really talking to me. It wasn't in my head. I saw them. I heard them."

Max understood. He guessed that if he said the word *ghosts* directly, she might shut down, so he tried to be clever. "Is that why you got so angry with Dad when he started seeing things?"

That frightened girl returned to her face. "Either I spoke with things that spoke back or I was crazy. Neither of those was good for a mother. I needed to be your rock, your guiding light, your everything. That's the job of a mother. How could I do my job if my own mind couldn't be trusted?

"But I also realized that those things I saw and heard as a child had never followed me through life. It seemed all children went through an imaginary friend phase. I figured mine was more real, but I couldn't be the only one. There had to be others that saw real things, and they must have outgrown it. I had outgrown it. You understand? The whole experience disturbed me, yet I came to see that none of it changed me. I was determined to be a good mother at your side, one that could guide you to being an adult. You would be fine, and that's all I cared about. Whatever happened in my head when I was little didn't matter."

"You've been a great mother."

She eased back with a flash of satisfaction. "I don't know about *great*. I only ever tried to do good for you. When your father first confessed to me what was happening in his head, I knew I had to stop this craziness. I wanted to let him know what I knew. I wanted to ease his mind. But if anybody overheard us, if your father went to a bar and drank his mouth loose and word got out that both your parents claimed such outrageousness, the state would surely take you away. Or your Aunt Jane would come in and take you from me."

"That's why you turned on her. It wasn't religion."

"Well, being an atheist didn't make me trust her, but the idea that you might be stolen from me, raised by her, all because of things I saw when I was a kid. And I don't know what I saw. Maybe I did have an overactive imagination. Once I stopped seeing and hearing these pretend friends, they never came back. So, how could I believe it had ever happened?" She pulled on his arm, bringing him closer. "And yet, I do."

"You don't need to worry about the afterlife."

"What if they're waiting for me? What if they're angry that I ignored them, that I couldn't see them?" Tugging at her blanket, she scowled. "I sound ridiculous. It's being in this hospital. It's got my brain all flummoxed." She closed her eyes as if willing away her memories. When she looked at him again, her voice weakened. "But with your job, with … with …"

"With the kinds of cases we work on?"

"That's why I need to hear it from you. All this talk of moving on, but what if none of us move on? What if we're just roaming around like those I saw as a child? I don't want to be some kid's imaginary friend."

He smiled. "You won't. You'll be fine. I guess this means you believe Sandra and I now."

"You don't understand."

"I do."

"You can't. Try to remember this, though. When you're old, when your end arrives —"

"Stop talking like that."

"— then you'll know what I know." She looked beyond Max's shoulder. "Maybe I'll be able to see it all again."

A dark cry rose from her chest. She lurched forward, her eyes bugging with horror, and Max caught her in his arms. As her tears flowed, Max stroked her staticky hair and rubbed her boney back. She curled into him. Holding her, listening to her sorrow, he couldn't decide what part of their conversation had been lucid and what had been delusion.

He could still feel her small frame and smell that sterile hospital room. Standing in the hallway of his home, staring at his mother's bedroom door, he could still hear her final whimpers. He thought she had settled down, cried it out, and perhaps would fall asleep. He recalled the relief he felt knowing he would have a few hours of peace before she woke.

But she never did.

He should have done more, have said more. There must have been some combination of words that would have eased her mind. On her deathbed, she only sought peace about the thing that he was a supposed expert in, and he had offered nothing but what everybody already knew — *go into the light.*

With a chill, he stood in his hallway and glanced into the bathroom, the living room, the kitchen. Since his mother's passing, he had noticed these moments of cold in the house. Sandra promised that his mother had moved on. Drummond had confirmed it. Neither of them saw any sign of her ghost. Yet he still felt the frosty touch of the dead.

Days after Mrs. Porter had passed, J arrived from school for the funeral. It was a small ceremony. A quiet one. Not so much a ceremony as an acknowledgement.

Max, Sandra, J, and Drummond stood at the edge of the grave in silence. Max's mother didn't even get the full family. Over the few days leading up to this, each member had tried to contact PB, but none succeeded. Wherever that young man was, he could not be reached.

Max's phone chimed, and his heart leapt against his ribs. Fumbling out the device, he rushed by the troubling door and entered the kitchen. He could breathe in there.

"Hello?" He never bothered looking at the caller's ID and prepared to hear a request that he participate in a quick survey that also entered him in a chance to win a vacation or that the FBI had an arrest warrant in his name for outstanding fines unless he bought a few thousand dollars-worth of gift cards to cover the cost.

Luckily, it was Sandra. "We've found something."

He perked up at the sound of her enthusiasm. "Can't wait. I'll get Drummond and meet you at the office."

"Sorry, hon, but you men will have to come here. The books we're using are not allowed to leave this library."

An unsettling lump formed in his gut. "What library?"

"Haven House."

Chapter 5

TWENTY MINUTES LATER, Max leaned against his car and stared at the old house in the woods. Haven House. Drummond floated nearby. A soft drizzle tapped out eerie rhythms on the leaves, and the air lacked the natural aroma of a forest. Rather, a moldy scent lingered like something had died long ago yet the trees never quite got rid of the odor. Not hostile, but not welcoming.

Certainly, not welcoming to Max. Filled with the nerve-wracking dizziness of its twisting halls, endless configurations of its book stacks, and the constant vibrations of cast spells, Haven House had left its mark on him. The few times he had been required to enter that building, he always worried that he might not make it back out. He glared at the house, crossed his arms, and let loose a long sigh.

Drummond had the opposite problem. The witches of Haven House had warded the building so well, he could never get in. Every visit, he remained stuck outside, unable to help his partners, forced to hover and wait. For a man like Drummond, it was a special kind of torture.

"Do we really need to be here?" the ghost said, pacing the air at Max's side. "Your wife could take notes and share it with us later."

Unfortunately, Max had to admit that the place served as the greatest library of ancient witch texts and tomes collected in the United States. Possibly in the world. The three witches running things had taken a liking to Sandra, and more than anything, that fondness protected Max.

"Why are you angry with Sandra?" Max asked.

Drummond rustled his long coat. "I'm not."

Lately, whenever you're mad at her, you refer to her as *your wife* or *that lady you married.*"

"Let's not worry about my word choices and focus on the problem — we're at Haven House and that's never a good thing."

"Relax," Max said, feeling his neck muscles tighten another notch. "Sandra wouldn't call us out here unless it was necessary."

"Or if she wanted to show off."

"That's not like her, and you know it."

Shoving his hands in his coat, Drummond shook his head. "I shouldn't have said that. I don't even think it. This place, though, it gets to me."

"I feel the same."

"Sometimes I wish our cases came with warning labels. This one requires battling poltergeists. That one involves a spell to turn you into a squirrel."

"Yeah, it seems like they . . . hold on, you were once turned into a squirrel?"

"Get me drunk enough and I'll tell you about that one someday."

"You can't get drunk as a ghost."

"Then I guess I won't be telling you about that one."

The longer they waited, the more uneasy Max felt. The shadows of the house darkened, and he couldn't blame it all on the differing clouds, the time of day, or even the numerous trees doing their best to block out the sunlight. After a minute, Max said, "Why do you care about this headless ghost anyway?"

"Why do we care about any of our clients? They pay us."

"This ghost isn't going to pay us."

"Maybe she will. She's got her coven. They could pay."

"You mean the one that threatened to curse me?"

"What are you worried about? We always find the money at some point."

"Easy for you. Ghosts don't have to pay bills."

"Then I'll make sure Pauline pays us. Or her coven. Or somebody. We've got a ghost to help, so can we focus on that?"

"But that's my point. Other ghosts have tried to hire us before, but you often turn them away. Why this one? Wait a second — was she a waitress?"

While Max snickered, Drummond didn't even smirk. The ghost pulled his Fedora low. Max's amusement died in the drizzle.

With genuine concern, he said, "I know you hate talking about this kind of stuff, but I'm your friend. You can trust me."

"It ain't about trust."

"Right. It's all that manly-man crap you grew up with. You don't have to be a stoic rock anymore. Those 1940s attitudes are long gone. Heck, you're dead. What does any of it matter now?"

Drummond turned his head an inch, watching Max with a side-eyed glance. "You don't understand. It's because we're friends that —"

A loud whine cut through the woods as the front door of Haven House opened. Madame Novak stepped out. Though she looked in her fifties now, Max had seen her appear far older in the past and knew she defied age entirely. Inside that house, he had viewed photographs of Madame Novak and her witch sisters dating back over a hundred years. Whenever he thought about that, he wondered what price they had to pay for their long lives. Regardless of her age, the rest of her remained a short but formidable lady, like a chubby grandma who only wants to bake cookies but will throw down with anybody who gets in her way.

"Hi, Max." She wiggled her hand as a wave before gesturing him toward the house. "Your sweet, darling wife is ready for you. Come on in."

Max looked at Drummond. The ghost glowered hard at Madame Novak and said, "I'll be right here. If anything bad happens, I'll get inside. Whatever it takes."

The harsh grimness in Drummond's voice promised he would do as he said. Even if he destroyed himself bashing against the Haven House wards.

Max threw out a brave clap of the hands. "It won't come to that. They love Sandra."

Drummond grunted. Not the response Max had hoped for as he walked toward the door.

When he entered the house, his heart jumped gears. The

witches had changed everything. Instead of the familiar lobby with a counter like one would see at an old bed and breakfast, Max stepped into a stone lodge. A large room with exposed beams and a wagon wheel chandelier providing dim light. A fire crackled in a hearth on one side of the room. Heavy wallpaper with a maroon and yellowing-white lines making a geometric design helped close the room around visitors. Far from a cozy place to research.

Madame Novak said, "Stay close to me." She headed through dark wood double-doors in the back.

Max followed. "What happened to the old entrance?"

"Madame Weir loves to redecorate from time to time."

"Madame Weir?" He tried to picture the monstrous witch that haunted him worse than any witch he had ever met in this new light. It hurt his brain.

"Oh, yes. If you get her and Madame Fein talking about changing rooms in this house, they'll go at it for hours. They love to redesign the flow. When that whole feng-shui fad started, they really went crazy. Seemed like every morning I awoke to a different house."

"But that sounds more like redecorating. This looks like an entire restructuring."

"For you." She chuckled as she led Max down a long hall of warped wooden shelves filled with books of various sizes. "We witches can do a lot more than concoct poisons and cause trouble. I think they like to do it to keep busy, but then they also love helping people find whatever books they came here for, so maybe my sisters redecorate in order to force people to need us."

She veered off to the right, and Max swore they had doubled-back toward the entranceway, yet the halls continued to stretch out. This place could be a labyrinth under the best of circumstances. Add in witchcraft, and he guessed it was best to ignore physics.

Madame Novak halted and stared at a framed photograph on the wall. She blushed. "I'm so glad they kept this one."

Moving closer, Max looked upon a black-and-white photo of a young woman posing in front of a Buddhist temple. "Is that you?"

"During the Korean war. I volunteered as a nurse. My sisters were furious with me. Witches have enough threats to our lives without jumping into more. We tend to stay out of political conflicts unless they're witch politics. Even then, most of us want to be left alone. We're a very individualistic group." Tracing her face on the wall, she said, "More than the politics, my sisters were angry that I had left for a man. They've always been jealous that I get more of the attention in the romantic department than they do. Vernon took this photo while we both were on leave. The fact that they hung this here means a lot. I think they're starting to get over it."

As Madame Novak walked onward, Max followed. He didn't know which thought disturbed him more — that Madame Novak participated in the Koren war, that she was considered the catch between her sisters, or that the other sisters, particularly Madame Weir, had desires for romance. The old woman picked up her pace as she rambled about Vernon's cute, pudgy face and his warm, generous heart. "He was the kind of man that had me considering a baby."

Max swallowed back his nausea.

Down one hall, a flash of orange light and the stench of burnt cabbage wafted his way. A puff of thick smoke billowed over the walls. It moved like a languid river, a gentle trickle that still managed to block the passage. It entranced. When Max finally broke away, he looked back toward Madame Novak.

But she was gone.

He rushed ahead and reached a T-junction. Looking both ways, he saw dark halls stretching into emptiness. Pictures had been hung sporadically and dust floated in the dim light.

Max's gut clenched. He went to the right. No particular reason except some direction had to be chosen, and he had been in Haven House enough times to know that going back would not help. No matter how well he mapped his movements, they never matched up on the return trip.

Passing a boarded door, he stopped. A cold spot. The back of his neck prickled. He swore the temperature had dropped. All signs of a ghost.

But that wasn't possible. The house wards prevented ghosts. That's why Drummond never could enter. Unless ...

Would Drummond lie to him?

Max slapped his cheek. This house could cause strange thoughts. He had to remember that. He had to remember that he knew Drummond better than anybody — other than Sandra — and that old ghost would never lie about something so important.

But that didn't change the cold spot. Maybe another ghost, one stronger than Drummond, had found its way into the house. Or perhaps a ghost had been haunting the place before the wards went up, and it got stuck in here. Max wasn't sure that could happen, but he needed an explanation for that cold spot.

"A draft, you idiot," he muttered, adding Drummond's gruff delivery for good measure. Of course. A draft. That made the most sense.

But logic did not ease his mind.

He walked further down the hall. The familiar sensations of fear — throat drying, heart racing, back sweating — rushed through him like a squall. Though he opened his mouth to call out for Madame Novak, he forced his lips closed. She wasn't the only one in this house. Some of the others were dangerous. Not just Madame Fein or Madame Weir, but there were strange things living in these walls. Max could feel them. Hear them scraping along the wood. His stomach groaned as the scraping grew louder, pressing the air. Scratching and scratching. Itching into his ears. The hallway swiveled, and he put out a hand to keep from falling.

His fingers dropped onto a doorknob.

All grew still and quiet. He didn't recall that he had continued walking, but gazing along the hall, nothing looked familiar. This was not the same hall he had been in. Without windows to see the forest or his car or Drummond, he couldn't be sure he stood in the same house.

A voice called his name. It sounded like Sandra. Yet even as his mind pointed out that no sound had been heard, that the voice had been in his head, he turned the knob.

Windowless, covered in thick, red velvet drapes, the room reminded Max of a fortune teller's tent at a traveling circus. Incense coated the air. A violin played some somber tune as if through an ancient radio. In the center of the small space, a round table had been placed with two chairs opposite each other and, naturally, a crystal ball perched in the middle.

Max waited, half-expecting a woman clad in endless scarves and jangling jewelry to sweep in and bid him welcome. She would talk of her gift to unlock the mysteries in the spirit world, mysteries she would share for a nominal fee. But nobody entered.

The longer he waited, the more he felt as if he did not belong there — which, granted, he didn't. But he remained. Part of him had the urge to leave, but more of him wanted to stay. More of him wanted to step closer to that table, to that crystal ball. Just a peek. That's all. Just a teeny peek at whatever the future may hold.

He slapped his face again. The sting burned along his skin, yet he did not halt. His eyes locked onto the ball like an addict itching for that fix.

He shook his head. That made no sense. He had never believed in fortune tellers, never used their services in a serious manner — well, maybe for a case, but even then, he didn't really buy into it. Sandra had said that people who claimed to have such gifts rarely did. But then again, if any crystal ball was real, the one in Haven House would be it.

As he debated with his mind, his feet continued their slow shuffle across the room. As he argued against these actions, his body bent over the table. As he silently screamed within, his face closed in on the ball.

He looked in.

From the world of movies and television, Max assumed he would see swirls of mystical smoke that might part in the center to reveal some relevant moment in the future. It might be cryptic — almost certainly would be — but in time, its message would become clear. What he got was a flipped image of the table and the room beyond the ball. Maybe he didn't have the "gift" fortune tellers had. Or maybe …

Two eyes appeared in the crystal ball. Old eyes. A woman's eyes.

Max's breath caught. The distorted view in the ball made it difficult to identify the person, but who else could it be? Only one person in his life had died recently. Only one person had gazed up at him before her life left her body.

"You see anything?" a craggy voice said.

From the other side of the table.

Max popped straight up to find Madame Novak hunched over and staring into the ball. "Only you looking back at me."

She snorted. "Sounds about right. Madame Weir bought this thing a few years ago and insisted it would work, but we've yet to find anybody capable of making it do anything." She folded her arms like a mechanic trying to understand why a car won't start. "I've never been a believer in prognostication — at least, not this kind. During our last house redecoration, we made this room. Madame Weir promised that the ball never worked because the environment wasn't welcoming to it." She gazed at the curtains. "Waste of valuable space, if I'm being honest. But it makes her happy, and we sisters must sacrifice for each other to keep the peace. You live long enough with somebody, and you learn that fact. I don't have to tell you, though, you and your dear Sandra have been together quite a while. Lots of sacrifices in your history, I'm sure."

Lacing his hands behind his back to hide the adrenaline shake, Max said, "Are we close to her?"

"We'd be there already if you hadn't gone wandering. You should know better."

"It wasn't intentional."

"This house can get confusing. I understand. Now, stick close, and I'll have you there in a jiffy."

True to her word, Madame Novak managed to reach the room with Sandra and Brenda in only two short turns. Max wondered if they had been circling their destination all along and that Madame Novak had been waiting for Max to get lost. That kind of paranoid thinking wouldn't help him, though. Not now, anyway.

When they entered the room, Max found his wife seated at a wide table with ornate carvings along the legs. Old books covered most of the available desktop, and Sandra's notes covered the rest. Both ladies had their heads buried in their work and only glanced up when Madame Novak cleared her throat.

Sandra's face opened brightly, and in that small moment, Max felt grateful. She was the most important person, always had been, and he squeezed her tighter than his usual hugs. Then he kissed her cheek, holding his lips against her for longer than the normal peck.

"I've figured it out," she said, and Max knew it was time to get back to work.

Chapter 6

SANDRA STRODE TO THE CENTER OF THE ROOM, her confidence evident with each word spoken. Max loved watching her act so fearless. Especially when his own gut quivered at the mere smell of the musty books surrounding them. Hearing her, focusing on her, helped quell his churning stomach.

"We knew we were looking for an ancient spell," Sandra said, not bothering with any preamble. Max would have preferred more build-up — it was the way he liked to tell these things — but her process was more important than her presentation. He cared not only because he found it fascinating, but because doing so served as a check that no steps had been overlooked or missed entirely. It was why he did the same when relating his own research to the team, and he appreciated her efforts now. She continued, "Like a lot of ancient spells, this one clearly involves blood."

Madame Novak sniffled. "I'd say taking off the head of a witch is more than a little blood."

With graceful patience, Sandra said, "Of course. That is why Brenda and I decided to come to Haven House. If this had been merely blood magic, my own library would have sufficed."

"Oh, deary, don't go thinking you have all the knowledge on blood magic. We have books that no human hands have touched since the author finished writing them."

"Exactly the reason we came here."

Brenda made no attempt to hide the edge in her voice. "Decapitation ain't normal witch behavior so we've come to where there ain't normal witch books."

"I'll take that as a compliment." Madame Novak lifted her lips in an ugly sneer.

While Max feared this veering into dangerous territories, he trusted Sandra. She had a healthy wariness of the Haven House witches and knew when to hold her tongue. Brenda, too, had enough experience to avoid a tussle with witches over a century old. However, none of the Haven House witches could be considered fully sane. While Madame Novak presented herself as the most reasonable and aware of the three, Max would never presume to anticipate her reaction to anything.

Hoping to refocus matters, he said, "Obviously, we're dealing with something far more dangerous than usual. It's a good thing you called on Haven House for their assistance."

As Madame Novak's sneer slipped into appreciation, Sandra offered Max a grateful wink before using the opportunity to push onward. "The texts we were looking for had to be either older or more obscure than anything I'd ever seen. We needed to find a spell that required ingredients beyond simple blood. Even death as a catalyst might not be enough. Rather, we were looking for offerings to go along with the sacrifice."

"You are learning well," Madame Novak said. "*Offerings* is the perfect word."

As Sandra and Madame Novak shared a nod that suggested peace had been restored, Max glanced over at Brenda. She looked like a mouse cornered by a hungry cat. The cat — that was Haven House. Max understood all too well, and the way she looked at him, a fleeting moment of understanding passed between.

Sandra gestured to her student. "Would you like to explain how we found the spell?"

Brenda shook her head. If anything, Max guessed she refused because she wanted to vomit more than speak.

"No problem," Sandra said, clearly noticing Brenda's discomfort. "With Madame Novak's help, we were able to narrow things down to the books you see on the table. Unfortunately, none of this has been digitized, and the books lack indexes in the back. They don't even have a table of contents."

"Of course not, deary," Madame Novak said. "These books

were written by people trying to share knowledge with those to come later while keeping secret everything they were writing down. If they got caught and a judge or a priest or whomever saw a table of contents reading *Spells to Rot a Victim's Lungs*, that might go poorly for the author, don't you think?"

"Those days are long gone, and these books are disintegrating. You really need to modernize."

Noticing Madame Novak bristle, Max said, "Even when it is digitized, that doesn't always help. Sometimes you're still stuck going through everything line by line."

"In this case," Sandra said, "we have the added problem that most of it's not in English. Normal texts from centuries ago tended to use a very old version of English or French or German alongside Latin and Greek. Google translate helped some with that. The more sensitive information would usually be in one of the homemade witch languages, but since these books predate all of that, they are in languages long dead that I never heard of. Madame Novak helped us there."

With a bashful wave of the hand, Madame Novak said, "I don't think I was that much help. I'm quite rusty when it comes to Namariti."

"But you did bring us those red books. They were key with cross-referencing and with some of the rougher translations."

"As a librarian of Haven House, I'm here to serve."

"What's the spell?" Max said.

Sandra walked behind the desk and lifted her notebook. "It's called *veoloxal*."

"Better," Madame Novak said. "It's Vee-oh-HOCKS-el. Not *locks* but *HOCKS*."

Max snickered. "Sounds like a medication applied to an indecent rash."

"It has only one use that I can figure out," Sandra said. "To make objects in the spirit world become real in the physical world."

Max's amusement slashed away. His heart sank, and his lungs deflated. His muscles twisted inside of him. He felt like a wet towel being wrung out.

"It's a very dangerous spell," Madame Novak said. "Highly unstable, too."

"It's also highly secretive." Sandra turned a page, placed her notebook on the table, and lowered over the words. "Whoever figured this spell out wanted to make sure that most witches could never use it. Many spells have an ingredients list like a recipe. In this case, the regular ingredients are listed, but then they're followed by three lines — each one in a different language."

Max thought of Madame Ti and her coven. They included witches from all over the world — witches that would know many different languages. And he had firsthand knowledge that The Coven of Ti had already experimented with ancient magic, unstable magic.

He looked at Madame Novak. She probably knew from the start that this was the book Sandra had wanted. Of course. It's probably the only one in existence, and that meant Madame Ti would've had to come to Haven House to find this same spell.

Sandra made a small motion with her hand to still Max. How did she know he was about to open his mouth to accuse Madame Novak of playing both sides against each other? How did she know a small hand gesture would be enough to stop him? Well, she was his wife, after all. He shouldn't have been surprised.

"This is what we've translated," Sandra said. "The first is written in an invented witch language used during the Dark Ages. It reads: *the head of a cursed witch in decay.*"

Max said, "I take it that's Pauline."

"I certainly think so. This second line is in French. *The head of a man who does not exist in dust and bone.*"

"What does that mean?"

"No clue. The last is in a 19th century Southern dialect with traces of Creole. It reads: *the head of the newly reborn, fresh and full of lost life.*"

Max sat back and crossed his arms. "Three heads."

"And whoever's doing this has one already. We can expect two more."

"Not if we stop them first."

Closing her notebook, Sandra said, "Then it's back to the office."

"Absolutely not," Madame Novak said. "There are rules."

"Right. Sorry."

"These books stay here. And don't even think about snapping pictures with your phone."

Max looked to his wife. "You wrote down everything we need, right?"

"Hon, I learned how to research from you."

"Then you can keep your books, Madame Novak. We've got work to do back at the office. That is, if you'll kindly escort us out of here. I'd hate to take a wrong turn."

Madame Novak grinned without any pleasure.

Chapter 7

DURING THE DRIVE BACK to the office building, watching Sandra and Brenda in the car in front, Max used every relaxation technique he knew to release the overbearing tension created from visiting Haven House. Nothing worked. That is, nothing worked until Drummond appeared in the passenger seat. Bringing the detective up to speed and listening to his cranky comments loosened Max's shoulders and deepened the laugh lines crinkling his eyes. By the time they parked and climbed the stairs to their office floor, Max had returned to normal — still stressed, but a normal stress.

Much of the office layout remained the same as it had been since they first moved in — a large open area with Sandra's desk by the window and Max's more toward the center, a bookshelf on the far wall that acted as a library for Sandra's witch tomes and as a home for Drummond, and a discount couch and chairs with a coffee table on a circular rug hiding the casting circle beneath. A short hallway led to a conference room, a break room, and the most important, a bathroom. Little by little, however, details continued to change and evolve. The newest addition — a whiteboard Brenda had installed on the wall opposite the couch. Not only could they write on this, but it was magnetic which helped create visual layouts of their cases.

Max thought it a bit dramatic, but Drummond loved the idea. "Back in my day," the ghost had said, "we were stuck with chalkboards, corkboards, or nothing but a pencil and paper. This sort of thing is real good for us visual thinkers."

Even as Max repeated the ghost's words for Brenda's benefit, something he and Sandra now did as a matter of habit, he had bit his tongue that day. The idea that Drummond had learned about *visual thinkers* deserved a comment or two. In fact, thinking about it now, Max snickered.

"What's so funny?" Drummond asked as he drifted toward his bookshelf.

"Nothing important."

Sandra sat at her desk, laptop open, but Brenda took her laptop to the couch, stretching her legs as she wriggled into comfort. Max went down the short hall to the bathroom, and on his return, he offered coffee to everybody.

Floating in circles around the ceiling, tapping his chin, Drummond said, "A witch, a group of witches, or an entire coven want to take something from my world of existence and turn it into a real object in your world. There are only two groups that I can think of who have attempted to wield such drastically powerful magic as that — the Brotherhood and Madame Ti."

Max said, "I doubt the Brotherhood is up to the task. Even when they were powerful, they never could pull off something like this. We haven't heard a peep since we pretty much destroyed them."

"Then it's Madame Ti."

"She's certainly capable of dreaming up such a terrible idea."

Sandra said, "And she's got plenty of people in place to help her along."

Brenda said, "Then why are we sitting here? Let's go confront Madame Ti."

Though Max recoiled at the idea, Sandra raised a warning hand. "I'd agree with you, except we don't know for sure. If we're wrong, we don't want to put it in her head that this is even a possibility."

Sitting at his desk, Max opened his laptop. Sandra had sent a copy of the spell to everybody. As he looked over the ingredients list, he thought about how the first line related to reality. *The head of a cursed witch in decay.* Written in a witch language.

Max looked up at Drummond. "Is our headless client with us?"

"No. Want me to get her?"

"According to this spell, you need the head of a cursed

witch—"

"That's her. They cursed her, then cut off her head."

"Yeah, but she's supposed to be in decay. They killed her. They didn't dig her up from the grave and remove her decaying head."

Sandra said, "You think they got the first step wrong?"

"Maybe. We need to ask Pauline."

Raising her hand, Brenda said, "Maybe you're reading the word *decay* wrong. If she was dying already, if she had a disease — something that could be considered decaying."

Drummond clapped his hands once. "Be right back."

"He just left, didn't he?" Brenda said. To Max's surprised look, she added, "I think I'm getting a feel for the shifts in the room when a ghost is here and when one isn't."

"That's good," Sandra said. "You're really improving as a witch."

Max looked at his laptop again. "If they have the wrong witch head, none of this matters. The spell won't work, and we don't have to worry. But, if they have the right head, then they are moving to the second step. Let's focus on that for now."

Brenda pushed up from the couch, crossed to the whiteboard, and grabbed a marker. Using a different color for each line, she wrote out the three phrases Sandra had copied from the witch book at Haven House:

The head of a cursed witch in decay
The head of a man who does not exist in dust and bone
The head of the newly reborn, fresh and full of lost life

Turning their attention to the second line, The Porter Agency buckled down, each member focused on their own path of inquiry. Over several hours, Max tried to decipher how a person could not exist yet still be real enough to have a head that could be removed. Since Sandra and Brenda most likely explored avenues involving witchcraft, Max decided to take a more practical, mundane approach.

He came up with two possibilities for a person not to exist.

Either they were a fictitious character, or they were once real but no longer existed — as in once alive but now dead. In both cases, particularly the case of a fictitious character, the best way to have a removable head was a statue. Of course, if the person in question had been real and no longer lived, then there might be a grave to dig up; however, the ingredients specifically state that the head did not exist *in dust and bone*. The skull — especially a decomposing skull — would be nothing but dust and bone. A sculpture, however, would be neither.

After spending a lengthy amount of time sifting through images of one North Carolina statue after another, Max had yet to find any that struck him as noteworthy for the purposes of this spell. There were sculptures and busts of important figures in history, but nothing about them ignited his researching instincts. Nobody connected to witchcraft or old magic or strange legends. No person or story that would grab a witch's eye for this unique spell.

He acknowledged that such a connection was not a requirement. But there was no practical way they could intercept Madame Ti or whomever if they had to protect every statue in the state.

As a precaution, he checked the news for the last several months to make sure no statues had been violated with a decapitation. Nothing showed up, thankfully. He then turned to other types of depictions that could have the head removed — photographs and paintings and such. No luck, though.

From the frustrated frowns on Sandra and Brenda's faces, Max surmised they had not fared any better.

"I've got your answer," Drummond said as he slipped out of the bookshelves.

"You know where to find the second head?" Max asked.

"How would I know that? I've been in the Other trying to find our client. Then I spent time trying to work out what was wrong with her before she died. Cancer, by the way."

Sitting up in the couch, Brenda said, "That's not really decay, is it? Cancer is a multiplying of cells that gets out of control."

Sandra stood, taking advantage of the break in their studies, and headed toward their small kitchen area attached to the hall. "*Decay* is the closest word I could come up with in translation. Don't forget, all three of these descriptions are from other languages, and in the case of the first, we're dealing with an ancient witch language never even given a name."

"Then *disease* might be a good word, too?"

"Or *sickness* or *illness* or anything that relates to something slowly killing a person. Even *rot* might work."

Max jumped to his feet and rushed over to the whiteboard. Tapping the second line, he said, "This one was originally in French."

Leaning on the entrance to the hallway, Sandra said, "That's right. Why?"

"It suggests that those involved in the creation of this line were French. Probably from France. Or that the original victim was French. That narrows down the possibilities of people involved."

"To all of France," Drummond said. "Great thinking."

"It better not be France, if our local witches want that head. These lines must have an interpretation that works here in the United States or they're going to have to steal a head in some other country and smuggle it into North Carolina. I don't see that happening in the middle of a witch war."

"Like I said, you're doing some great thinking. What does this tell us?"

"The French had some presence in early American history — we would never have won the American Revolution without their help — but I'm willing to bet that the number of bizarre cases in our state involving a French person is going to be slim."

Max hustled over to his computer and hit up his favorite websites to search for the bizarre and strange in North Carolina. The others waited and watched. If they tried to speak, Max raised a single finger to hold them off, buying himself another five minutes before the next attempted interruption. When Drummond came in for disturbance number three, Max said, "I think I found something, but I need to make sure. Let me finish this, and then I promise I'll tell you what I know."

Fifteen minutes later, he sat back, hands laced behind his head, and kicked his feet up on his desk.

Drummond said, "You better start talking or all three of us are going to turn you into the next victim of the spell."

"Gather around," Max said, enjoying the satisfying release that always accompanied successful research. "I'm going to tell you the odd little story of Peter Ney."

Chapter 8

SANDRA SAT AT ONE END OF THE COUCH as Brenda scooted her legs out of the way. Drummond slid through the air, landing nearby. They waited for Max to take the hint. He would not be telling the tale of Peter Ney from his desk armed with a cocky grin. Groaning as he rose to his feet, he gathered his notes and joined the group by the whiteboard. He didn't plan on using it. Not his style. Although, Brenda had purchase different colored markers for it, and that appealed to his researcher brain. Organizing and compartmentalizing different types of data helped uncover connections often overlooked. Maybe the whiteboard would be a good idea, eventually. But not today.

Sticking with the tried and true, Max planted his feet in front of his audience, pulled together his final thoughts, and planned the best order in which to share what he had learned. As usual, he chose chronological. It always made the most sense to him.

Clearing his throat, he said, "In 1769, a man named Marshall Michel Ney was born in a small town in France."

"Sheesh," Drummond said. "You're starting with the man's lineage? We don't have all day."

Sandra repeated Drummond's words and Brenda laughed.

Max shot the ghost a look. "Just listen. He had a normal upbringing — at least, nothing unusual enough to be reported — and in 1787, at the ripe age of eighteen, he enlists in the French Army. The military turns out to be a perfect fit, and his career moves fast. He remains in the military when Napoleon takes over. As Emperor, Napoleon even is recorded as praising Ney for his courage and sharp mind. In fact, in 1804, Napoleon gives Ney the title Marshal of the Empire. That's a big deal."

"We kind of figured that out," Drummond said.

"Ney also showed himself to be a man of great honor. In 1812, when France attempted to invade Russia, they were forced into a horrible, tragic retreat out of the country. Ney earned the name *Last Frenchman in Russia* because he stayed with the rearguard until all his countrymen escaped. According to other sources the name was given by Napoleon and was actually *the bravest of the brave.* "

"Don't gloss over that," Drummond said, drifting closer. "The Russians decimated the French during that retreat. I believe more French died trying to get out of the country than died trying to fight their way in."

Max nodded, happy to see Sandra and Brenda had been hooked in as much as Drummond. He went on, "This isn't about the French-Russian war. If you want the details on that terrible experience, Tolstoy wrote a famous book on the subject — it's long but a good read."

"Quit showing off," Sandra said.

Shaking off the accusation with a smile, he said, "The important part here is that suffering through that carnage, Ney had started to doubt Napoleon. That doubt festers and two years later, Ney emerges on the scene again, this time helping lead a military revolt that restores Louis XVIII to power. For this, Ney earns the title of Duc d'Elchingen."

"You're butchering that French," Drummond said.

"Can you pronounce it better? No? Then I'll continue. In 1815, one year later, Napoleon is back. Ney's long history and deep feelings for the man have Ney join Napoleon once again. Those men had a complicated relationship, but here's the thing — Napoleon's comeback doesn't go well. He's defeated, and Ney is arrested for treason."

Drummond said, "I'm surprised they didn't nab him earlier."

"Even if they had wanted to, they really couldn't get away with it. Not when Ney was the poster boy for being a great solider."

"But now he's charged with treason."

"Yup. And on December 6, 1815, Marshall Michel Ney is executed by a firing squad."

Sandra said, "I take it that he got somebody pregnant shortly before his death."

"Not that I know of." Max grinned. This was where things got strange and interesting. "But about five years later, a man pops up in America working as a French language teacher, and he moves into the town of Cleaveland, North Carolina. His past is murky, which only pushes the bored to start digging, hoping to find something that would stir up trouble. They found it in this strangers name — Peter Stuart Ney."

"If you're saying —"

"Hold on. I'll get there. Now, Peter Ney was a solitary man, but in a small town in the 1820s, even the best hermit can't avoid the townspeople's notice — let alone their gossip. It's pretty clear that Peter loved to read every newspaper he could find, and he took special interest in anything involving France or Napoleon. He was a heavy drinker, too. Plenty of times he would get so drunk that he would talk of his old days in the French army.

"One day, he found out about a French fencing instructor who lived nearby in Mocksville. They did not like each other, or perhaps Ney wanted to prove himself, or maybe there was a woman involved. It's unclear, but they had a duel. Ney won. Barely broke a sweat, apparently.

"Two more things happened that drew people's attention. First, when the papers reported that Napoleon had died, Peter supposedly was so distraught, he tried to commit suicide. Second, since many French veterans of the Napoleon era had immigrated to America, it was not uncommon for some to pass through Peter's small town. Every last one that did, remarked on the uncanny resemblance between Peter and the beloved military man, Marshall Ney. It didn't take long from there."

With the enthusiasm of a kid engulfed by a great story, Brenda said, "Then they were the same person."

"A lot that points to the possibility. But there's more. When Marshall Ney was executed, many didn't believe it happened. There was widespread gossip that the whole thing had been faked. Ney was a Freemason, and it was thought that the Freemasons would never execute one of their own. Since many of those who ran the trial and the eventual sentence were also Freemasons, it was thought that they faked the execution.

"Peter Ney knew what people said of him, and he would laugh it off, mostly. One of the problems for him, though, was that Americans at that time were really into the entire France situation. A toppled monarchy and the fall of Napoleon fueled a lot of imaginations. Also, a lot of grifters. People would impersonate being exiled French aristocracy, exchanging a night of false stories from France for a hot meal and a warm bed.

"But the absolute dynamite that blew this rumor into the stratosphere came in 1846. On his deathbed, Peter Ney said, *I will not die with a lie on my lips! I am Marshall Ney of France!* At least, that's what was reported."

Drummond said, "That's quite a story. How exactly does this help us?"

"I'm glad you asked."

"I'll be gladder when you answer."

"There's a cemetery in France where Marshall Ney was buried. There's also a church here in Rowan County where Peter Ney was buried." Max pointed to the second line on the whiteboard — *a man who does not exist in dust and bone*. "If Peter Ney was Marshall Ney, then Peter Ney never existed. Either one of those graves is empty, or it's filled with somebody else bones."

Sandra said, "What if Peter Ney was really just a guy named Peter Ney? What if the report of his dying declaration is a lie?"

"Then we're back to square one. But no other story about a French person in North Carolina fits. I mean, there's no shortage of bizarre things that have happened around here involving a French person, but specifically a man, specifically one that somehow doesn't exist, specifically that —"

"We get it. This is the one."

Drummond said, "I suggest a road trip. Max and I should go out to Rowan County and find the man's grave. We can confirm the story. Worst case, we find out Max's is completely right but we're too late and the head is gone."

After hearing Sandra repeat the ghost's statement, Brenda said, "That's a good idea. Sandra and I can work on deciphering the last statement."

"Before we do that," Sandra said, "we should prepare a spell for Peter Ney's grave. Regardless of the truth, our culprit might still come for his head. I should be able to create something simple that could protect Ney's corpse. It won't stop a witch for long, but we could get a warning from the spell."

After a few minutes longer of planning, The Porter Agency split off to their assigned tasks. Max had no idea if they were any closer to stopping this spell and those behind it, but they were moving in a direction. Sometimes any direction was better than no direction. With any luck, even if they missed the target, they headed the right way.

Then again, nobody should trust Max's luck.

Chapter 9

THE THIRD CREEK PRESBYTERIAN CHURCH was a brick building just south of Statesville. Max found it with little trouble. Drummond stayed quiet most of the drive, which Max found disconcerting, but he let the ghost mull in peace. No point in wasting some pleasant silence.

Crap. Maybe more of Drummond's old ways had been rubbing off. Max had to be careful or he might end up a stoic tough guy.

The church's attached cemetery spread over several acres of grassy land. Short rows of graves marked families and eras, but much of the land lay untouched. A farm stretched to the north and a vineyard to the west. Woods formed a wall in the distance except on the eastern side, where a thin layer of trees separated the church from a stretch of homes. Add a parking lot and a simple, rural road, and this place screamed of small-town religion.

Before they exited the car, Max could tell Drummond did not want to be there. Cemeteries and hospitals were filled with ghosts. For Sandra, it could be disorienting, claustrophobic, and overwhelming. For Drummond, as far as Max understood, it was more akin to standing in Times Square on New Year's Eve without all the happy partying. Just crowded, noisy, and annoying.

Yet Drummond acted as if he were ready for a lovely stroll, about to enjoy the cooling evening air. Without looking at his partner, Drummond said, "More land than graves, and it looks like most here have moved on. All in all, this is the nicest cemetery I've visited in years." He tipped his hat to some ghosts Max would never see.

At least, locating Peter Ney's resting place turned out to be easy. A red brick shelter had been erected around the entire grave. Glass windows allowed mourners and visitors to peek in. The tomb had a brick piece that bore a plaque which read:

> *In memory of Peter Stuart Ney, a native of France and soldier of the French Revolution under Napoleon Bonaparte, who departed this life November 15, 1846, aged 77 years.*

"That's interesting," Max said. "If Peter was actually seventy-seven, then go back from 1846 and you end up right at 1769."

Drummond said, "The year Marshall Ney was born."

The sun lowered in a burst of pink hues as Max scanned the graves for any dusk visitors. "I hate to ask," he said and waited for an old pickup to rumble by.

"Let me guess — you want me to stick my head into that tomb, see if ol' Petey is there."

"That's why we came out here, isn't it?"

"Was this your plan from the start? Make sure I come along so you don't have to get your hands dirty?"

"I suppose I could get a shovel, break the glass, and start digging. Hopefully get the answers we need before I get arrested for grave robbery."

"No need to be a smartass about it."

Max pulled back. "Sorry. I thought we were doing our normal bit of banter."

Resetting his hat, Drummond shrugged it off. "Nothing funny about disturbing a corpse. Why don't you, at least, get Sandra's warning ward going?"

"I was going to, but there's no point if there's nothing in that grave to protect."

"I said I'd go down and take care of it. No need to be so pesky."

"First, you didn't say that. Second, this case is clearly important to you. It's got you twisted up tight. Now, I don't want to pry, but is this headless witch somebody you knew?"

"It's nothing like that."

"You can tell me. It might help."

"What'll help is if I get us some answers." Drummond turned to face an empty area at the side that Max presumed had some onlooker ghosts. Drummond confirmed this by removing his hat. "You'll have to forgive me sirs, ma'am, but I'm sort of an officer of the law, and I'm afraid I need to do a rather unpleasant task. You may wish to look away."

With that, Drummond slipped into the tomb and dropped his head into the dirt. Max stepped toward a different grave and bowed his head as if lost in some deep memory about the deceased — just in case a caretaker poked out of a shed or some kids walked out of the surrounding woods. He knew it was unlikely, but Max thought it better to keep the habit than get caught slacking on the job.

When Drummond returned, his dreadful gaze told the whole story. "The good news is you were right. Bad news is we're too late."

"No head?"

"It would've been a skull, but yeah, Ney's skeleton is minus an important part."

"Damn."

Max looked through the tomb's window at the flat patch of earth. To remove that skull, a person would have had to break into the tomb, dig up the coffin, and crack it open. That would have created a huge mess. Yet he saw no dirt, no glass shards, nothing to indicate any damage. If, however, the thief was a witch and used a spell to extract the skull, then perhaps she could have taken the skull without leaving any trace behind. Or she had help. "You think somebody in maintenance might be in on it, too?"

"It's possible," Drummond said, "but why go to that trouble? If we can assume that whoever stole the skull is also responsible for murdering a witch and cutting her head off, then our culprit didn't show any fear about leaving a dead, headless body out in the open. Why would they care about cleaning up evidence from robbing a centuries-old grave?"

"That barn was not easily found."

"But it would've been found eventually. The person doing this doesn't care about how things look afterward."

Max drummed his fingers on the glass as he gazed inside the tomb once more. "We're dealing with at least two people then. Like you said, the person who killed Pauline and cut off her head is brazen. They don't care about evidence or leaving behind clues. None of it. But Peter Ney's skull — that's different. That was carefully extracted."

"I can agree with that. We're definitely looking for at least two."

"Then there's no bribing the maintenance staff."

"This was done with a spell. Had to have been. Sandra could rattle off a dozen that might've been used. Don't know if that's important now, unless it'll help us find the bastard, but it should at least ..." Drummond gazed across the plot of land toward the parking lot. "Will you look at that?"

Max spotted the oddity right away. A woman dressed in filthy, incongruous layers leaning against a Mercedes and tapping away on her phone.

"How did we miss her?" Max said.

"She must've just arrived."

"No. We've been keeping track, checking our surroundings regularly."

"Well, she's there, ain't she?"

"I can see that. Maybe she's a ghost and materialized like you do."

"Is that car a ghost, too?"

"Then how do you explain her?"

"Evidence says we screwed up at some point. Probably when you were distracting me with all your yapping."

They watched as the woman lifted her phone in front of her face. She kept her focus in their direction. Max peeked at his partner.

"Yeah," Drummond said, "I get it. She's taking pictures of you."

After a moment, she pocketed the phone, stared directly at

Max, then walked down one of the short rows of graves. The Mercedes drove off. Max had never noticed a driver, and as he headed in the direction of this woman, he made a mental note to start working on his situational awareness again. Like most skills, he could get rusty if relying purely on muscle memory.

If he had been tailing with the intent of not being seen, this would have been a horrible place to do so. Few of the gravestones reached a height above the waist and most of the cemetery lacked trees or any other objects to hide behind. But he had no need to hide. She clearly knew he was there. She even glanced back a few times, seemingly to make sure that he followed. When she reached the end of the row, she continued across the empty field.

"That's not good," Drummond said.

"Should we let her go?"

"We won't learn what she's doing here, and if she doesn't know something about Ney's missing head, I'll quit this business."

"Then we keep going."

"But be cautious."

Max trudged forward into the thickening grass. The chittering of evening insects formed a constant background noise. This was stupid. He considered turning around and driving home. Once he explained to Sandra what and who they had found at the cemetery, she could offer some perspective. Together, they could return and march out into this field to figure out what this woman had wanted.

Or he could drive home and leave Drummond to spy on the woman. After all, whenever she looked back, she only motioned toward Max. If she could see a ghost, she played up her ignorance quite well.

But no. He would not abandon his partner, and he would not run away to his wife. Failing to soothe his dying mother had been enough for one year. Drummond and Sandra needed to know Max would hold his side up strong, and at the moment, that meant finding out how this woman ducking into the tree line connected to this case.

The temperature dropped in the shade of the woods, but it did not account for the chill Max felt as he walked further away from the openness of the cemetery. That brought an amused snort. He never thought he'd wish to be in a cemetery.

Up ahead, the woman moved with surety, darting around trees and over large rocks as if she knew the path well. When she finally stopped and faced Max, the air grew even colder. She was younger than he had thought. Younger and fiercer.

"Don't move," Drummond said.

Max wanted to point out that she couldn't hear the ghost, but then he understood — Drummond was talking to him. Max halted. His eyes searched for the threat beyond the woman. When he saw nothing, he narrowed his focus upon her. What had Drummond seen?

"I've heard about you," the woman said, her eyes wide and wild. "Max Porter and, I assume, your pet ghost is here, too."

Drummond bristled — as much as a ghost could. When Max saw what kept his partner at bay, he tried to keep his composure in check, too. A small witch's casting circle had been dug into the ground, and the symbols of a spell lined the edges. Just large enough for this woman to stand inside.

This woman, this witch, had come into these woods either before Max's arrival or from another direction, prepared the circle, left the woods unseen, slipped into the parking lot, and took a picture of Max before luring him to this spot. Thinking through it, Max wondered about that photograph. "You're working for somebody. Sent my picture to them."

"Working with my sisters is no work at all. Isn't that the grand advice for life? Love what you do, and you'll never work a day."

Max faked a chuckle. "Sisters, huh? What coven are you with?"

"You don't need to know anything but this — stop pursuing your case."

"What case is that? We often have more than one."

A soft glow emitted from the circle at her feet. "You shouldn't have followed me here."

"You lured me here." Max planted one foot behind him,

ready to launch at her and disrupt her spell.

She shook her head with dramatic flair. "My world does not center around you. Leave here. I have my own business to attend."

"I'm not sure I believe you."

"Leave this alone. When we're done, the witch war will be over and peace will be restored. Keep meddling, and your wife will become a widow."

The light of the circle brightened. Drummond dashed aside, yelling, "Take cover!"

Max jumped behind the nearest large tree as the area splashed with stark light. As if at a professional photo shoot, flashes strobed the forest. Trees and shadows cut into Max's view like hard stills from a low-budget horror film. A crack of thunder erupted though the clouds had been clear, and a crisp odor of charred leaves drifted in the air.

Peeking from behind the tree, Max saw a lot of smoke and no witch. Drummond emerged, too, looking around the casting circle. Whatever she had done, the circle had burned into the ground.

Max pulled out his phone and snapped a shot of the spell. Sandra would be able to piece it together later.

"Who the heck was that?" Max said.

"Never seen her before."

"At least we stopped whatever spell she was going to do. I doubt her plan was to take us into the woods, have a chat, and disappear."

Drummond gestured to the casting circle. "I'd be more concerned that this is the second time your life has been threatened today."

"One thing I've learned from you — when the threats start coming, it means you're on the right track."

"Absolutely, partner."

Walking back towards the cemetery, Max sent the photo to his wife. He added a text suggesting they all meet up for dinner to compare notes. Just because a witch thought he was on the right track didn't mean he knew anything at all. The Porter

Agency had to catch up. Based on the rising threats, they needed to catch up fast.

Chapter 10

THEY MET AT XCARET, a Mexican restaurant on 4th Street in downtown Winston-Salem. While the food was reliably wonderful, the décor had been created in the fever dream of an artist with no regard for the word subtle. Bright, bold colored vistas of Mexico — the coasts, the villages, the people — had been painted on the walls, benches, and tables. The steady waltz of mariachi music pumped out of strategically hung speakers. Sizzling fajitas blended with the rumble of conversations, and the luscious aromas filing out of the kitchen blended with the strong scents of the plates set before eager customers.

Max, Sandra, and Brenda attacked their food, ignoring the server's warning about hot plates. Nobody in the group had a meal since breakfast. For the next several minutes, they each focused on eating. Drummond floated above the table — the packed restaurant offered no other space for him without causing somebody an icy brush with the dead.

"You could have had this food delivered," the ghost said.

"What's it matter to him?" Brenda said after Max shared Drummond's comment. "We need food, we need a change of scenery, we need a break. This checks all those boxes."

Sandra had already devoured half her massive burrito as she said, "He can still smell the food and see it, but he can't eat it. If we were back at the office, he would be able to hide in the bookshelf until we finished."

"I don't hide from food," Drummond said.

"Watching us eat is bad enough, but here he is stuck smelling and watching everybody else's meals, too." Peeking upward, she added, "But we rarely put him in this position, so he should know that we don't take it lightly."

"Doll, I'd never blame you for being inconsiderate. I'm sure this was Max's idea."

Wiping his mouth, Max told the ladies about Peter Ney's grave and the witch they found there. He pulled out his phone and located the picture of the spell in the woods. "Did you come up with anything about this?" He slid the phone to his wife.

Sandra munched on a tortilla chip as she studied the picture again. Max squirmed when a glob of salsa fell off the chip and narrowly missed his phone. Before he said anything, though, she cocked her head and became far more engrossed in the picture. She then handed the phone to Brenda.

"It looks like an illusion spell," she said.

"An illusion?" Max said. "She didn't disappear to somewhere?"

"She was probably standing right in front of you, holding still so you wouldn't hear her."

"How come our chilly friend didn't see her?"

Drummond said, "Ghosts don't get magic sight. Not like that, anyway. And call me your *chilly friend* again, you might find out how cold I can make you."

"From what I've learned," Brenda said, "actually transporting is much harder than you'd think."

Sandra nodded. "The interesting thing about this spell is that it's still very old magic. There are modern transportation spells. Extremely difficult magic — I can't do it — but it is possible. But this witch used a casting circle with the symbols and configuration that suggest a spell from the days when witchcraft was beginning to step out of the pagan, ritualistic era and into a more formalized study. My guess is she was out there practicing. Getting in touch with this kind of magic."

"She just happened to be at the cemetery with Peter Ney and us?"

"Maybe she took the head. Maybe she followed you to take your picture. The spell part though, that looks like practice to me. You don't go collecting heads unless you're planning something big. The witches involved need to be at their best."

Pocketing his phone, Max said, "Bringing us right back to the

Brotherhood or Madame Ti."

"I've been thinking on the Brotherhood," Drummond said. "I don't care how stupid they might be, if they've reorganized and want to get back in the action, they'll wait until this witch war is over. They jump in now, they'll be too weak. They're likely to get destroyed."

"Then just Madame Ti."

With an unconvinced shrug, Sandra pushed aside her plate. "Brenda and I worked through the third ingredient line, and we think we're on the right track."

Brenda said, "The line reads: *The head of the newly reborn, fresh and full of lost life*. We worried this referenced a baby, but they aren't *reborn*."

"Also, baby sacrifices are mostly a myth. Something dramatic for movies and stories and tales to scare kids into behaving. Even if such things did happen in the past, witches don't go around stealing newborns for sacrifice anymore. If we did, people would notice. Dead babies are too salacious a story. And with the internet today, the entire world would know."

"We tried a few other ideas, but we finally cracked it when we thought about how in some religions, when you join, they treat it like a birth."

Max said, "We're looking for a born-again Christian?"

"A born-again witch."

Sandra crunched another salsa-drenched chip. "Some covens treat new members as if they have been reborn a witch."

"The line says *newly reborn*, so we think it's talking about a witch new to one of these covens. The rest of it *fresh and full of lost life* means the head can't be from a corpse that died years ago. It's got to be new, fresh."

Drummond said, "They'll have to cut that head off during the spell-casting."

"Exactly. Whoever the next head belongs to, she's still alive."

"Then I'm going back to the Other. If I can find a newly dead witch that belonged to a coven, we'll know that coven is seeking a replacement — a newly reborn."

After Drummond disappeared — probably thrilled to get

away from the tantalizing aromas in the restaurant — Max said, "Even if he finds a witch or two in the Other, their covens would have to believe in this rebirth idea."

"A lot of them do," Sandra said. "Too many to narrow it down that easily."

"Then we've got plenty of research still to do tonight."

Rubbing her eyes, Brenda said, "I'm sorry to do this to you, but I have to work in the morning. You know, so I can pay my rent, this food, electricity."

Currently, she handled clerical duties at a real estate office. Max and Sandra wanted to find the money to hire Brenda, but with the prices of everything rising, they couldn't pull together enough to make it worthwhile for her. Someday, they promised themselves. Hopefully, Brenda wouldn't leave them before they had the chance.

Max didn't think she would. She loved witchcraft, and Sandra was a good teacher. But then, nothing was permanent. Life was change.

Reaching across the table and clutching his wife's wrist as if to hold her in place, he said, "Looks like it's just the Porters tonight."

Sandra chose to drive home, and Max had no choice but to follow. He would have preferred going to the office. Or another restaurant. Or, heck, a roller rink. Anywhere but home. He pictured that closed bedroom door and shivered. Yet shortly after leaving Xcaret, he stood in his kitchen and set up a workspace at the table while Sandra cracked open a bottle of pinot grigio.

"I know you're still going through a lot about your mother," she said, after they each finished a glass. "I've been trying to be supportive."

"It's appreciated."

He kept his head in his laptop, focusing on searching through the internet for anything that could help them. Of course, witch covens did not advertise on Facebook, so he had to be more creative in his search techniques. He also had to push away the thoughts invading his mind — mainly, what was Sandra trying to say by bringing up his mother?

The longer they clacked at their keyboards, the greater the tension grew in the air. Whether he imagined that tension or she felt it, too, didn't matter. He had to know.

Pushing his laptop away, he said, "You have something you want to say. What is it?"

Years of marriage stopped her from a fruitless denial. Instead, she sipped her wine and looked upon him with care and concern. "You need to deal with your mother's death. Fully. Her door — that's not a good idea. Even if we had a bigger house, even if we had a mansion and one room made no difference, I wouldn't like it. There's a bad energy that consumes a house if you let a room become a tomb."

"It won't be forever."

"That's why I didn't say anything. You need to grieve in your way. But I don't want you to get lost in that grief. I want you to talk about it with me. Y'know, that's part of what marriage is for."

"This case is helping. Gives me something to focus on."

They returned to their research. Max clicked on a few links but eventually conceded that the basic internet would not provide any answers. That meant turning to the dark web. While he expected that accessing the dark web — surprisingly easy once he had learned how — would provide better results, he also loathed the idea. Some of the most useful sites regarding the activities of witches also catered to other, more disturbing interests. Max had never clicked on any of these perverse links, but reading of their existence, knowing that there were people eager to click into those depths, always left him feeling tainted.

While he surfed those treacherous waters, Sandra dove into the witch dark web — a dark web within the dark web. Waters he wouldn't dare enter. Peeking over the lip of his laptop, he saw her concentrating as if studying for a math test — focused, determined, but at ease. Just some serious work that needed to be done.

"I wish I could be as casual as you," he said.

Sandra snapped her attention at him, her face bruised with shock. "Nothing about your mother's death has been casual."

"What? No, not about —"

"She wasn't my mother, and we had a strained relationship, at best, but that doesn't mean I'm heartless. You'll have to forgive me that I'm not as distraught as you, but I love you, so when you hurt, I hurt." She gulped the remainder of the wine in her glass and poured more. "I think Drummond had the right idea. We should bury this in work. I'm guessing that's why he found this case."

Max's eyebrows raised. "You think he went looking for a headless ghost?"

"He cares about you. Ever since your mother passed away, he's been acting a bit more stoic than usual. Her death didn't only touch you. It hit us all."

"Not you. If not for me, you wouldn't care."

Her jaw clenched. At a measured pace, she said, "Just because I'm your wife and I'm the one willing to put up with your crap while you go through this hard time, don't think that gives you permission to say any stupid thought you have."

"You're not denying it." Heat flashed through him as he pushed back his chair and crossed his arms. "When she died, it felt sudden. I know she was with us for a long time, but that last MS attack was like any other. She should have been fine. Yet in only a few hours we went from taking her to the hospital on another run to me holding her as she stared into the unknown. Except it isn't unknown. We know, don't we? We've seen some of the afterlife. At least, the parts that get left behind here."

Taking a deep breath, Sandra put out her hand. "I know how hard it is to lose a parent. I've lost both. You never really knew your father that well, and after all that Aunt Jane business, I get it — your mother was the closest blood family you had. But your family isn't over. I'm here. PB and J are out there in the world, succeeding, because of us. They are our family. Even Drummond is our family."

"She was your mother-in-law. That made her family to you,

too."

"She hated me." The words banged into the walls, startling Max with their vehemence. Sandra went on, "We pretended to tolerate each other at times, but she absolutely, one hundred percent, no doubt about it, despised me. If I were dead now and she was alive, she would have been thrilled to be rid of me."

Max wanted to object, but Sandra stood and placed a hand on her hip. "And your mother never hid it from me," she said. "From the first time I met her, she decided I wasn't good enough for her precious boy. You saw some of it, but most of her disdain she held in check until you weren't around. I didn't want to tell you any of this, I didn't want to ruin your memory of her, but I refuse to let her death be her way of making a final attack on our marriage. Yes, honey, she hated me, and I hated her. You'll have to forgive me for not feeling the least bit sad that she's gone. I only feel bad for you. I hate seeing you suffer for her when she caused so much strain to our relationship."

Breathing hard, Sandra lowered to her seat and returned to her laptop. She spoke softer, with care. "I shouldn't have said any of that. I love you. I just don't want to see you hurt."

He didn't know what to say. His mind had locked, overwhelmed by Sandra's passionate flood of words. Without a clear path forward, without a clear thought to guide him, he opted for the familiar, the useful, the safe — he returned to the research.

In the silence that followed, he could feel Sandra peek over at him periodically. Her eyes weighed on his chest, his shoulders, his mind, but he couldn't say anything yet. She needed to hear that he forgave her outburst, that he understood what she had meant, and though it was harsh, he accepted that she had spoken from her heart with love for him. Yet the longer he said nothing, the more guilty he felt at putting her in a tough position. That would come out, too, if he spoke. He would say he was sorry, but he did not want to apologize for anything.

An hour of tense silence crept by. When Sandra finally spoke up, Max braced for another dive into this argument. Instead, she said, "I think I found something."

Chapter 11

MIDNIGHT NEARED. As they drove across the city and headed north on Route 89 in the direction of Hanging Rock State Park, Max reviewed the research in his head, double-checking their conclusions. If he found any mistake, he could turn around and forget this risky move. After all, knocking on the door of a coven unannounced and on the cusp of the first witching hour begged for trouble.

But he couldn't find fault in Sandra's work. The witch community — specifically the North Carolina witch community — maintained databases of all known, active witches and covens. This website had been established back in the days of the Hull family's dominance over magic usage in the state, and several witches decided to keep it running. Nobody knew who these tech-savvy witches were, though Sandra suggested it might be Madame Novak and her sisters at Haven House, but most agreed that the database was a good thing. Even the witch community had to accept surveillance in the modern world.

Max understood the thinking a little. Throughout history, witches had operated in isolation. When they found each other and formed covens, those covens kept secret, hidden, buried. It was too dangerous to reveal the truth about any of what they knew. People tended to react poorly when they learned that magic existed.

But this database allowed a measure of contact that felt safe. In the past, if a witch had trouble with a spell and lacked the ability to get to Haven House — if she even knew Haven House existed — she might struggle for years, reinventing techniques that others had perfected long ago. With the website, she could locate those who knew, reach out, and hopefully, get answers or guidance. Since the website marked witches that welcomed queries and those that wished to remain alone, nobody would be bothered that didn't want to be.

"From this," Sandra had said back in the kitchen, "I drew up a list of covens that were either newly formed or had a new member in the last six months."

"I guess that includes the Lennon coven."

"Pauline's death did create an opening, but nobody's filled it yet. Not according to what I can find."

"That's good. I'd hate to deal with Madame Lennon when we haven't solved the first part yet."

"That's the thing I realized — the second part of the line: *fresh and full of lost life*. We assume that means the death of the witch and the cutting of her head must be freshly done. But a lot of witch books have lines like this in multiple layers."

"As a security measure?"

"Exactly. We write in dead languages and languages we invented to protect our secrets from misuse." To Max's doubtful expression, she added, "At least, misuse as defined by us."

"I take it that giving the written spells multiple layers of meaning is another way to shield your knowledge from unwelcome readers."

"If we accept that the lines about these heads might also carry layers of meaning, then *fresh* might refer to more than the severed head. I think it might mean the coven itself."

That alone would not have been enough to get them in a car heading into the woods late at night, but Sandra took that idea and put it against her list of covens. She found three that had been formed in the last two months. But Max noticed something that plucked at his mind.

"What about incomplete covens? Are they in this list?"

"Like covens looking for members?"

"If we want the freshest, newest coven, we need to find one that has twelve members and is about to add the thirteenth to be completed. That would be a new coven and a reborn witch."

A few clicks and Sandra smiled. "Only one fits. The Astrum coven."

"Let's go."

"Now?"

Max glanced around the kitchen. "You really want to stay here?"

And so they drove through the dark, allowing the chilly night air to prickle their unease. He had suggested they leave the house to put distance between them and their fight — as if they could escape themselves. He tried to push away those thoughts, let the miles clear his head, but that left him thinking about where they headed — a coven.

He had encountered enough covens to know one truth — no two were alike. Some acted like a lost hippie commune. Others reveled in the accumulation of secret knowledge. Some sought access to power and riches. Others harbored violent tendencies. As Max turned onto Dodgetown Road and headed into a more remote area, he only knew that this coven hadn't been around long enough to establish a reputation. They could be anything.

When the GPS had them turn onto Pitzer Road and then make a sharp right onto Duggins Road, Max discovered a narrow cut of pavement through the forest, yet no signs of people. No homes. No service stations. Not even powerlines.

They made a left off the paved road and off the official GPS map. Trees leaned overhead while branches slapped the side of the car. Moving slowly to avoid the larger holes in the dirt, Max wanted to make a U-turn and leave this place behind. But there wasn't room for such a maneuver. More than that, though, Max noticed how Sandra sat forward, her face close to the windshield as she devoured every detail of their approach.

To her, a new coven must have seemed exciting. All the reasons Max had for fearing this new gaggle of witches were the same reasons Sandra's fingers tapped her knee, the same reasons her eyes grew wider.

"There," she said, pointing to a clearing off to the left.

Max entered a small parking area in front of a stone and wood building that reminded him of Haven House. Other than a floodlight covering the lead-up to the house, there were no lights on. Sandra exited the car, and as Max followed, he inhaled the rich aroma of a campfire filtering through the trees. Orange firelight danced on the leaves and tree trunks behind the house, and a melodic chanting drifted with the scents in the air.

"Looks like the coven is busy tonight," Max said.

"It is the witching hour." Sandra gazed upward. "There's almost a full moon, too. I imagine a lot of covens are busy tonight."

She started off toward the side of the house, but Max reached for her arm.

"We don't know what we'll find back there." His heart clutched in his chest. "Look, in case things go bad —"

"Max Porter, are you afraid?"

"Absolutely. You should be, too."

"After everything we've faced over the years, I'm not too concerned about a new coven."

"You are not invincible."

"Don't worry, I take this seriously. I won't let my guard down."

He shuffled his feet as he searched for the right words. "About earlier."

She kissed his cheek. "We were venting. Or I was. Mostly. It's part of dealing with a major death, and I'm sure it's not our last scuffle over your mother."

Max wanted to leave it at that. It sounded good. But he saw the twitch in her eye. Sandra was nervous, too. "I'm sorry that I pushed your buttons," he said. "I will get through this, but I need things to be right between us."

"They were never wrong."

"You know what I mean. There's a lot I feel bad about. I don't know if I was a very good son with all this MS stuff."

"Hon, you brought her into our house. You took care of her. Pushed her to live a life in her final years instead of sitting there waiting to die. You cleaned up after her, you bandaged her, and I can't even count the number of times you took her to the hospital. On top of that, we paid for most of her bills. I think you've done plenty."

"Then why couldn't I give her any peace? She was so

frightened at the end."

Sandra looked toward the coven house and the firelight flickering in the back. The singing grew louder. "Maybe we should go home. Talk through this some more."

"You know we can't. If this coven is the right one, they need to be warned what's coming. I feel guilty enough about my mother, I don't need a decapitated witch on my conscience, too."

She wrapped her arms around him. "You've done nothing to feel guilty about. You were a great son to her, better than she deserved, and while I was never emotionally close to her, I do feel sorrow. For you. Because I love you."

He kissed her. "I'll never stop loving you."

"That's the right thing to say. Always." She stepped back and faced the house. "Now, let's go talk to some witches."

Chapter 12

STROLLING AROUND THE SIDE OF THE HOUSE, Sandra linked her arm with Max. He had always enjoyed the feeling of having her on his arm. It gave him a boost — in warmth, in strength, in confidence. He could walk anywhere with her and sense that he had won the lottery when he met her. All the proof hung on his arm at that moment. Even as they turned the corner and saw thirteen witches dancing around a fire, Max felt shielded by Sandra. However, another part of him warned that courage did not equate protection. No matter how good Sandra proved at witchcraft, they still walked toward thirteen other witches. Not a fair fight, if it came to that.

The witches wore black cloaks with red inner-linings. Some wore nothing else. Others draped themselves in flowing white gowns that glowed with the intense light from the fire — not a simple campfire but a bonfire to rival many high school beach parties. While most of the women looked young, some barely in their twenties, one woman stood tall with her back to the flames, her wrinkled skin stark in the shadows. She wore the same black cloak, the same white gown, but she had the front folded down to reveal her sagging, aged chest. Symbols had been painted across her skin.

This would be the head of the coven, and Sandra dropped Max's arm as she strode ahead. Max held back. Traditionally, witchcraft belonged to women, and though he could hear their conversation, he was not an accepted participant.

"Sandra Porter, welcome," the older woman said.

The rest of the coven stopped dancing and singing. Silhouetted by the shimmer of firelight, backed by the crackling wood, they stood straight and watched. The old woman approached with the stern expression of a nun forced to teach math to a bunch of grade schoolers.

"I am Mother Sun," she said, gazing down. Max thought she must be six-and-a-half feet tall. Her nose curved toward her mouth which only made her downward eyeline more severe. She went on, "I guessed that our little coven would one day grab your attention, but I did not think it would be so soon."

Sandra said, "Why? Are you planning something that would involve The Porter Agency?"

"I was under the impression that your work involved the more ambitious covens. We're not like that. Not yet." She tilted her head to glance behind Sandra. "You must be Max."

"The one and only." Max kept his face as stern as Mother Sun's.

At the snap of her fingers, one of the women scurried forward, adjusting her cloak to cover her bare body. "This is Sister Mercury. She'll be happy to get you a drink or a late-night bite while you wait."

"Wait for what?"

"This evening's work isn't done."

Sandra said, "We don't need anything. But we have an urgent message, and then we'll be gone."

Since Mother Sun had barely moved her face during the entire exchange, when her eyes narrowed, the act felt as if a massive shift had occurred. "Do not mistake my coven's youth for inexperience. We are not weak, and we will not take kindly to threats."

The sisters moved forward like an army ready to defend their general.

Sandra held her ground. "I didn't say anything about threatening you."

"No threats from us," Max said. "But you are in danger."

With sharp stabs of her hands, Mother Sun said, "Sister Mars, check that the house is locked. "Sister Jupiter, Sister Venus, revisit our wards. Make sure they're intact." As the sisters hustled off to satisfy their orders, Mother Sun returned her powerful glare to the Porters. "What is this danger?"

"There are powerful witches," Sandra said, "and even more powerful covens who may be involved in the casting of a highly dangerous, unstable spell. Old magic. Beyond blood magic. The spell is called the *veohoxal*, and —"

"We're not concerned with what other covens cast."

"You should be. Because this spell requires the severed head of a new member to a new coven. We've done the legwork to know that the Astrum Coven is most likely a target. Who is your newest member?"

Without looking back at her witches, Mother Sun said, "That would be Sister Moon. But she has nothing to fear."

"I promise you, she does. These covens are serious."

Max said, "Are you aware there's a witch war going on?"

As if annoyed by a fly, Mother Sun said, "Living in a remote area doesn't mean we are backwoods people. We are intelligent and informed."

"Then you know Madame Ti and her Coven of Ti have already killed witches. They won't hesitated to slaughter everyone here in order to get to Sister Moon."

"The Coven of Ti is incomplete. Mine is not. We have more strength than her."

"We're not sure who is behind this," Sandra said. "And if the database says that the Coven of Ti is incomplete, that doesn't make it true. Madame Ti might be withholding that information so covens like yours fail to see her true menace."

Taking one step closer, looming over, Mother Sun said, "That's possible, but true or not, I'll take that witch over you, Mrs. Sandra Porter. You and your husband have quite a reputation in our community. You've caused us a lot of harm."

"We've helped free you from the shackles of the Hull family, and we've helped to protect witches from public scrutiny."

"That hardly negates the witches you've had a hand in killing. Or the spells you've blocked. Or even your unwelcome intrusion into our world's politics. You dare hide behind a few helpful nuggets you've thrown at us when the truth is that you and your Porter Agency have caused witches far more damage."

Max stepped between the two women. To Mother Sun, it

probably looked like a chauvinistic move, but spells took time to cast. During all this talking, Max suspected the other coven witches prepared their own spells. He wanted Sandra to have a chance.

"We didn't come here to fight," he said, noting the closed eyes of several witches — probably chanting up some way to rip out his entrails. "This was a courtesy. We don't want to see any of you die, and we didn't know if you were aware of this ancient spell or that it involved cutting off the heads of witches. If you don't want to hear it or you don't want to hear it from us, no problem."

"We'll handle it ourselves."

"We weren't offering to help. Only to give you a heads up — no pun intended."

Mother Sun's nostrils flared. She appeared to play out an argument in her head, but perhaps she also prepared a spell. However, before Max could interrupt her train of thought, she spoke directly to Sandra. "While your agency has a disturbing reputation amongst us, I have also heard many things about you and your witchcraft — things that demand grudging respect. Like you, the Astrum Coven has no wish to fight. If your purpose here is what you say, then you have delivered your message. You can go."

Max raised a warning finger. "You need to believe us. One of your witches might die."

"We all care greatly for each other. You do not need to worry."

Off to the side, standing at the edge of the group, one woman in a white gown looked less sure than the others. She had an oval face and dark hair that accentuated her fears. She was the one. Sister Moon. Max had no doubt. He moved towards her, but Mother Sun blocked his way with one step.

"No matter how strong a witch your wife is, no matter how much respect she has earned over the years, don't start thinking she's untouchable. Thirteen of us will destroy one of her. And you — what can you really do?"

Tightening his fists, he thought he might answer her with a

strong blow to the jaw. But a soft hand touched his shoulder. Sandra said, "Come, hon. It's time to go."

Max locked eyes with Mother Sun, hoped to make her feel unsteady, but her stoicism never wavered. Sandra applied pressure on his shoulder until he backed away. Each small step pounded as hard as his heart against his chest. They kept their eyes on the coven. Max did not trust these ladies and watched their hands with extra care. If he spotted any glow of magic, he would — well, he didn't have much of a plan other than running, but at least they wouldn't take him by surprise.

Once he and Sandra reached the corner of the house, once they were out of sight, they whirled around and bolted for the car.

Chapter 13

BREATHING HARD as he slammed into the driver's seat, Max fumbled out his keys. Every bottled nerve released with a growled swear. Sandra flopped down next to him as she yanked the door shut. When the engine turned over, he flicked on the headlights. Sister Moon stood in front of the car, her hands out begging them to stop, her eyes shimmering with the same terror Max felt pulsing through his veins.

They gawked at each other. The idle of the car the only sound. Until the witch rushed around the side and opened the back door. She slid across the seat, situating herself in the middle.

Sandra shifted to face Sister Moon, but Max remained forward with his hands sweating on the wheel. He peeked at the rearview mirror and had to remind himself to keep breathing, keep thinking.

"Please, stay here," Sister Moon said, her voice silken, like the kind of person who wanted other to think she used the word *summer* as a verb.

Max said, "We're not exactly wanted."

Folding her hands over one knee, Sandra leaned back like they were college friends hanging out. "You're the new member, aren't you?"

"I am, so don't lie to me. This veohoxal spell — is it real?"

"Very real. At least, it's real enough that it was written down. Whether it will perform as promised is always an unknown with spellbooks and spells as old as this one."

Sister Moon peeked out the left window, then the right. "But somebody is trying to cast it. They're coming to grab me, take me somewhere, and cut off my head, right?"

"That's why you should be with your sisters."

"They barely know me." Sister Moon poked Max's shoulder. "Are you ever going to drive? We should get out of here."

Max said, "I thought you wanted us to stay. Now you want us leave?"

"I want whatever's going to keep me alive. Either go back and convince Mother Sun to listen to you or take me to somebody who will listen."

"You need to trust your coven," Sandra said. "They're your family now. They'll protect you."

"You've obviously never been in a coven."

Max said, "Just because my wife hasn't been in a coven, doesn't mean you shouldn't listen to her. We've had a lot of experience with this kind of thing."

"If my coven is so wonderful and protective, then how come nobody's come out front to see where I am? See if I'm okay? I'm sure there are covens that are sisterhoods of great strength, but not this one. These women act more like a mean girl sorority. They spend their time hazing me. When they're not doing that, they gossip about sex. I'm not even sure they all believe in any of this." She slumped back and looked out the side. "I don't know what it was like for you, but when I first discovered magic, saw how wonderful, how powerful it could be, I knew I had to find a coven. I needed witches that could teach me. I know they exist. I've read about them. But this one — Mother Sun is too selfish. I think she formed the coven to focus on her, to celebrate her. Whatever coven she came from screwed her up, and she's going to do the same to the rest of us."

Flashes of light dazzled from behind the house. Between the surrealness of those lights and the whiplash swing from meeting the coven to meeting Sister Moon, Max sat in the driver's seat unsure whether to shift into drive or turn off the car.

Sandra must have felt the same because she said, "If these women are so horrible to you, then why join them?"

"Any coven is better than no coven."

"It may feel that way, but plenty of witches never belong to a coven and are fine. I'm one of them."

"You've got a husband, a career, a life beyond being a witch.

Not me. If I leave this coven, where else will I go? Witches are not welcome in the world. Never have been. At least with this coven, I know where I stand. They're bitches but they're my bitches. And I'm theirs. That's the way it's supposed to be."

"But I'm a witch, too. I'm proof that you don't need them."

"Do you walk around wearing a T-shirt that say *I am a witch*? When you fill out forms that ask your occupation, do you say you're a witch? No. You're no different than the rest. You hide your true nature. But in a coven, you can be yourself. You can be whole."

Max said, "Yet you're sitting here."

"Begging you to come back."

"Or drive away."

"I'd rather you come back, though. Get Mother Sun to listen to you. I don't want to die, and I can't exist without my sisters. They need to take you seriously. If you leave here, I'll go back to them and they'll go on treating me like the new girl who deserves to be picked on and they'll think everything's okay. Until I'm gone, murdered, and without my head."

Though Sister Moon's eyes looked at Max, his mind saw his mother. The desperation, the confusion — a mixture that harbored more than fear. A dreadful unknown hung over this woman, a trepidation at the thought of the afterlife, and Max's head nodded.

"Really? You'll talk to Mother Sun again?"

"Of course." He turned toward Sandra. "If the worst happens, that'll be all three heads."

Sandra had already opened the car door. "We're never going to abandon you. We'll try with Mother Sun one more time. If that fails, don't worry. We'll figure something else out."

The brightest flare of light from behind the house erupted alongside a deep thud. A plume of smoke rose high along with a shrill scream. Before the ground stopped vibrating, Sister Moon had shot out of the car and raced around the side of the house.

"No," Max said, but she kept running.

Sandra rushed after the witch. "C'mon," she yelled back at Max. "Or we'll be too late."

Chapter 14

THROUGH ALL THE YEARS that The Porter Agency had dealt with witches, they experienced numerous cases involving the violence one witch could enact upon another. There were even a few times when they had witnessed a battle between multiple groups or specific covens. But neither Max nor Sandra would ever have claimed to have walked through the aftermath of a battlefield. They were not soldiers. Yet the backyard of the Astrum Coven could have been a snapshot from a war movie.

Thick smoke blanketed the forest, burning the back of Max's throat. Flames teased the edges of the clearing in small patches. Sandra gasped at two large areas that had been scorched. The first marked where the coven's ritual fire had burned. All its wood had been spread outward towards the tree line, some still glowed with embers. The second area formed a blast radius from a blackened hole in the ground like the impact crater of a tiny meteor.

Bodies were strewn across the charred land. Half the coven. Maybe more. But no cries of pain. No movement of any kind. They were all dead.

Max tried to comprehend what he saw. No stranger to the dead but this — this was monstrous. Sandra wiped at her eyes as Sister Moon darted from one corpse to the next.

"Sister Jupiter? Sister Venus?" the young witch cried out.

On shaky legs, Sandra walked to the hole in the ground. She narrowed her eyes, narrowed her focus, clearly trying to blot out the horror around her so she could do her job. After a moment's attention on the blast, she said, "Definitely magic."

Coming alongside, hoping he could do the same, Max said, "Looks like a bomb to me."

"I can feel the energy manipulation pulsing off this area. If you dare take a sniff, there's nothing that smells of explosives or guns or anything I would associate with a practical weapon. But I do smell ozone." Her voice cracked. "And burnt hair."

Trying to breathe through his mouth, Max said, "I'll take your word for it."

From the second floor of the house, green and blue lights flashed. Sister Moon jumped to her feet. "They're still here."

"Wait," Sandra said. "We don't know how many witches attacked your coven."

"Mother Sun is in there and any other sisters I still have left."

Sister Moon shot towards the back door. Max and Sandra hurried behind. Not much else they could do.

As they neared the house and put the revolting backyard behind them, Max recalled the many times he had promised to get better at firing a handgun so that he could safely carry one. He always remembered it when he needed it but would forget to follow through when life calmed down. This time, he hoped, he would finally put it to the top of his to-do list — assuming he survived whatever they found in that house.

Many witches — perhaps most of them — hoarded like folklore dragons. Except where dragons sought gold and other riches, witches tended towards the oddest collection of useless trinkets and disturbing debris. Something as simple as a collection of old magazines brought with it mold and dust and scribbled notations that read like madness.

A coven of witches — thirteen all living under one roof — left Max wondering how they managed to find space for everything. Each step through the ceiling-high maze of collected trash encroached on any sense of security or well-being. The place was a death trap. Any of these piles of papers or clocks or oddly-shaped novelty glasses could tumble over and cause serious injury. Worse, the smallest lick of a flame would torch the house.

The air reeked with a stuffy blend of sweat, decay, and incense. Lots of incense.

Sister Moon left the kitchen and guided them through the

living room. Towers of romance novels from the 1950s, boxes labeled cassette tapes, and piles of clothes outlined a flatscreen TV. Perhaps the weirdest part of the room — Max noticed a PS5 hooked up with the controllers ready to go. He wanted to crack a joke about witches playing *Dark Souls,* but a lightning crack from upstairs reminded him where they headed.

Whispering, he said, "You two should prepare some spells before we go up there."

"No time," Sister Moon said. "Mother Sun is not as powerful as she brags about. I've seen her studying at night when she thought everybody was asleep. Not the kind of studying you might do or witches I've heard about — more like cramming for an exam. There was a desperation in her."

"All the more reason to prepare. If she can't handle whoever's up there —"

"That's why we have to go now."

Stepping out of the living room and into a hallway covered in portraits and framed photographs, Max saw the staircase at the opposite end. Sandra reached back to clutch his hand. A small gesture, but one that assured him she understood how fast things were moving and that she would do her best to be ready. It was as much as he could hope for at this point.

They neared the foot of the stairs when they heard a high screech. Mother Sun flew backwards, tumbling down the staircase, landing flat on her back in the hallway. Photographs dropped off the walls, crashing against the stairs and floor, spreading bits of glass. Sister Moon sprinted to Mother Sun's side. Even from afar, Max could see the blood seeping into every crease and wrinkle on her face. The bruises around her neck. The scorched hair, and most of all, the smoke snaking off her body toward the ceiling.

A husky yet feminine voice shouted, "You will rot for this."

Max, Sandra, and Sister Moon lifted their gazes. Stomping feet rushed across the upstairs floorboards followed by a hard smack and an even harder thud against the floor.

Tears streamed down Sister Moon's face as she said, "Sister Earth."

A different voice spoke, and Max knew her — the witch from the cemetery. "We've destroyed your coven. Your Mother is dead. Give use your newest, your reborn, and you'll still live."

"You ignorant asses," Sister Earth said. "You've already killed her outside."

A third voice answered. A smoother voice. One with the certainty of leadership. "I am impressed with your loyalty. If I had met you sooner, I would have invited you to join our coven."

Max shared a look with Sandra. No doubts anymore. They were dealing with another coven. Although this woman did not sound like Madame Ti. Max frowned, but Sandra had no answer beyond a shivering shrug.

"The problem," the coven leader said, "is that all your loyalty won't save you or your sister. I know she's still alive, just as I know that you are not her. I see the colors around you, those that surrounded your sisters, and I knew that none were the one we want. But I will find her. The burden you now carry is how many more innocent people will have to die because you won't tell me where she is."

Sister Earth said, "She's gone. Far from here. We were warned you would be coming."

"You don't even know who we are," the cemetery witch said.

The leader sniffed. "I'm sure you've heard of me, though. Soon, you'll hear of my coven."

"Sorry." Sister Earth sounded on the verge of laughter. "I don't know about any delusional, psychopath witches."

Max braced to hear more violence. Instead, the leader gave an amused chuckle that shook with anger.

She said, "I am the greatest living witch. I have cast spells most witches think are only fables. I am the witch with no fear. I have swum in the waters of madness, and I have climbed the summit of enlightenment. You don't know me? You will. The entire world of magic will know me. I am Sister Sadie, and I claim my right to rule you all."

Max never heard what was next said. His brain couldn't process words right then. It barely had the space to keep his heart pounding or his lungs filling with air. All his mental capacity diverted into disbelief. *Sister Sadie?*

The Porters had thwarted her plan to escape an insane, ravaged body — a prison of flesh — when they disrupted her spell at a winery barn. They knew she was still alive, knew she might find another spell to free herself, but the veohoxal spell was not about that. Unless she was dead. Could that be what this was for? If Sister Sadie had died that night at the barn, then perhaps her acolytes were trying to bring her back.

But Max couldn't hear or see any ghosts except for Drummond. How could he be hearing Sister Sadie? He stepped toward the staircase.

"Don't," Sandra said.

"It can't be her."

"Of course, it can. We know all we need right now. The rest we'll figure out. But if we stay, if they get Sister Moon, then this is for nothing."

"I'll take a peek. That's it. I've got to see." He glanced at Sister Moon hunched over the dead body of Mother Sun. "Take her to the car. Be ready to get us out of here. I won't let them see me up there, but better to be prepared."

"Hon, don't go up there."

Max drew Sandra in a hug. A short, hard kiss, and then: "I have to look. I have to know."

Perhaps she heard the anguish in his voice. Perhaps she recognized his need to face this past trauma. Whatever the case, Sandra gave a weak nod. "Don't die up there. I'm still a witch. I can ruin your afterlife."

He kissed her again. Slower. With more heart. Then, remembering Sister Moon, he turned to the young witch. "If the woman upstairs is the one I think it is, you are in far more danger than death. But it's up to you. Stay here, fight, and die, or come with us."

Sister Moon looked like an animal stunned into fear-laden paralysis. To her credit, it only lasted a few seconds. Her eyes relaxed, and her strength returned. The same energy that had led her to stop the Porters from leaving in the first place. She placed her hand in Sandra's as she stood.

Max gave his wife one final nod. "Get to the car. I'll be right there. I love you."

Bravery did not factor into his actions. Nor courage. Rather, Max approached those stairs with foreboding. He had told Sandra the truth — he simply had to know. That determination overrode his natural sense of fear — heck, his natural sense of self-preservation.

Lying low, he crawled to the top. Sweat discovered new crevices on his body to soak as his pulse learned about a faster gear to kick into. Each creak of wood amplified in his skull. Each mote of dust endangered him with a coughing fit that would reveal his presence. When he reached the final stair, he peeked over the lip.

The cemetery witch stood in the back, watching the action as Sister Earth cowered on her knees. Blood dribbled down the young woman's face. Her left eye had swollen shut, and like the hallway, her clothes had scorch marks all over.

Hanging over this abused woman, the main witch in charge, the one claiming to be Sister Sadie, glowered at her victim. In another setting, she would have been considered a classic beauty. Tall, golden haired, with plump lips and a charming, youthful figure. But the hatred seething from her pores and the devilry painting her eyes sharpened her features, turned her from a sweet damsel to a damned soul. Despite this monstrous visage, Max could not be sure she was really Sister Sadie.

But then this would-be ruler, hooked a finger under Sister Earth's chin. "I can hold more spells in my head than any other witch alive. Do you understand? I can repeat them inside my mind like singing several songs at once, like a choir of magic, and that means I don't need to waste time with casting circles and drawing symbols and chanting forever. I simply let one go free. Like the one I'm singing now that will send jolts of green fire out of my finger and into your jaw."

"Do it," the cemetery witch said, her eyes lustful, her mouth grinning wide.

"Sister Ruth thinks I should. But if you tell me where the witch I seek is, then I can stop your suffering."

To Max's amazement, Sister Earth summoned the will to spit. In that moment, that half-instant before the fire ignited, Max saw the shock and rage on the torturer's face.

And he knew.

He had seen those eyes before. He had felt the pressure of the insanity behind those hate-filled eyes. Like a soldier enduring a sudden flashback to war, Max saw that woman's eyes, and he suffered a second of being trapped in a barn, unsure if he would live through the night, unsure if he would stop this crazed witch from possessing a new, healthy body. All doubt left him as his heart banged against his ribs in a panicked urge to rip free and run.

This was Sister Sadie.

Chapter 15

FROZEN TERROR, MIND-NUMBED HORROR, SHEER PANIC. They coursed through Max abandoned from logic or rationality. He simultaneously saw the lovely woman in front of him and the twisted fiend she had once been.

Stumbling down the stairs, his heart threating to arrest, he clutched his chest. The body of Mother Sun stared up at him with her accusing and shocked expression. He put one hand to the wall to steady his wobbling gait. Several portraits knocked askew. One photograph fell to the floor, shattering the glass facing.

From upstairs, Sister Sadie said, "Who's there?" Then to Sister Ruth: "Go already."

The next several minutes blurred — running down the hall, bumping into walls and furniture, desperate to find an exit, knocking over several pillars of junk, getting lost in the maze of collections, then a pierce of light cutting through the dark outside, racing towards it, slamming into the front door, bursting outside and feeling the touch of cold air, hearing Sandra at the idling car, screaming *Drive!,* diving into the passenger seat, tearing down the street, putting distance between them and that house, that woman. By the time Max could piece it all together, they had hit the main road and headed back towards the city.

Through gasps, he said, "It was her. Different body, different person, but it was really her."

Sandra said, "I believe you. Calm down."

"That woman is the definition of criminally insane. Honey, listen to me, believe me, she is more powerful than before. She's like some kind of super-witch."

He heard the words babbling out and marveled that Sandra

didn't have him committed right away. Even as he repeatedly peeked at the side mirror for a glimpse behind them, even as tears shimmered in his eyes, he expected Sister Sadie to come flying through the air, cloak flapping behind like crow's wings, and ram the car off the road.

"Take a deep breath." Sandra spoke in a placating tone as she merged with traffic on 52 South. "We have dealt with many powerful witches before. Including Sister Sadie. We beat every single one. We beat her, too. Remember? It was difficult but not impossible."

"This is different," he whispered.

"It always is. But together, we find a way through. As long as we're thinking, we'll figure it out. You need to relax, regroup, and start that big brain of yours."

Max listened to the wisdom of his wife. He inhaled deep and slow, held the breath to a count of five, before letting out the air in a shaky but calming release. Twice more he went through this procedure.

She was right. They had faced many vicious foes. They could do this, too. Together.

"You okay now?" she asked.

He nodded. "Sorry." Glancing back at Sister Moon, he added, "I'm not usually like this."

"He's telling the truth. He's often the one who keeps his cool."

Sister Moon didn't respond, but Max caught a doubtful look cross her face.

"I guess I thought Sister Sadie had died," he said. "Or, at least, was stuck in her old, ruined body. I thought we'd never have trouble with her again. I mean, I suppose I wanted to believe that. But I knew we'd see her one day. Just wasn't expecting it like this."

Sandra patted his hand. "You're sounding more like my husband. Good. Because we have to keep this woman alive and stop Sister Sadie from finding any other newly reborn witches to decapitate."

"And here I thought we'd finally get a good night's sleep."

Sandra glanced at Max. Max glanced at Sandra. The two laughed.

Sister Moon said, "You two sound like the crazy ones."

Max and Sandra paused to digest this comment which only sent them into further hysterics.

Managing a cleansing breath and wiping at her eyes, Sandra said, "We'll be okay. The first thing to do —"

With a swift motion, Drummond popped through the front seat console. "What are the two of you thinking?" He whipped his hat off and jammed it in their direction to punctuate his points. "You run off to a full coven of thirteen witches to take them on? Without bringing me as your backup? Of all the stupid things you could do, the moronic and idiotic and imbecilic and any other synonym I can think up, you risk your lives without me. Why?"

"We're sorry," Sandra said. "We didn't think —"

"You certainly didn't. We're a team. That means we do these things together."

Max said, "Last we knew, you went off to the Other. There was no time to get hold of you. Not when Sister Moon might have already been abducted."

"That's a line of bull and you know it. What the two of you did — going out there without me — that was personally and professionally reckless. There's no excuse."

Sister Moon said, "If you want my opinion, I agree with the ghost."

All three members of The Porter Agency looked at her dumbfounded. Drummond said, "You can see me? Hear me?"

Wrinkling her brow, she shrugged. "I see and hear most ghosts. As long as they know they're dead." She nudged her chin towards Max. "Everything your ghost is saying makes me think this was a mistake getting in your car."

"Don't worry," Max said. "We'll keep you alive. And we'll figure out what this spell is going after. We know what it does — brings something from the ghost plane into our plane — but we need to concentrate on the target. We figure that out, and we can stop it."

"I already know that."

Sandra screeched the brakes. If it had not been past midnight, she would have caused an accident. Instead, she pulled over to the side of the empty highway. Turning around in the driver's seat, she said, "You know who they're targeting with that spell? Sister Sadie and her coven? You know who they're after?"

"That's what I said."

"Well?" Max asked.

"Simple. She wants the gold."

Drummond clicked his tongue. "Well, well. Greed strikes again."

Chapter 16

SISTER MOON GAVE THE BACK SEAT A PETULANT KICK. "Can we get moving? I'd rather not die because you can't drive and talk at the same time."

"You got a mouth on you, kid," Drummond said.

"I can cast spells on ghosts, too."

"Everybody calm down." Max ignored the irony of his previous manic state. To Sandra: "Let's get back on the road. Sister Moon, please tell us what you're talking about. What do you know about this spell?"

After a pause in which Max thought Sandra might argue, she put the car in drive and returned to the highway. Only then did Sister Moon peek out the back window, turn back with an unsteady sigh, and slump in her seat. Tough — Max had enough to know that — but as tough as wanted him to believe.

"I never heard about the specific spell before," she said, still finding the strength to sound strong. "Not until you two showed up at the coven house. It was probably you that led Sister Sadie to us."

Drummond re-situated his hat. "Kid, I'm the one that gets to call out my partners on their stupidity. Not you. I taught them well. No way were they followed. And while they may be dumb enough to jump into a risky situation without me, they did it to save you. So, show some respect."

Max doubted Drummond believed half of what he said — certainly not the part about his partners being smart enough not to be followed. Still, Max appreciated the support.

"If you didn't know about the spell," Max said, "then how do you know that the target is not a person? That it's gold?"

Sister Moon said, "If you would shut up, then I can tell you what I know, and you'll be able to figure out the rest."

When no one spoke another word, Max finally gestured to the witch. "We're waiting."

"When I first moved here," Sister Moon said, "I tried to learn as much local folklore as I could."

Her focus locked on Drummond as if he was the only one in the car. Max fought the urge to point out that she had a living audience right in front of her. If she needed the attention of a ghost, then so be it. Besides, he was too frazzled to be petty beyond a fleeting thought.

"I wanted to join a coven, and I thought if I knew more of the local world than any other potential sister, I'd have an edge."

Max said, "Why come to Winston? There must have been covens wherever you lived."

Without looking his way, she scratched at her arm as if her secrets crawled near the surface of her skin. "I've not lived in any one place for long. All the towns I spent time in tended to have covens that acted like book clubs — excuses for bored people to congregate and drink. I wanted a coven devoted to witchcraft. I wanted the real thing. I met a witch that told me about Winston-Salem. She said it like the city was made by magic. She said it was one of the central points of magic in America."

Drummond said, "Been that way for a long time."

"Among the many stories I heard and read, I came across this one a lot — that there is an entire system of secret tunnels beneath the city. Some are connected. Some are not. They were put in at different times for different purposes, and many are now walled-off for safety reasons. Others have already collapsed. But they do exist."

Max raised a questioning glance at Drummond. The ghost said, "First I've heard of it. Doesn't mean it isn't true. Even the smallest city can hold secrets."

"A bunch of these tunnels," Sister Moon continued, "were designed by the Reynolds family. You know? Like Reynolds Tobacco?"

"We're familiar with them," Max said.

"The main story is that Reynolds had the tunnel system built to stretch throughout the city. It centers around where the company headquarters was and reached out to their factories. It also went to Wachovia. That's where the bank was. Reynolds used the tunnels to avoid the public, but he also had minecarts of gold coins pushed through. These coins would be passed around to employees on paydays or special occasions. They also rolled bags of cash to the bank and such. These carts were always accompanied by guards carrying machine guns. Oh, and there is a hidden lake somewhere as well. I don't know why they built a lake under a city, but that's what they did."

A firetruck screamed along the road in the opposite direction, Max remembered seeing an avalanche of old newspapers tumbling to the floor during his escape. Plenty of ways it could have caught fire, and he suddenly knew without doubt that the coven house would burn to the ground before the night ended.

"There are lots of other tunnels. His wife had a bunch built beneath Reynolda Village because she didn't want the power lines and water lines and such to be seen. There are the sewers built by the Moravians when Winston was first formed, and there are some tunnels under a high school. I think those are bomb shelters or something."

Drummond put words to a thought in Max's head. "You expect us to believe that you just happen to know the exact bit of lore we're looking for? And in such detail?"

"I only knew a little when I met Mother Sun. I mentioned it one night at dinner, and that's when she got real interested in me. That's when I learned that covens are expensive to run. With so many competing right now, with nobody in charge and this witch war going on, things cost even more. She told me that there were spells we could use to find any of those gold coins that may still be down there, but I needed to be sure. I spent the last few days looking into it. That's why I know what I know."

Max said, "Mother Sun wanted to use the veohoxal?"

"I hope not," Sandra said. "She would've killed herself trying."

Sister Moon said, "I don't think she planned to do anything. She was a lot of talk and a little magic. That's what I've been thinking lately. I mean I looked into these tunnels, but if there was gold, a simple location spell could have found it. She didn't even want to try that. I'm not sure she could."

"You think she was a fraud."

A sharp sniffle, and Max caught Sister Moon wiping at her eyes. "She meant well. I think she was a frustrated witch that wanted to be so much more. I think she started Astrum Coven so she could be near more powerful witches. In a way, she probably took the *Mother* part of her name more seriously."

Drummond knuckled his hat back. "What about —"

"That's enough," Sister Moon said, her voice catching. She nibbled her fingernails as she stared at the lights of Winston-Salem streaming by.

Max had more questions, and he wanted to do some research to confirm what she claimed. But that could wait until they reached the office. For now, Sister Moon needed to digest all that had happened. And mourn all she had lost.

Chapter 17

OVER THE NEXT TWENTY MINUTES, as they drove to The Porter Agency office, Max used his phone to research these alleged tunnels. He also asked Drummond to search beneath the city for direct proof. Sister Moon sat quietly, only uttering a sniffle or a muted cry a few times.

He confirmed the main thrust of the Reynolds story right away. While it had been the kind of story teens told to dare each other into risky behavior, enough years had passed for some of those teens to become reporters in their adult lives. Max found an article from the Sentinel in 1982 that interviewed a man named Phil Archer who worked for Reynolda House when the tunnels were in use. He explained how Mrs. Reynolds "wanted to give the feeling of an English Hamlet or little English kind of village, so she didn't want to see any of the utilities." Thus, she had tunnels built underground. Much of that work had now collapsed and all the entryways were sealed off to prevent accidents.

"And liability," Max muttered as he swiped on in his search.

Another source was a man named Tim Flinchum. He claimed to have worked for Reynolds Tobacco in the 1970s, specifically in the tunnels. A few taps and Max uncovered records from 1975 that put Flinchum exactly where the man said — living in Winston-Salem under the employment of Reynolds Tobacco.

Flinchum said that he serviced utility lines in those tunnels which all threaded their way to the Reynolds Headquarters. Pulling up his maps app, Max found that the building now belonged to the Klimpton Hotel. The part that lured Max deeper in — Flinchum said, "When Mr. Reynolds built them, when he paid people from one plant to the other, he actually transferred the money from the Reynolds building to where they were working at through those tunnels." Even stranger, Flinchum confirmed the existence of a large pond — not a lake — meant as a water source in case of fire.

Max located another piece of evidence with ease. He used YouTube. A video of two young men standing outside a tunnel entrance grabbed Max's attention. The video showed an arch of old masonry with a keystone brick engraved with the date 1880. The men walked deep in, almost twenty minutes of walking, and found that the tunnel functioned as a drainage run-off. This rather mundane result did not lessen the fact that Max had discovered plenty of corroboration for Sister Moon's story.

Finally, he pulled up a 2011 video clip from WXII, the local news station. The piece covered the same ground as the others Max had read, but it also included an interview with Mr. Oscar Dubicki. This man asserted that he had been a gunman assigned to protect these minecarts of gold coins. At 97-years-old, it was possible. If Dubicki had worked in his early-20s, then Reynolds would have been dead for over a decade, but the company continued. Many of its practices would have continued as well. Max couldn't find a record of the tunnels being discontinued, but certainly by the end of the Great Depression, the practice of distributing gold coins and paying via secret tunnel would be over or on the way out.

Sandra parked the car, the lack of movement bringing Max back from his research. He shared what he had found as they escorted Sister Moon up the stairs to their office. She hugged herself as she meandered through. When she saw the couch, she dropped on one side looking more like a refugee than a witch.

Slipping out of the bookcase, Drummond pushed back his hat and rocked his chest forward. "If this don't beat all — she's telling the truth. There are a lot of tunnels under the city. Easy to miss because they're all dark. If you don't know what you're looking at or looking for, it blends in with the rest of the ground."

Max said, "I found reports that confirmed her story, too."

"Yeah, but I bet you didn't find any mention of a certain

section of one tunnel under the downtown area that's got ghost wards on it."

"Wards?" Sandra lowered to a chair facing the couch.

"That's right, doll. A witch or a bunch of witches went down there already and cast a few spells to stop nosey ghosts or brilliant detectives from poking around. There were more wards than just that, though. I could feel them, but I couldn't tell what they protected against."

"Probably making sure other witches can't spy on that tunnel or even locate it."

Max said, "I'm willing to bet that section of tunnel has a minecart track on it. Sister Sadie is going for those gold coins."

"Maybe," Sandra said.

"She's got at least one follower — Sister Ruth — and we know she wants to rule over all the other witches."

"Revenge, too," Drummond said. "She's not the forgiving kind."

"She'll need a coven for all of that, and Sister Moon pointed out that a new coven requires substantial cash. Sister Sadie doesn't strike me as the kind to sell her services for people with petty gripes, and she certainly won't be making love potions for income."

"That's another reason to start a coven. She could make the others work regular day jobs."

"But those gold coins bypass that. They'll fund the coven and her bid to rule magic in the area. If she succeeds at getting that gold with such a difficult spell, a spell that required ruthlessness as well — she'll have every witch in the South frightened of her name."

Sandra said, "You might be right about that, but don't be fooled by her new body. She's still Sister Sadie. She's still as insane as ever. This whole thing could easily be without any sensible purpose."

Max walked over to the couch and lowered into the unoccupied chair. "What do you know about this?"

Scrunching her shoulders, Sister Moon said, "I never heard of Sister Sadie until tonight."

"I meant the tunnels. You did the research for Mother Sun, and whether or not you thought she could pull off the actual spells, Mother Sun pretended she could."

Catching Max's direction, Sandra perked up. "She had to have a way in. Drummond said he couldn't find one, but there must be."

Sister Moon said, "Maybe she planned to teleport."

"Mother Sun couldn't even come close to a spell like that, even if one exists. No, she had some practical way in."

"I told you that she couldn't do the spell anyway. Why would she plan to get in the tunnels if she knew she'd fail at the spell?"

Floating overhead, Drummond said, "Because, kid, she would have to put on a show for the coven. Make it look like she tried. As long as every witch worked hard at it, you'd feel like you put in the best effort. Spells fail sometimes."

Max said, "She could make all sorts of excuses, too. Blame it on your research or the translation of the spell or the phase of the moon. Whatever she wanted. The coven would have accepted it, gone back to the drawing board, and maybe tried again in a few years. By then, she'd either have figured out how to cast it properly or she'd find something else to distract your sisters. You'd move on to a new spell, a new problem. Anything."

"Mother Sun wasn't like that." Sister Moon snapped the words.

Sandra pressed closer. "Come on. Tell us. Did she show you how to get into the tunnels? If we're going keep you safe, we need to know. Those wards, too. What do you know about them?"

"Nothing." Sister Moon rocked in place, her mouth tightening, her fingers vice-gripping her shoulders.

"Did Mother Sun put them in place? That's important. If she did, then Sister Sadie didn't, and that would suggest that Sister Sadie's target is not the gold. If she's going after something else, we've got to know. Otherwise, we're focusing on the wrong thing, and that could put your life in danger."

"Shut up!" Leaping to her feet, her hands shot to her sides, clawed and turned forward as if ready to throw out a prepared spell. "You're all users. You don't care about me or Mother Sun or my dead sisters. You're only helping me for yourselves."

Max watched for any magic arcing between her splayed fingers. His heart hammered. From the corner of his eye, he saw Sandra rise to her feet as Drummond lowered into view.

He had time for one thought.

Crap.

<h1>Chapter 18</h1>

MAX SET HIS FEET FLAT ON THE FLOOR, ready to lunge forward and tackle the witch. He trusted that Drummond prepared to freeze the girl unconscious, if necessary. Sandra — she made a small hand motion to keep Max and Drummond at bay. For now.

"We're not going to hurt you," she said. "We're not trying to use you."

"Everybody says that." Sister Moon gasped the words out. "And I always get hurt."

"Not this time."

Sister Moon's eyes shifted from Drummond to Max to Sandra like a wounded bird trying to find a safe branch to land upon. "You'll say anything to get what's in my head."

Max aimed for a friendly voice. "So that we can save your life. Sister Sadie is out there, and she wants to cast that spell."

Pointing to the whiteboard, Sandra said, "This spell. And this last line — that's the reason we think she wants to take your head. Whatever else you may want to accuse us of or suspect us of, this part can't be denied. The veohoxal spell is what she's doing, and you are the final ingredient. I know you're afraid and you don't know who to trust, but you're not protecting anybody by holding back on us. In fact, you're endangering yourself more."

"You came to us," Max said. "Part of you knows we want to help."

"He's right," Drummond said. "I've watched these folks take on incredible odds to protect others. Let them do it for you, too."

Sister Moon hesitated. "What I know is worthless to you."

"That's not true," Max said. "I have spent my life researching old history and reading the idle thoughts of hundreds of people throughout time. I've read their diaries and their journals, and I promise you, there are no idle thoughts that are worthless. Please, talk with us."

She looked toward the exit. She licked her lips. Then a slight shake of her head. Then a defeated slump. A long breath as if giving up her last rebellious thought. "I was raised by my mother. My father died when I was little. I don't remember him at all. But my mother, she was my first introduction to witchcraft."

"Your mother was a witch?"

"For a time. Not long. She jumped around from interest to interest. I doubt she studied enough or even took it seriously enough to make any spells work. Didn't really matter because somebody convinced her that she was playing with the Devil. Then it was on to Christianity. Like lots of people who convert, she dove in far deeper and more serious than those born into the religion. When you do that, you discover how self-contradictory the whole thing is. It's basically impossible to live a good life if you follow those teachings."

"People find a way."

"People find a compromise. Or they ignore the bits they don't like and cherry pick the parts they do. I don't really care how they justify it. I'm a witch. At its core, if you take out the actual magic, it's nothing but an offshoot of pagan religions."

"That's debatable."

"Do you want to debate me or hear what I have to say?"

Max gestured for her to continue.

"Christianity didn't help her much, anyway. She spent a little time trying to be a Muslim, then a Hindu, and in the end, she dropped religion and searched for meaning in alcohol, drugs, and sex. Made a great role model."

Sandra said, "Is that the real reason you sought a coven? Your mother couldn't raise you, you discovered a knack for witchcraft or that part of your life made sense to you, so you gravitated towards finding a coven. A family."

"Isn't that essentially what I said in the car?"

Sandra didn't take the bait. Instead, she adopted a stronger yet warmer stance. "Your mother betrayed you. She should have been there to raise you and guide you, and instead she used you. Didn't she?"

With her hardness returning, Sister Moon said, "Absolutely she betrayed me. Growing up, she told me it was us against the world. My father had died, and I was all she had left. But that was a lie. She had her religions, her men, her booze, anything she hung onto to give her an out from dealing with me."

"Even if she couldn't express it well, I'm sure she loved you. It takes a lot for a mother to overcome her instinct for love."

"Love me or not, doesn't matter. She let me down. And the covens I've dealt with — no different. Each one of them has let me down. You don't think I knew Mother Sun was using me? I knew. I could see all the ugly wrinkles under the makeup of that coven. It was never going to amount to much. But that doesn't mean I wanted them dead. It was just that ... like my mother, they only cared about what they could get from me. You're no different."

Drummond descended through the air, hands in his pockets, and a half-grin wrinkling his face. "You know, kid, I'm over a hundred years old. Well, I would be if I had stayed alive. I've seen a lot. Max and Sandra here — some of the best people I've ever met. They're honest and good. They do remarkable things. Selfless things. They make me want to be a better person — better ghost. You can trust them."

Sister Moon's clawed hands finally relaxed. With the timid nod, she allowed Sandra to gently bring her back to the couch.

"Good," Drummond said. "Now, maybe because your daddy died, you never had someone to smack a little sense into you." Max cringed but Drummond went on, "You listen to me — you got screwed over by your family and friends. It happens to everybody. Heck, governments, the whole world, screws everybody over. Nature is not altruistic. Stop expecting it to be. If you want to live through this, we're the ones trying to ..."

Drummond reared his head back and frowned.

"You okay?" Max asked.

A bang at the door. Metal whined. Wood creaked. Perhaps a major storm had hit. Max checked the window — all clear.

Another bang. Sandra and Sister Moon flinched. Max stepped back.

"I'll take a peek," Drummond said as if he already knew he would not like what he found.

He started forward but never got beyond the couch. The door blasted open, screaming one last time, hinges pinging as they broke free. Several feet inside the office, it tipped over and thudded hard onto the floor.

Sister Ruth entered. Her hair jittered on end while her muscles twitched and spasmed. Spellcast energy bristled off her. Opening a hungry mouth, she said, "Give me the girl and you'll live. For now."

Chapter 19

WITHOUT A LOOK OR A WORD, Max and Sandra stepped in front of Sister Moon. Moving in a wide arc, clearly trying to avoid his icy presence from giving him away, Drummond positioned to flank this invader. They watched Sister Ruth like chess masters contemplating the next several moves and counter-moves.

Sister Ruth tilted her head toward Max. "Sister Sadie hasn't forgotten you. When she cast her spell to find the girl and she learned the Porters were involved, you should have seen her delight. I thank you for that. I've never seen her so excited. It was a pleasure to witness, and I think it'll be even greater when she has time to truly hurt you."

"Not making me want to help you," Max said.

"I don't need your help. Only your compliance."

Sandra said, "Should we call her Mother Sadie, now?"

"That's not her way." Sister Ruth's pride filtered between the spell energy she carried. "She wants to create a coven of equals. Not one dependent on an individual. A coven to last forever."

"How overly-ambitious. Nothing ever goes wrong for witches like that."

As Sister Ruth responded with a litany of the horrors Sister Sadie intended for the Porters, Max's attention fell behind the witch. A casting circle had been drawn in the hallway. He didn't want to think about how long Sister Ruth had spent out there building up the power sizzling off her now, or how she had evaded Sandra's wards and warning systems. That casting circle designated the source of Sister Ruth's current strength. Break the circle, break her spell.

Max caught Drummond eyeing up the same target. The ghost threw him one quick wink. It was all he needed.

"Now." Max barked the word as he crouched to attack.

Sister Ruth tried to throw some kind of energy at him, but Drummond has already swooped in and stunned her with a fist of ice into the brain. Rushing forward, Max hauled off an uppercut that landed hard on her chin. She crumpled to her knees.

Leaping by her, he burst into the hallway, banging the opposite wall, and whirling around. He caught a glimpse of Sandra ripping back the rug that covered her casting circle as she lowered to the floor to start a spell. He swiped his foot across the casting circle in the hall, breaking the chalk lines and destroying Sister Ruth's spell. They had the upper-hand for the moment, and Max delighted at how well the team had worked together.

But then he peered down one end of the hall. Two more casting circles. Then the other end. Two more. Four more spells.

Dashing down one end of the hall, he swiped through one circle, then the next. Heart pounding, he sprinted back. As he glanced into the office, he raised his hand to warn Sandra. "She's still got two —"

Fire burned against his side as his body propelled through the open doorway. A flash of blue splashed around him. His cheek bashed into the floor, and he slid further. Not on fire. Just the burn of magic.

But when he rolled onto his back, he saw Drummond dodging several attacks. Sister Ruth persisted near the fallen office door and threw one blast of orange after another. When Drummond evaded the next shot, the ball of magic put a hole in the wall. It burned away to the plumbing and wiring behind the brick. Smoke drifted off the seared edges, but like Max's side, the fire disappeared. It was enough to damage but not set the place ablaze. When were they ever going to keep an office in one piece?

Drummond evaded another attack. This time, Sandra's desk took the damage — splitting it down the middle. The two sides fell into each other, splintering wood and metal.

Looking at the hole in the wall and the wreckage of the desk, Max made a quick assessment — blue magic would hurt, orange magic would kill. He checked Sister Ruth's hands — no color, for now. She needed to recharge or cast something new. Didn't matter. She had nothing in her hands. That left an opening.

He launched to his feet. The sudden change in elevation spun his head. He stumbled toward the witch, and he saw her wry grin.

As she lifted her hand to strike, the entire office grew blindingly bright. Sandra. She had cast one of her fastest spells, one Max had experienced many times, and while the simple flash wouldn't prevent the attacks, it did a good job of creating confusion. It should buy them time. Not much, though.

Drummond soared down from the ceiling, his fist drawn back. When he swung, Sister Ruth raised both hands — not in cowering defense, but rather, casting another of the hallway spells. She uttered one sharp, witchy word, and Drummond's body arched as if punched hard. He flipped over and careened through the wall.

Sandra attempted to put together a second flash spell, but Sister Ruth whirled around and thrust her hands forward. With a shout, Sandra was tossed out of her casting circle, banging into the whiteboard. Her head rolled, dazed, as she tried to regain her focus.

Forming an orange ball of energy in one hand, Sister Ruth cocked her head at Max. "I only came here for the girl. Give her to me, and I will leave."

Max glanced around the office. No sign of Sister Moon. "I think she bolted."

With one menacing step closer, Sister Ruth said, "There's no other door out. The windows are closed, and we're not on the first floor."

"I don't know what to tell you. She was here when you barged in, and I've been a bit busy to notice where she went."

"I'm not going to waste time debating this." Speaking louder, she said, "Wherever you're hiding, you can hear me. Show yourself, or I'll kill this man. If you still don't come out, I'll kill his wife. And then I'll shred their ghost to ribbons."

Max looked to Sandra. She was in no shape to stop this. Drummond was peeling out of the wall, looking groggy and unfit to fight on. Estimating the distance to Sister Ruth, Max didn't see how he could land a punch or even simply bump her before she'd blast a burning hole through him.

"Last warning," Sister Ruth said. Then she turned a pitiful eye on Max. "I'm sorry. Sister Sadie won't be happy that I had to ruin her vengeance against you, but I think she'll find a way to harm you in the afterlife."

"You don't have to do this."

Her gaze upon him embodied the Southern phrase *Bless your heart* as she raised the energy above her head. A metallic ping rang out alongside a flash of white light. Max squinted. When he could see clearly again, Sister Ruth's pitying expression had turned to shock — pure, physical shock.

A thin line of red formed across her neck. She gurgled. The line thickened until blood ran down like a bursting dam. With a final choked utterance, her head tumbled off her body and rolled against the bookcase.

Max could not move. His mind struggled to catch up with what his senses told him had happened.

Drummond swayed in above and clicked his tongue. "Can't say I'm sad to see that."

Falling back to sit on the floor, Max shuddered before he looked at Sandra. He knew her explanation, and he couldn't deny its truth. He was about to be killed. Of course, Sandra would do anything to protect him. Yet he had not expected such a violent action. Not from her.

But her face locked forward, staring at Sister Ruth with the same petrifying shock he had felt. Her eyes shifted towards him while the rest of her remained motionless. She didn't do this. She couldn't have, Max's brain finally recognized. Not because of some grand moral choice — there simply hadn't been enough time to cast a new spell. Not for her.

As if stepping from behind an old green screen in a cheap movie, Sister Moon appeared. Only a few steps from the couch. Only feet from Sandra.

"Well, well," Drummond said.

Sandra, recomposing faster than Max could, turned to Sister

Moon. "That's why they want you. You're no ordinary witch."

Sister Moon flushed. "I cast a spell. That's all."

"You cast an illusion to protect yourself, and you cast that attack. But I don't see a casting circle other than my own."

"That's right," Max said, finally catching up. "And before, you were ready to fight us with some spell you had prepared in your head."

"They're all in her head, hon. At least three we know of. How many more do you have ready to go?"

Sister Moon said, "I'm no threat to you."

"That wasn't the question." Drummond moved closer.

Her eyes flared like a cornered mouse. Max hustled forward.

"It's okay," he said. "You know we won't hurt you."

"Then why are you threatening me?"

"We're not." Max glanced over at Drummond and Sandra, urging them to back up. "But you've been lying to us this whole time. I understand why. You had no reason to trust us. Not much, anyway. That's done, now." Nodding at Sister Ruth's body, he said, "I can't think of anything clearer to show we're on the same side. Now, it's your turn. How about you tell us your whole story again. Only this time — the truth."

Chapter 20

WITH A SIMPLE SHIFT OF HER EYES, an easing of her shoulders, and an awkward turning of her knees inward, Sister Moon lost the presence of a powerful witch capable of slicing apart another powerful witch and became the youthful, lost little wannabe that joined the wrong coven in search of a family she never had. If it wasn't so calculated and frightening, Max would have been impressed. Instead, he hoped Sandra recognized the risk. The fact that Sister Moon and Sister Sadie had shown themselves capable of holding one or more spells in their minds or that the late-Sister Ruth could cast numerous spells in a short time proved how dangerous they were.

"We can talk later," Sister Moon said. "There's a body near your front door, and with the extensive noise we made, it won't take the police long to show up."

Max said, "I doubt that. Nobody cares about this area. How else do you think we could afford such a large office?"

"There's nobody in the building this late at night," Sandra said. "Nobody but us. You don't have to worry." She cocked her head as if she had uncovered the one oyster with a black pearl. "Please, tell us who you really are."

On the surface, Sandra appeared to be nudging Sister Moon toward opening up, but Max knew his wife too well. Skimming just below, she wanted more than Sister Moon's story. Sandra's desire to unlock all of witchcraft matched how myopic Max could be when deep into research. Encountering witches so much stronger than herself, she had to know how they had achieved their abilities. On the outside, she displayed motherly care, but deeper within, she stalked forward like a jaguar ready to pounce.

Maybe Sister Moon knew this, too. Or maybe she only sensed trouble. Either way, she hesitated.

Drummond dropped his voice into a thick, gentle blanket. "You won't survive this alone."

Slowly, the witch found her way to the couch once more. She toed the casting circle Max had carved into the floor. Her head snapped toward him, her mouth open. "You did this?"

Taken aback by the swing in attitude — though Max chastised himself for not getting used to her quick changes already — he said, "When your wife's a witch, you do what you can to support her."

Sister Moon looked back at the circle. "Nobody's ever done something like that for me." She wilted into the cushions, head down, hands in her lap. "Here's the truth — I've known for a long time that I had a talent for spells."

A quick prod from Sandra broke Max's intense focus. His wife walked to the shambles of her desk and started sifting through the remains. As Sister Moon continued to talk, Max joined in the office cleanup. Though Drummond couldn't help without causing himself pain, he drifted aside, giving Sister Moon some distance so that she might feel more comfortable.

"I first noticed," she said, "when my mother dabbled in witchcraft. That part about her was true. She brought home books from an occult store, and most of them were nonsense. Full of spells that would never work or stories that had the slimmest touch of truth in them. But one day, a friend of hers shows up with a cardboard box. This friend's mother had died, and she found a box of old witchcraft books. I remember her saying that she never knew her mother was into the occult, but she thought my mother might find something interesting in there. Right away, I knew that these books were different. They had a liveliness about them. They pulsed. Do you understand?"

Sandra brought out a broom and dustpan. "You could feel it, hear it — like a heartbeat."

"Those were the first authentic witch tomes I ever saw, and I could almost taste the energy coming off them. I didn't know how I knew, but I felt the click inside me. I looked at those books, and they made sense to me. My mother struggled for weeks to use them. She never got anywhere. It frustrated me to watch her when I saw the answers clear as a fresh rain, but I stayed quiet. Whenever she wasn't in the house, I raided her stash of those books, and I practiced. I wouldn't say it was easy, but it came naturally."

"Isn't that the way of a great talent? Through hard work and practice, they can perform feats that the rest of us only dream of. And they make it look effortless."

"But they put in more effort than anybody else. I don't know if I'd put myself in that kind of league. I simply love witchcraft. Back then, I craved any moment I could get with those books. I don't want you to think I'm lying or exaggerating, so don't get the wrong idea. My first spells were minor, simplistic things that would take me days to figure out. But even from the beginning, even when the spells failed, I could feel the energy inside of me. It was like I'd become an electrical wire, but I still needed to learn how to hook up properly to make the power flow. When I finally lit a candle from across the room with nothing but a spell, I was dancing. As I got better, I got cocky and impatient."

Max understood that. The way his brain connected bits of researched history looked obvious to him. Sometimes, he would get full of himself about it or irritated at others for not seeing what he did. He tied off the first of many trash bags he'd be dealing with the rest of the night and listened closer to Sister Moon.

She went on, "One night, I had it with my mother. She didn't understand that the symbols had to be exact, that the syllables she sounded out had to follow the correct rhythm, that the candles had specific colors for specific purposes. I could go on and on, but basically, she didn't understand any of it. I grabbed the book from her, drew the spell — it was a location spell she wanted to use for a lost earring — placed down my mother's hasty sketch of the house, and in a few minutes, the spell marked a glowing green light on a spot under my mother's bed." Sister Moon grunted a bitter noise. "I actually thought she'd be proud. Or, at least, pleased. The horror on her gaping mouth — she looked at me like I was a freakish monster. She was afraid of me. Her own daughter. By this time, she'd already started thinking about Jesus. Maybe I should've seen it coming, but I was sixteen and suddenly I'm being sent off to a Catholic boarding school."

"Really?" Max said.

"Why's that surprising?"

Keeping his attention on clean up, he said, "Oh, well, I thought ... I mean I made an assumption from the way you talked about growing up, but I was wrong."

"You thought I was poor."

"Maybe not well-off anyway."

"We were never rich. I know my father had a life insurance policy that kept food on the table. Beyond that, I was a kid. I didn't pay attention to how the bills got paid. All I know for sure is that the electricity never got cut off, and somehow the money was found to send me away. That last part isn't so hard to figure out. She feared me. She probably would have pawned every last possession to get the money for boarding school."

Drummond said, "Consider yourself lucky. Plenty of the witches I knew when I was alive got thrown out of the house with nothing."

"She would've loved to do that, but it'd have been bad for appearances. None of it mattered, though. I went away like she wanted. The Church and I didn't get along. Shocker, I know. You don't need those details. The important part is that I got fed up with the nuns, so I left. Ran away. It was easy, and I doubt the school or my mother looked very hard for me."

Max and Sandra filled two more trash bags before the office showed a glimmer of ever being presentable again. The hole in the wall needed replacing. They would have to purchase a new desk, too. Not to mention getting rid of the corpse.

"I refused to stop studying witchcraft," Sister Moon said. "That's when I bounced from coven to coven. But they ended up the same. Happy for a new, eager young woman to join their ranks until someone discovered that I had serious power."

Sandra said, "That challenged their authority."

"And the other sisters. If they didn't hate me out of jealousy, then the coven mother would try to exploit me. Mother Sun was the most honest about it, though. For all her faults and lack of ability, she could sense power within others to an uncanny degree. When she invited me into the coven, she made it clear — the coven needed money without debt or strings. She promised that if I would help cast spells to get that money, she would make me her second in command."

Drummond said, "I'm sure your coven sisters loved that."

"They didn't know. Mother Sun said I'd have to wait until I cast a big spell — something undeniable. Then she could promote me without causing a rift in the sisterhood. I thought it made sense at the time, but now, I think it was just another betrayal by another so-called family. She never intended to do anything but use me." Sister Moon surveyed the office. "Looks clean enough. Can we get out of here before Sister Sadie finds out what happened?"

Glancing at the dead body, Drummond said, "You seem plenty tough. Maybe you don't need to run from Sister Sadie."

"I'd rather not test that idea."

"Yeah, but if you get rid of her —"

"I'm not a blood-thirsty monster."

Sandra said, "Of course. Drummond forgets that humans see killing and death a bit different than ghosts."

Before Drummond could rebut, Max jumped in. "Honey, you take Sister Moon. Drummond and I will finish cleaning up and dispose of the body."

"Where?"

"I'm sure there are plenty of dumping grounds this old ghost knows about."

"Hey," Drummond said. Then: "Maybe a few."

Sandra said, "I meant about Sister Moon. Where should we go?"

"You need to hide somewhere."

Max added, "Don't let me know until we're ready to regroup. I hate to admit it, but Sister Moon is right about Sister Sadie. At some point soon, she'll realize things went wrong. Once she knows that we're directly responsible for her failed plans again, there's a good chance she'll go ballistic."

A few minutes later, Sandra and Sister Moon had left the building. Max tossed the trash bags in the alley dumpster before pulling his car around so that the trunk faced the doorway. When he returned to the office, he stood over the dead witch.

During the initial cleanup, he had pinned a towel over her neck to stop the blood from staining the floor. Looking at her now, he would need a lot more than a towel.

"This is not going to be easy, is it?" he said.

Drummond floated over the body. "Not one bit."

Chapter 21

DRUMMOND GAVE INSTRUCTIONS FROM THE SIDELINES like a coach smoking while complaining that his team was out of shape. Max gritted his teeth. A lot. But he followed his partner's advice.

Using the circular area rug meant for covering Sandra's casting circle, Max rolled the corpse up. If not for Drummond, he would have forgotten to stick the head in, as well. That small comment saved Max plenty of time and disgust. After taping both ends, he hauled the load to the car.

"I know she's getting heavy, but don't quit," Drummond said.

She was more than heavy. As if by magic, she had become solid rock. Dead weight, indeed.

With a hearty roar, he heaved the carpet roll into the trunk, slammed the door down, and sat on the bumper to catch his breath. Patting the sweat off his forehead, Max said, "When I said that you knew some dumping grounds, I figured you dealt with enough cases that those things would have come up. Not that you've ever actually dumped a body. But you sure know the necessary steps. Have you done this before?"

Lower and colder, Drummond said, "I've been around a long time. I've seen things."

They stayed outside in silence. Once Max felt ready, they returned to the office for the final cleaning — starting with the blood. While Max scrubbed the floor, Drummond hovered by the window, gazing into the night.

The three o'clock witching hour neared.

Max worked at the blood harder.

"You think Sister Sadie knew we'd get involved in this?" he said, wringing out the saturated water before attacking the floor again. "I mean look at this case. She gets an acolyte in Sister Ruth. Promises her all kinds of power — *when we rule magic* kind of stuff. She must have found another spell that put her into a new body."

"She could have used the same spell she used at the barn. We just never heard about it."

"That spell took her years to get working. After a taste of freedom, I doubt she felt very patient once back in her old, failing body. Doesn't matter, though. However she did it, she did it. With the success of getting her new, healthy body, the devotion of Sister Ruth is cemented. Any hesitation she had is gone. Sister Sadie has proven she's a powerful witch."

"She might've sent Sister Ruth out to recruit."

"Possibly. Even if they don't add to their numbers yet, the big problem doesn't change. Starting a coven, running a coven, takes money. A lot, apparently."

"That's why she's doing this crazy spell."

Max frowned. "Yeah, but this is the part that's bugging me. Sister Sadie needs money for her coven, and instead of working for it, selling her skills, or heck, even stealing it, she decides to use an ancient spell that may or may not work. It also requires her to murder people. It's insane."

"So is Sister Sadie."

"Yeah, but Mother Sun wanted to use the spell, too. Why?"

Drummond gave the question some serious thought. "Could be the spectacle. You said that by pulling off the spell to get a new body, she probably won over any doubts Sister Ruth had. But now, if she appears to a potential coven member, what can she say? *Trust me, I was once a decrepit old lady crazy witch but I'm so powerful I jumped into this new body.* Who would believe that if they didn't see it firsthand?"

"You think she wants to do this spell like an advertisement?"

"And a threat. And a money maker. If she can find the ghost of the man who pushed the gold or someone who was involved in transporting it through those tunnels, if she can make that minecart of gold coins appear, solid and real, taken from the whisps of a ghost's memory, there'll be no question that she's one of the strongest witches around. Maybe the strongest. Even more, others will know what lengths Sister Sadie is willing to go to get what she wants."

"She won't have to fight to become the ruler of magic, the other witches will give it to her."

Snapping his fingers and pointing, Drummond said, "That's what this is about."

"Not vengeance, then."

"Maybe a little thrown in for spice. Maybe that's a bonus."

"Wonderful."

Max gave the office a final look. He couldn't hide the fact that something had happened, but nobody would see broken furniture, strewn supplies, blood, or a dead woman. At least, not without a blacklight and a DNA kit.

With less struggle than hauling a corpse into his car, Max lifted the front door off the floor and set it in place. From the hallway, it appeared normal. He'd have to get new hinges and remount the door first chance. The rest of the fixes could wait, but not the front door.

"Drive south," Drummond said once Max got in the car. "It'll be a half-hour or so. Back when I was alive, I had a friend, Leroy, he lived out there."

"You've talked about him before. I think we even went out this way once."

"In my day, the area was all forest. Leroy lived in a tiny cabin, far from a road, very remote. There are some good spots for us down that way. Places you can take the time to dig a grave without getting interrupted."

They stayed quiet the rest of the drive. The hum of the road and the stillness of the late hour blended into a muted drone that lulled Max's weary body. Adrenaline could only keep him going for so long, and he suspected his exhausted mind had already reached the point of poor decision-making skills. More than ever before, he relied on Drummond to make the right calls — an idea that both comforted Max and terrified him.

"Over here." Drummond pointed to a dirt road that cut into the thick of the forest.

Minutes later, Max stood at a patch of earth nestled between the triangle of three oak trees. He wanted to keep the headlights on, but Drummond said that only made sense in the movies — so the audience could see what was going on. In the dead of night, however, those headlights would stick out.

"Bright lights in the middle of the forest? Any cop driving by will notice."

"How about my phone? Is that too much light to ask for?"

Max leaned the phone on the car bumper and had its flashlight mode shine — enough light to dig by. Armed with a shovel and a pickax, both tools grabbed from his house on the way south, Max set into the arduous task.

The first shovelfuls went easily enough, and he had a glimmer of hope that this wouldn't be as difficult a job as he expected. Reality dashed those hopes. Once he got deeper than the surface level soil, he hit North Carolina's infamous red clay. This wasn't the first time he had to deal with digging through the thick and unforgiving clay, and it never got easier. Switching between strokes of the heavy pickax to break up the clay and shovelfuls of the loose results, Max spent over an hour creating a place for Sister Ruth to rest.

After dragging her out of the car and tossing her in, he then had to fill it back up. Another twenty minutes. As he patted the ground with the back of the shovel, Drummond informed him that the job wasn't done yet.

"The extra dirt that's been displaced by her body — it's got to go somewhere."

Another fifteen minutes went by as Max spread the leftover earth throughout the forest. He then had to gather sticks and rocks to scatter over the grave. It wouldn't deceive a close inspection — probably wouldn't fake anybody walking by — but from a distance, it helped sell the idea that there was nothing worth seeing over this way.

Soaked in sweat, Max finally leaned his back against the car. "I've had my fill of graves."

Drummond crossed his arms and contemplated the ground.

Clearing his throat, Max said, "You see, right now is one of those times when you should drop that 1930s stoicism and start talking."

"About what?"

"My mother. Did you really think I meant I was tired from all the graves I've had to dig this year?"

"I knew what you meant, but I don't see what I could say that I haven't already said."

"I'm not trying to talk about her death for me. I've talked enough about it. I'm dealing with it." He thought about her closed door in the house. "Mostly. But you —"

"What about me?"

"You knew her. She even was involved in some of our work. I can't be sure, but it seems like you might have some thoughts about her passing." Max wanted to face Drummond, but he had learned that men from Drummond's era preferred to speak side-to-side, both gazing out at the land, rather than actually look at each other. If they had beers to hold, so much the better.

Tightening his arms, Drummond said, "I don't want to upset you —"

"You won't. I'm your friend and —"

"Can you close your mouth for more than a few seconds? Let a man build up when he's got something to say. You people nowadays want to spew everything out. Sometimes a man needs a preamble to find the right level of comfort."

"Sorry." Max mimed zipping his lips.

"This isn't an easy thing to say, and when I say it, you'll want to speak. I know you will. But I beg you, keep it shut. Just let me get through this. Okay?"

When Max nodded, he made sure not to turn his head. He didn't want Drummond to feel viewed under a microscope.

The ghost paused long enough to itch at Max's desire to fill the silence. But before Max said a word, Drummond drifted forward. With his back to Max, he removed his hat.

"I'm sorry, partner. I told you I didn't see your mother's ghost. That wasn't exactly the truth." He raised a hand to stop Max from talking. "Don't worry. She did move on. That was true. But for a few moments, I saw her before she found her way onward."

"You really saw her?"

"For a second. Maybe two. We were in the hospital, and I was floating down the hall toward her room — you were in there holding her — and when she died, she looked confused and betrayed, as if she had expected so much more from the afterlife. But when the light shined on her and she moved on, the last thing I saw was a trembling smile. So, maybe it worked out okay for her."

"That's not bad. Why didn't you tell me about this?"

Drummond's broad back sagged. "It has nothing to do with you. Or your mother. It's what I saw in her eyes. That confusion. That betrayal. I'd seen it before. With my mother."

Both men grew silent again. This time, however, Max waited. He didn't fidget or make small noises intended to get Drummond talking. He looked at the freshly dug ground with its sparse covering of sticks, and he waited.

At length, Drummond said, "When my mother was put away in an institution, they weren't helpful places back then. The one I managed to get for her was among the first to try healing patients instead housing the unwanted. I had hope for her. The doctors did, too. They would report to me on her progress and promise she improved daily. But whenever I visited, the truth was undeniable. She would never get better. Not to the point of getting out of that place."

"You did the best you could for the time."

"Maybe. But maybe I didn't look hard enough for a better place. Can't change it, though." The ghost scratched his cheek before tilting his head to the side. He didn't look at Max directly but now spoke in profile. "Little by little, her mind started to go. I don't mean in the mental institution way. Rather, it was a matter of age. One of the last times I saw her, she had no idea who I was. She talked with me like meeting a stranger and becoming friends. She boasted about her little boy, and I played along. Seemed to make her happy. When the time came to leave, she took hold of my hand, and she had no idea again who I was — not even recognizing the stranger she had met for the day. She looked scared."

Max's throat tightened. Drummond turned around, his stern face desperate to hide the upset shaking beneath.

"The worst part, though, was when I pulled my hand free. For an instant — like the instant I saw your mother before she moved on — my mother returned. Her understanding of who she was, that light in her eye, she was herself again. Her fear turned into confusion as she tried to figure out where she was and what her son was doing there, too. She never spoke, but that confusion flashed into an accusation. *Betrayal* is the only word I've ever come up for it. Seconds later, she returned to being that other woman who didn't know me."

Memories swept through Max — youthful days arguing with his mother, later years annoyed by her intrusions in his life, caring for her during her decline, holding her in her final moments. "You know you didn't betray her. Right? You did the best for her that you could."

"Isn't that what we all do?"

One last silence consumed them. Drummond drifted back to Max's side as they gazed into the dark forest. Finally, the old ghost clapped his hands once. "Let's go."

Though Max could already predict Drummond's complaining, he felt the need for one final comment. With the shovel, he pointed to the recent grave. "At least your mother had somebody to mourn over her. Nobody will know what happened to Sister Ruth. Even if they did, they won't ever find her. But I don't think anybody's going to be looking."

From behind them, a crackling, sing-song voice said, "Don't be so sure."

Chapter 22

THE WOMAN IN THE WOODS had scraggly, black hair and a wide, flat face. In another setting, she would have been somebody's eccentric aunt or an overly artistic neighbor. But in the dark night, in the cold forest, no mistake could be made.

"Another witch," Max said, tired of saying the word that day.

"Sister Gold." The witch performed a slight bow.

"Let me guess," Drummond said. "You're from the Coven of Metals, along with Sister Silver and Sister Copper. Since when did all these covens start naming with a theme?"

Squeezing the shovel handle, Max said, "Did Sister Sadie send you?"

"If she had asked, I would have come, but she didn't need to. Our coven cares about our own. Sister Ruth told me she was fixin' to get the girl from you. I offered to help, but she said it was too dangerous — I'm not as far along in my studies, you see. Now, I sat in my room and waited, and I started thinking that the real reason she didn't want me along was because she wanted to impress Sister Sadie on her own."

"Sibling rivalry?"

Sister Gold tapped her finger on her crooked nose. "Not very kind thoughts for me to have, I know, but I am human. A little jealousy is to be expected in a coven. But when she didn't come home, hour after hour, I realized something may have gone wrong. She did say it was dangerous, and I guessed she could do with a little sisterly help."

"You cast a location spell?"

"This is the 21st century, Mr. Max. I tracked her phone."

Drummond glared at Max. "You didn't empty her pockets before you buried her?"

"You didn't tell me to."

Sister Gold turned her head toward the empty space to Max's left. "I see the tales of you having a ghost partner are true."

Max pointed to his right. "He's over here."

"Pleasure to meet you, Mr. Marshall. Unfortunately, it is clear that my dear Sister Ruth is no longer among the living. That saddens me greatly."

"You look real upset."

"Oh, don't take my outward composure to be callousness. I loved Sister Ruth. She helped me to gain so much power and to understand so much of witchcraft. I'll forever be indebted."

Drummond snickered. "Her tears must be in a jar somewhere."

As much as he appreciated his partner's levity, Max couldn't be so at ease. He watched this witch's hands, observed her body language, paid close attention to her eyes. But it was dark and the light from his phone made everything outside its beam even darker.

"If you want Sister Ruth, she's buried right there." Max gestured to the ground.

"I'm not here for her."

"You're not?"

"I want the same girl she came for, of course. Sister Moon. I thought that'd been obvious."

Max feigned innocence. "Don't have her. Don't know where she is."

Wagging her finger at him, she said, "I expected better. Acting tough won't get you far. We both know that killing Sister Ruth had to have been luck. She was an accomplished witch. Likewise, I doubt you underestimate the strength of our dearest Sister Sadie. Yet you act like I can't or won't hurt you."

Drummond eased closer in her direction. "I'll stop her, if I have to."

"I know you can hurt me," Max said. "I also know that you aren't like your sisters. You haven't been holding a couple spells in your head while we've talked. I'm not sure you can. It's difficult."

Sister Gold clawed her hands. "You think you know what's happening because you don't see the energy building between my fingers? I assure you, there are plenty of spells that do not reveal themselves that way."

"Yeah, but the ones you need for a fight do."

"You think you know about witchcraft?"

"I'm married to a witch far better than you. I've learned a lot."

With a huff, Sister Gold whirled away. Max set his feet in a balanced stance in case he was wrong, but her tensed body did not spin back to assault him with magic. Instead, she relaxed as she looked at Max's car.

She sauntered to the side door and opened it. Max reached into his pocket for the car's key fob, but it was too late to click the lock. The inside lighting gave him a clear view of her. He wished the light went out. Her hair had plenty of gray, and her skin sagged off the bone. There was a deadness to her. If a witch could call the dead to rise, then he guessed they would look like Sister Gold. And if such a thing were possible, Sister Sadie would be the one to try it.

Living or undead, Sister Gold leaned into the car and lifted something off the headrest. Max couldn't make it out, but from the way she pinched the near-invisible object, he knew — a hair. Sandra's hair. With a hair in her possession, Sister Gold could easily cast a spell to find his wife.

Or worse.

Like an enraged bull, Max charged. He grunted and growled, the fire within burning hotter. He reached the witch in time to see her arrogance drop. Her arms went up to protect her head as he smacked her in the side.

But she was no child cowering in fear. After the initial surprise wore off — seconds only — she balled up a fist and struck back. Nailed him straight on the chin. His turn to be surprised. Stunned long enough for her to follow up with a harder punch to the gut. She stepped back — perhaps to admire the pain she caused or to offer a threat.

This brief pause created an opening, and Drummond zipped in to take advantage. Max silently cheered the ghost, ready to see the witch fall in frozen perplexity. No such luck.

Sister Gold whipped a necklace from her pocket and thrust it into the air. Dangling in the middle — a well-crafted ghost ward. "I know you're there. I feel your cold."

With Drummond cautiously approaching to get an idea of how strong the ward was, Max had no choice. He shook off the pain in his ribs, strained for some air, and blitzed forward. If he could tackle her to the ground, he'd have the advantages of size and weight.

She must have heard him — not that he had been stealthy. As he closed in, she kicked forward, catching him between the legs. Momentum saved him. With his legs pumping, she missed a direct hit. But getting kicked in the thigh and having that kick rise to where the leg joined the groin ditched Max into the dirt. He held still on all fours. Pain radiating from the strike point, constricting his lungs, forcing his gut into his throat, twisting his insides.

For the duration of a labored breath, he could not move or see or hear. His senses shut down in an effort to protect him. The next breath brought the world back into focus. A little, anyway. The next breath, a little more.

Max guessed he had been on all fours for a solid ten minutes. But when he saw Sister Gold running off, taking advantage of his compromised state, he decided it had been mere seconds.

"I'll get her." Drummond lowered like a sprinter at the start of a race.

"No. Wait," Max said, the words thin and weak. Using the car's side as a crutch, he managed to stand. A few deep breaths — all the time holding out one hand like the weakest police officer commanding a perp to halt. Then: "Go find Sandra. Warn her."

"But Sister Gold —"

Max wrenched open the car door, feeling stronger with each second. He lowered to the passenger seat and yanked the glove compartment release. From inside, he grabbed his 9mm handgun.

"I'll take care of Sister Gold."

Chapter 23

TRUDGING THROUGH THE FOREST, Max panted as sweat soaked through his clothes. He needed to finish this fast. Not only to protect Sandra but because the cold would soon chill his wet skin.

He tried running. After a few strides, his groin complained with a sharp stab that reached up his neck and into the back of his head. Too dark anyway. Run for long and he'd end up tripping on a root or smacking into a tree trunk.

With his phone's flashlight, he opted to walk as fast as his body would allow. He didn't worry, though. Sister Gold cut a clear path for him to follow. She didn't run, either. Too dark for her as well. Too arrogant, also.

Weaving around one tree and another, he closed in. She had walked away from the dirt road that led out to the main highway. At first, Max guessed she had lost her sense of direction — easy enough to do in the woods during the day, almost guaranteed at night. Yet the longer she sauntered ahead, the more blatant her path became.

He thought of Sister Ruth at the cemetery. She also had walked through the woods, seemingly aimless, yet had led straight to a casting circle. Max increased his pace.

Staggering between the trees, he felt unprepared when he spotted Sister Gold up ahead. She sat on her knees and clutched a small but thick branch. He darted behind the nearest tree. Probably unnecessary — her back was to him — but he held a strong suspicion of what she had done.

Peeking around the tree trunk, he watched her digging in the ground. Another casting circle.

Apparently, Sister Sadie had a thing for teaching her coven

sisters to cast their spells deep in the woods. Not uncommon for witches. At least, for witches from the 17th century.

Taking on a proper grip of his weapon, Max moved in closer. Despite the pain running up his inner thigh, he kept a good stance.

"Mr. Max, it amazes me you've lived this long. You are so predictable."

Keeping his trigger finger flat on side of his handgun, Max said, "Stand up and back off."

"Certainly." Sister Gold got to her feet with a hefty groan. She stepped forward, making sure not to disrupt the lines of her casting circle, and with the circle between them, she turned around. A big, devilish smile painted her face.

"I can't let you cast that spell."

She waited, but when Max said nothing more, she stepped back into the circle.

"I'm warning you," he said.

"A gun is only a threat if the man wielding it is willing to pull the trigger. You are not."

"That doesn't mean it's not a hunk of metal I'll use to bash you in the skull if you harm my wife."

She raised her hands in mock surprise, followed by a serious though disappointed look. "You keep thinking the worst of me. I have no interest in your wife. None of us do. We want the new witch. Nothing more."

Jerking her hand, her fingers splayed outward. Max jumped back, covering his face.

Nothing happened.

Nothing but her laughter.

"You were right. It's very hard to keep a spell prepared in your head. Someday, though, I'll do it."

Licking salty sweat off his lips while exhaling a shaky breath, Max lowered his hands and straightened. Then he had a simple thought, and a bit of his fears vanished. "You won't kill me, either."

"I think most witches would love to kill you."

"But you can't."

"You and your wife do hold a unique standing. I admit that. Some witches — powerful ones — they have taken you under their wings. Like pets. To kill you would incur their wrath. Also, I don't wish to start a war."

"There's already a witch war going on."

"That's true. Maybe I should kill you."

Max stepped closer. A few more feet and he could drag his heel through that casting circle. "Yet here I am alive. It's Sister Sadie, isn't it? Even if there wasn't a witch war going on, even if Sandra and I did not have the favor of other, stronger witches, you still wouldn't kill me. Because Sister Sadie wants her revenge firsthand."

"You'll find out for yourself when I take Sandra to her."

"That's not going to happen." Max stomped to the circle, ready to kick several feet back. But he reared at the last moment when the old woman dropped to the ground, crying in a familiar, weakened voice.

"Don't hurt me."

He heard his mother. He saw her. He could even smell her scent rising with the earth and leaves and trees.

"Is that really you?"

She huddled on the ground, covering her face with her hands as she wept. "How could you let me go like that? I deserved better."

Max fell back, his feet tripping on each other. He landed hard and flat, his head angled up to never lose sight of his mother.

It couldn't be her. That didn't make sense. Yet he saw her.

No, no, no. Sister Gold was there. Unless that had been her spell all along. The hair she pulled from Max's car — he had assumed it belonged to Sandra, but it could easily have been his mother's. Did Sister Gold resurrect his mother? Even if she just pulled his mother's ghost from the afterlife, or set up a communication with her like a medium could do, it would be enough to stall Max. Recognizing that possibility didn't change the fact that his mother was there. He needed to say something.

"Max? Where are you?"

Shaking his head, he tried to brush off his guilt. He had done his best to comfort her in the end, and he had failed. But after she had died, she would have learned the truth. Would she still blame him? Even after she had moved on?

Probably.

No, that was disingenuous. His mother had loved him. Had sacrificed for him. Despite the negative things he learned, she had done them out of love. Misguided love, but love nonetheless. Her bitterness and anger at the end evolved as she recognized that end neared. It grew from the pain of her MS. That horrible disease had robbed her of an easy, peaceful finale.

Returning to his feet, he moved to the edge of the circle. "I'm sorry."

"You have nothing to be sorry about."

That didn't sound like her. Even if she accepted his apology, she would make it clear that he had done the wrong thing. Once it was clear, she'd make it even clearer. "Tell me something that only I would know."

The woman did not respond. The longer he stared at her curved back, the more she no longer looked like a woman at all. That thought broke through the strange, turbulent energy in the air. Moonlight cut through the tall forest and landed on a large rock huddled in the center of the circle.

A rock.

He spun around, scanning between the trees, and into the distance. Sister Gold was gone.

Time continued to fight against him. Though still the same night, though exhausted by putting in twenty-plus hours, Max felt that time moved faster. Limping between one clutch of trees and around another, the night slipped from him. He had the distinct and unwelcome feeling — not a thought, but a feeling in his nerves and bones — that if he did not get to Sandra before dawn, she might not survive.

Not with Sister Sadie out there. Not with Sister Gold as her lackey.

When he reached the car, Max wanted to jump in and floor

it. But he had to clean up the grave site. After all the effort put into burying Sister Ruth out here, all the care in hiding her, he would be a fool to rush off while leaving a shovel covered in fingerprints and DNA behind. The pickax, too. He couldn't do anything about the tire tracks — not that he knew of — but he did scan the area for other signs that would rat him out.

The entire time, a short time that felt unendurably long, he thought of Sandra and begged her to hold on. Or perhaps Drummond had found her in time. She might have been prepared for a witch assault. She might have fended them off.

Satisfied that he had cleaned the minimum of evidence and hopefully a lot more, he managed a twelve-point turn and headed back toward the main road. Reaching pavement, he had a choice — left or right. He considered yelling for Drummond. But the ghost might be Sandra's main reinforcement. Sister Moon could be tough and vicious, but she had proven already that she had only one interest — Sister Moon. She was not Sandra's ally.

He dug his phone out of his front pocket. When he called his wife and the phone rang numerous times, his nerves returned. He pictured her collapsed on the ground while Sister Sadie's contorted face loomed overhead.

"Hi, hon," Sandra answered, calm and relaxed.

Taken aback by her casualness, Max said, "Are you okay?"

"For now. We're trying to get as many spells drawn as we can. Drummond's patrolling."

"Good, good. One question — where are you?"

"R.J. Reynolds High School."

"High school?"

"Sister Moon's idea. She thought there were tunnels under the school, and she was right."

Max turned left. "I'm on my way."

A muffled sound and Sandra's caught breath. Then: "They found us. Hurry."

Chapter 24

R. J. REYNOLDS HIGH SCHOOL sat to the northwest of Winston-Salem — about as far from Max as a place could be while still residing in the main part of the city. Even speeding in the final hours of the night, he had a long drive ahead. Close to an hour. Too long. The thought of losing Sandra was always a heart-wrenching thing, one that he encountered too often in this job, but after losing his mother — he wouldn't be able to handle it. He drove faster.

As he neared the edge of the city and faced crossing most of it via downtown streets, Drummond appeared hovering in the passenger seat. Max stayed focused on driving.

"Is Sister Sadie attacking her?" he asked.

"Don't know yet. Probably."

"Then what the heck are you doing here? Sandra needs you."

"Going right back," Drummond said. "How far out are you?"

"Look around for yourself." Max glanced at his maps app. "About fifteen, maybe twenty minutes."

Drummond gave a quick rundown of the school's layout and how to get to the tunnels. "Don't worry. Sister Moon's tough, and you know Sandra's the toughest. I'll get back, but we'll be fine." He paused. "You should hurry up."

"I'm going as fast as I can. Now get over there."

"I'm gone. Be ready for a fight."

"I didn't think they'll be having a tea party. Go already."

Drummond disappeared.

The school had one main building dating back to 1923, built in R.J. Reynold's honor by his widow. A thick wall of trees blocked off the highway behind, and several smaller annex buildings as well as a large auditorium spread across the property. The main school was an imposing structure in the way old government buildings projected authority and stability through design. The list of notable people who had walked its halls was impressive. From musicians like Ben Folds to politicians like Senator Richard Burr, tons of actors and actresses, as well as numerous professional sports figures. But if it meant saving Sandra's life, Max would burn the whole place to the ground without hesitation.

He banged the curb as he ripped into the parking lot and stopped next to Sandra's car. The back entrance to the school had been tampered open. Probably by a spell since he saw no sign of force. That, and Sandra's lockpicking skills were worse than his own. Once inside, he followed Drummond's instructions through the hallways until he saw the sign for an emergency shelter pointing to a stairwell. He rushed down and quickly found his way.

The square tunnel had brutally scuffed concrete flooring and cinderblock walls. Some sections had been plastered over and painted lime-green while others remained raw. Cables and piping trailed along the black ceiling. Well-lit from above, the types of lighting varied with the sections. Max guessed it depended on when each bit of tunnel had been constructed over the last century. A few junctions had tunnels filled with boxes or old filing cabinets, broken chairs or outdated classroom equipment. If not for Drummond's directions, Max would have been lost.

Making his final turn, Max slowed and listened. Quiet. Damn. If he had heard shouting or sounds of struggle, he could rush ahead, surprise the enemy, and maybe save his wife. But quiet — that suggested a dark outcome.

Wrestling down the desire to sprint ahead, he approached with caution. He didn't want to alert Sister Sadie if there was still a chance that he could help.

The humid air smelled stale. Dust coated the boxes.

Then he saw her.

Sandra sat on her knees in the middle of a hastily drawn

casting circle. A ghost-blue field encircled her, pulsing like a dying heartbeat. Her eyes were closed.

His stomach plummeted. "Sandra?"

Her eyes fluttered with the confusion of being drawn out of a deep sleep. When she recognized Max, she collapsed forward. He leaped ahead and caught her before she hit the hard floor. The protection spell surrounding her dissipated into misty whisps. A few feet to the side, Drummond floated — horizontal, head back, unconscious.

Pushing strands of hair from her perspiring forehead, he held her close. "You're safe now. You're going to be okay."

"Sister Sadie." She tried to sit up, but he tightened his grip.

"It's just me here. You held her off." He kissed the top of her head. "You are one tough-ass witch. I love you. Are you hurt?" She didn't answer, and his face twisted at the thought of returning to a source of pain, but he asked, "Do you need the hospital?"

"I'll be okay." She nestled against his chest.

With a relieved kiss and stroke of her arm, Max said, "That's right. You're okay. You're safe. I didn't lose you."

Her eyes snapped open, and she forced herself up. "Sister Moon. We lost her."

Max looked around as if the witch might have been misplaced behind the boxes.

Sandra uttered a defeated cry. "They've taken her."

Pulling her back into his arms, Max said, "Then we'll get her back."

Chapter 25

Dawn arrived as Max pulled into the driveway. Sandra sat in the passenger seat, cheek pressed against the window. Halfway home, Drummond had appeared in the back, rubbing his sore head and complaining about spell hangovers.

They zombie-walked into the house while Drummond floated behind. Sandra slumped into a chair at the kitchen table, and Max started up the coffee machine. Once that began brewing, he grabbed his laptop and fired it up.

"What are you doing?" Drummond said.

"I'm pretty sure it's self-explanatory."

"You're in no condition to fight Sister Sadie."

Max made a show of looking around the kitchen. "No Sister Sadie here. I guess I'm not fighting. I am, however, going to find where they are and stop them from killing a young girl."

Sandra opened her laptop. "We'll have a fight on our hands eventually. I'll be better prepared next time."

"Stop it," Drummond said. "Both of you. You're of no use in this condition. You need sleep."

"But —"

"I'm the ghost here, and even I feel beat. You're human. Without sleep, you'll be making bad decisions, and not like Max's usual bad decisions. Now go to bed. All of this can wait."

"It really can't," Max said. "We might be too late already."

"We're not. This kind of spell, one this big, is going to require a witching hour to cast."

"You're guessing, and this is not the time for guesswork."

Sandra said, "Drummond's right. Even the oldest, known spells require the proper timing. Anything powerful needs a full moon, at least. But this is more organized, so a proper witching hour is needed."

"It's only six in the morning. First witching hour is eighteen hours away, and you both won't be able to find anyone or handle anything if you don't rest your brains and your bodies. I'm here, and I'll keep an eye on things, so there's no need to worry about that. Now, quit wasting the time we do have, and get some damn sleep."

Without further comment, Max and Sandra shuffled into their bedroom. They shared one exhausted look in which they agreed that any bedtime rituals like brushing teeth, washing faces, or changing clothes would be suspended. The two flopped onto the mattress.

Max closed his eyes.

At two in the afternoon, Max awoke to the rich aroma of fresh coffee and delivery pizza. He entered the kitchen to find Sandra dressed in clean clothes, hair washed, and as perky as a college graduate on their first day of a new job. She kissed the side of his cheek.

"Go shower," she said, handing him a full coffee mug. "You smell like the bottom of a trash can." He looked at the pizza box. She tapped his nose with her index finger. "I promise I won't touch a slice until you join me."

Over the next hour, he cleaned up, drank coffee, ate pizza, drank more coffee, tried to ignore his mother's closed door, and finally settled on the living room couch with Sandra at his side. Drummond joined, hovering between the chairs opposite them.

"You look better," he said, winking at Sandra. To Max: "You look the same, but I didn't expect much from you."

Max said, "I'll admit we needed the sleep and the food, but we've lost a lot of time."

"Right," Sandra said, clapping both hands onto her knees. "First, the bad news — Sister Sadie now has all she needs to cast the spell. The good news — she can't cast it until the proper witching hour. The bad news — that's three o'clock tonight."

"But the good news — we know she'll be in that warded

tunnel."

Drummond said, "The bad news — we don't know how to get in there."

Max waited. When nothing more came out, he said, "Huh. I was hoping for some more good news."

"We've got twelve hours. What can we do with that?"

"Get more hands, for starters." To Sandra: "Give Brenda a call. I'm sure she can help."

Sandra said, "She absolutely could, but she also has a full-time job. The work she does for us is paid through my labor teaching her witchcraft. If we want to get more out of her, we've got to come up with a way to pay her."

"That's a problem for after we survive this night." Max opened his laptop and set it on the coffee table. "For now, I've got to go through the entire case again. Everything we've done and learned. Somewhere in all of this, I'll hopefully find how to get in that tunnel. Drummond, you should go underground again. See if you can locate that entrance directly."

"Sure, no problem," Drummond said as if he had been asked to scale Everest. "There's only a few endless miles of tunnels."

"Maybe you'll be lucky."

"Wait," Sandra said.

Max chilled at the hesitancy in her voice. "What's wrong?"

"I have an idea, but I don't like it."

Drummond said, "Spit it out or we'll think it's far worse."

Cringing, she said, "We should go to Sister Sadie's apartment."

"No, I don't think I could've come up with anything worse."

"It's bad, but not crazy. We know that after we beat her in that barn, she was returned to her old body. That body was in her loft downtown. Since then, she's obviously found a better spell and transferred into this new body. She seems more stable-minded."

"That's debatable."

"You know what I mean. That loft was fine for a crazy old witch, but not for an attractive young woman seeking power."

Max said, "Then shouldn't we look for where she's living

now?"

"We can try, but that's not what has my interest. Sister Sadie relies on old, old magic. It's her main way of doing things. Even things a more modern spell could handle."

Max shivered recalling the hex bags Sister Sadie had once used against him and the horrid hallucinations that they created. "What does that have to do with her old loft?"

"Before witches understood the strength of a casting circle, we had to use specific locations to create spells. Temples and sacrificial stones and unique spaces on mountains — that kind of junk. The casting circle freed us from those confines because it allows a witch to create magic almost anywhere she can draw a circle."

Drummond snapped his fingers. "But she doesn't go for the modern magic."

"Right. She'll use a casting circle, but she'll feel more comfort and strength in centering on a specific location."

Max said, "Isn't that why we need to find the tunnel?"

"But I'm not talking about that spell. I'm talking about the spell that allows her to be in her current body." To her team's confused looks, she said, "If that spell is remotely related to the original body transfer spell she once attempted, then her old body needs to be connected for a time."

"You're kidding," Drummond said.

"If her old body is still there, we could disrupt the spell and send her back right away. We'd save Sister Moon's life without ever needing to find the tunnel."

"We only have a limited amount of time."

"You were the one pointing out how we have a ton of hours."

"Yeah, to find a way into the tunnel. Not to make a dangerous situation even worse."

Rubbing his face, Max let out a resigned sigh. "I agree with Sandra."

"See?" Sandra said.

"But Drummond, too."

"See." Drummond crossed his arms.

"It seems to me that we have to do both. The only way we

can do that is to stop arguing and get moving right now. So, that's what we do." To Drummond: "If Sister Sadie's body is in that loft, then she'll have the place warded. No sense in wasting your time with us. Do your best underground, and if we need you, we'll call out."

"I don't like this," Drummond said. "But considering how much time I need to do a thorough job, I suppose your plan isn't too bad."

Offering more consolation than suggestion, Sandra added, "What about Pauline? She could help you, and that'll speed everything up."

"Can't hurt to ask."

Once Drummond disappeared, Max and Sandra headed for the car and the witch's loft. Max's stomach churned the entire drive.

Chapter 26

DESPITE THE DREAD hanging over anything to do with Sister Sadie, despite the desire to postpone this visit, it did not take long to reach the witch's loft. Max tried to think about other subjects while driving, but seeing her again, knowing it was her even in a different body, created trepidation within every thought. That disquiet must have pushed his foot harder on the accelerator because he did not want to be there. Facing Sister Sadie had been hard enough the first time.

Like many apartment buildings in the downtown area, this one originally had been a warehouse. Part of RJ Reynolds Tobacco, back in the day. At some point in the recent history of the building, it had been converted into loft apartments. Max and Sandra walked down a long hallway lined with doors and plenty of natural light flooding in through skylights above. Max didn't recall those skylights from a few years ago. Somebody cared about the building. Then again, whoever owned the building didn't mind having Sister Sadie as a tenant. They couldn't care too greatly if they let her in the place.

A tiny hope sparked inside him. Maybe the apartment had been emptied and rented to a new tenant. Maybe there was nothing to be found here. But then they reached the door with its handmade sign:

~ Promises ~
Full service invitations and announcements

Max read the sign repeatedly as if expecting the words to change. But no magic had created this sign. Only the hand of a mad woman.

Sandra reached over and knocked on the door. "Hello?"

"Are you nuts? You want to tell her we're here?"

"I doubt she's in there."

Indeed, nobody answered. Pressing close to the metal door to hide his activity, Max pulled out his lockpicks and got to work. As he tried to feel the pins being pushed upward, he noticed Sandra scanning up and down the hall. A good move by her, but it heightened his nerves, reminded him that they were in an apartment hallway and could easily get caught.

As if reacting to his thoughts, Sandra knocked hard on the door three times. He bolted straight, pocketing the lockpicks, and waited. An older gentleman with a frail poodle on a leash stepped out of his loft and shuffled down the hall toward the elevators. Away from them, thankfully.

When the man turned the corner, Max shot back to work. If he had been more skilled, he would have opened the door already. Unfortunately, he had yet to master lockpicking. Well, no fortune about it — he never put in enough practice time. Drummond would point out that having a ghost partner that could unlock the door from the inside made Max lazy. Max couldn't argue with that.

Okay, he thought, *I need to practice using my gun and picking locks. Anything else?*

He swallowed down a grander sarcastic tirade in his head for fear of tempting the Fates. Besides, he almost had the lock. Until the Fates responded with Sandra knocking on the door again as a young couple entered the hall. He hated to pull the picks out and have to start over, but what he attempted would be obvious to anybody if he left them sticking in the door.

The young couple walked toward them, the man with his arm casually slung over the woman. He nodded at Sandra. "Y'all looking for that old lady?"

"That's right." Tapping on the door sign, Sandra said, "She does wedding invitations."

"You're getting married?" the woman said.

A flash of discomfort on the man's face betrayed their whole story. That gave Max an easy way to be rid of these people.

"We're already married. But we want to renew our vows."

"That's lovely." The woman beamed warmth as she glanced toward her boyfriend.

He squirmed at everybody's attention. "Sorry to tell you, but she ain't there no more."

"Oh no," Sandra said. "Do you know where she moved to?"

"Heaven, I hope for her sake."

The woman slapped his chest. "Don't talk about the dead like that."

"She died?" Max glanced at the door. "What happened?"

Happy to get away from talking about marriage, the man said, "She was old, I guess. No foul play or nothing, if that's what you're getting at. Nobody knew 'til she started stinking up the place." The woman slapped his chest again, but he ignored her. "Police came and found her. Never seen a dead body before, but they wheeled her out and barely had her face covered. I think they wanted to get her gone fast. She was all blue and disgusting."

"How long ago was this?"

The man looked to his girlfriend. "Not long, I don't think. They haven't rented it out yet, so it can't have been too long. Maybe a few weeks." To his girlfriend: "That sound about right?"

She shrugged. "Maybe. I don't like to think about her like that. She could be creepy."

A few more words exchanged but clearly everyone had finished with the conversation. Except for the woman. She had a love for chatting, and it took some strong prodding from her boyfriend to get them further down the hall and into their apartment.

Once again, Sandra became the lookout, and Max returned to the lockpicking. No further interruptions came, and for good or evil, he unlocked the door. Sharing a final look with Sandra — one that posed the idea of never entering the loft, just walking back to the car and focusing on other aspects of the case, one that he knew they both rejected — he opened the door.

Chapter 27

Nothing had changed. The same high ceiling. The same open floorplan. The only enclosed room was the kitchen, and that only because the single bedroom sat atop it in the loft section. Stairs to the top had been built against one wall, no railing on the open side. Stylish but deadly. No furniture in the room but a stool. No hoarding of old magazines, boxes of cat toys, or stacks of playing cards. No piles of books. A vast open area that allowed the mind to bounce around unencumbered. Perfect for an insane witch.

"Anybody home?" Max said, his voice echoing.

The only aspect of the apartment that chilled the skin had also remained untouched. The walls and windows had been covered with white paper and canvas. Painted in red and black, Sister Sadie had drawn casting circles, ancient symbols, and weird images pulled from her confused and twisted memories. Sometimes, she portrayed her dark dreams. Sometimes, she captured the likeness of her enemies. Max hoped he wouldn't find paintings of Sandra or himself.

Pointing to the floor, he said, "It's empty. If there ever had been a casting circle around Sister Sadie or the stool, it's gone now. Any spell she had going either is done or broken."

"Unless it's upstairs."

"Then let's take a quick peek and get out of here. I don't want to be arrested for breaking and entering."

"You've done more breaking and entering for our cases than most thieves. I know Sister Sadie spooks you, but we've got a job to do. We need to be thorough. Otherwise, we'll end up back here to find the things we missed. Or worse, we'll fail and Sister Moon is murdered."

"Okay, you're right." He put out his hands as if presenting the apartment. "This was your idea. How do you want to do this?"

Sandra pointed to the kitchen. "You start there. I'll go upstairs. If we find nothing, we can do a once over on the main floor, but since it's empty, I doubt we'll get much there."

As she headed for the stairs, Max hopped into the kitchen. It was a cramped space that discouraged use. Probably the landlord's intent. After all, if tenants didn't use the kitchen, the appliances wouldn't break. Cheaper for the landlord. And in this kitchen, cooking would be nearly impossible. Nobody would enjoy laboring hours for a meal when every turn forced an elbow into the counter or a knee into a cabinet door.

While Max had no interest in breaking out pots and pans to whip up some pasta from scratch, he did take notice that there were a lot of drawers and that the cabinets went deeper than expected — plenty of places to hide things. He flicked on his phone's flashlight to look closer. Above, he heard Sandra rummaging around, and somebody shouted down the outside hall. Each little noise sent a jolt through Max, but he maintained his focus.

In the first few cabinets, he discovered nothing. Empty spaces with lots of dark areas the phone revealed to be empty still. But when he reached the corner cabinet and flashed his phone inside, he saw a tan lump in the back and to the side. Not an easy reach and difficult to angle his head for a better view.

He sat on the counter, turned his torso parallel to the wall, and stuck his arm in. The tip of his middle finger brushed something soft. Pressing his shoulder into the edge of the cabinet, he stretched further back. One touch. Two. On the third, he felt the object give way. His fingers rolled it into his hand.

When he pulled out of the cabinet, he already knew what he had found. The familiar weight of the leather pouch and the way the objects it contained poked at his hand told him everything. A hex bag. One of Sister Sadie's favorite delivery methods for her magic.

"I found something," Sandra called out.

Tossing the bag down, Max yelled back, "Let me take a wild guess."

In the course of twenty minutes, Max and Sandra scoured every dark corner of that apartment until they stood in the kitchen with five hex bags lined up on the kitchen counter. Dust mixed with sweat on Max's face and clothes. Nobody had cleaned the place. More than anything, this confirmed his suspicion that Sister Sadie, or someone, continued to pay rent. At least, for now.

With his arms crossed, he scrutinized the bags. Each one had a symbol on a wooden tag tied around the mouth. Sandra bent closer, sniffing the air above them.

"What do they do?" Max asked.

"Could be lots of things. Probably protection or an alarm system."

"Then Sister Sadie might know we're here."

"They also might be why we came. They might be part of what's keeping her stable in the body she now inhabits."

Max checked his watch. Almost four. "We could take the bags back to the office, and you could research the spells. But there's a big risk."

"If I'm wrong, and these aren't connected to her body, then we've lost a lot of that time."

"What if we open them? That would destroy her spell, right?"

"I'm not a hex bag expert. But under the circumstances, that sounds like the best choice. Fast and efficient. Risky, but I'm pretty sure there aren't hex bags that'll explode if opened."

"Great. We'll risk our lives on a *pretty sure.*"

Max didn't wait for a rebuttal. He grabbed the first bag, yanked the drawstring open, and dumped the contents. Two rocks, a small bone, and a dark powder that smelled of cinnamon.

They waited in a tense quiet. Listening to his heart thumping in his ears, Max watched his wife for any sign of something he could not perceive.

At length, she said, "If it did anything to her, we won't know about it here, but it didn't do anything to us. Let's open another."

Max snatched the second bag, opened and dumped it. A coil of hair, another rock, a few twigs of thyme, and a peppery odor. The third and fourth bags proved similar. A few rocks, a little bone, and a combination of herbs. When he opened the fifth bag, however, a startled scream raced out.

The sound blasted across the kitchen like the opening chords of a metal song through an overdriven amplifier. Max felt it hit his skin. The scream rose in pitch, distraught and anguished.

A strong energy soared around the loft, flapping the painted papers and canvases like flags on a windy day. Max didn't need to see it to track its movement.

"What is this? What do you want to do?" he asked Sandra.

Her head moved as if she watched this thing zoom from one end of the room to the other. Max couldn't track it, but then she often saw more than he did. She said, "Whatever that is, it's pissed off. We should get out of here before it decides we're the cause."

As this entity tore papers into confetti, Max and Sandra tiptoed to the door and into the hall. They rushed out to their car, got in, and caught their breath.

"I'm guessing that didn't work at stopping Sister Sadie," Max said, his heart racing. "Felt more like a trap for nosy paranormal investigators."

Sandra rubbed her hands against her knees. "I still think it was worth a try."

"We need to get back home and plan our next steps."

Happy to get away from the loft, he turned the car on. Before he could reverse out of the parking space, Sandra put a hand on his arm. Years of marriage communicated her intent. He turned the car off.

"I wasn't wrong," she said. "Not exactly."

He unbuckled his seatbelt and faced her. "Tell me."

"We came out here because I thought the spell Sister Sadie used to transfer her body would still have some connection to this loft. We forgot to ask ourselves a key question. Where did she get the younger body she's now in?"

As Max's head fell back against the seat, he said, "That thing screaming around in there — you think that's the ghost of whoever she body-snatched."

"I do."

He perked up. "Can we get her to shoot back into her body? Kick Sister Sadie out?"

"I imagine it's possible, but we don't have the time to research it, learn the spell, get whatever it requires, and perform it. Not to mention, we probably would need to have the body with us."

"And Sister Sadie's not going to walk into our offices and participate willfully. If there's nothing we can do, why are we staying here?"

Sandra glanced at the apartment building. "She's still there. Confused. Maybe in pain. That screaming sounded full of pain."

Opening the car door, Max said, "You want to help her move on."

"We've done it enough now that we know the routine. I can draw the casting circle in my sleep."

"Then I guess I'll be doing what I can to protect you from this ghost until you finish."

"Just talk with her. Keep her calm. We don't want her going poltergeist."

Chapter 28

THE WOMAN'S NAME WAS MARGO BRILL, and she had been a high school English teacher. She had no interest in witchcraft — heck, no knowledge of it — and simply wanted invitations to a bridal shower she was throwing for a good friend. Entering Sister Sadie's loft that doubled for her business front was the last thing Margo remembered. And remembering that brought with it the woman's vicious rage.

Max took the brunt of the abuse, but Sandra did not escape unscathed. When they shuffled into their kitchen at home and dropped into their chairs, both let out long sighs. They were bruised. Max had scratches on his arms and a shiner on his cheek. Sandra's disheveled hair hid the growing welt on her neck.

"I wish we could open a bottle of wine," she said. "Celebrate Margo having moved on and a job well done."

Max checked the time — 5:15 pm. "But the job isn't over yet."

"Yeah."

"Yeah."

She opened her hand on the table. He placed his hand on top. They sat. For a few minutes, at least.

Until Sandra squeezed tight and let go. "We hit the books?"

"I'll start the coffee."

Sliding her mug over, she tapped the side. "A lot of coffee."

Max tried to ignore the ticking clock in his head, yet it grew louder the longer he sat there reading through his notes. Not only did he feel the urgency, but he hated re-researching his work. His brain already knew the details and would often skip over parts without the rest of him realizing. Once he picked up on what he had done, he would have to go back and start over. It wasted time — a commodity they lacked.

Sandra triple-checked her notes on the veohoxal spell. She discovered, checked yet again, and finally confirmed that the spell specifically required the three o'clock witching hour and that they hadn't missed anything regarding the three heads. Location did not appear to matter beyond being wherever the ghost existed that the witch wanted to make corporeal.

"This is such a stupid way to make money," she said, flopping back against the cushions. "I get it that she's trying to show off her strength, but still."

"She's also insane."

"Not as much as you like to think. She takes insane risks, but from what we've seen, she does so with purpose."

"You don't think revealing herself as top dog and getting rich in the process is enough of a purpose?"

"Not for a witch. At least, not a witch like her." Warming to her thoughts, she bounced forward. "Look at her history with us. The spells she has cast have never been simple matters. They're always ancient spells that predate formal witchcraft. Unsafe, unstable things. Not only that but they've been spells that are violent. These are the kinds of spells that make people fear. Witch trials and burning at the stake — that wasn't for curing a hangover or making a love potion. People got afraid over this kind of crap. The kind of spells that, when they went wrong, people got hurt or killed."

"Doesn't that prove her elevator never reaches the top floor?"

"I know this will sound like a conspiracy theory, but what if she's got a bigger plan going on? What if she doesn't only want to be the leader of magic around here?"

"She wants to what? Rule the world?"

"I wouldn't be surprised if she considered that too small."

Max thought he saw where Sandra led, and he felt the chill spread across his body. "Ghosts?"

"She's already shown she's strong enough to hop into a new

person. That's an amazingly difficult bit of magic to pull off. That shows mastery over human life like most witches have never seen."

"Now she follows it up with taking control of the ghost realm."

"And not by capturing a ghost or using a ghost or anything like that. She's going one step further by pulling into our world an actual *object* connected to a ghost. If she succeeds —"

"Every witch around will bow down to her. Either out of fear or the desire to work for her, get some of that power. But she'll get more than our world."

"She'll have started to control the ghost world. A step towards any other worlds out there." With a faraway gaze, Sandra whispered, "She really is crazy." Snapping back, she turned to her laptop. "We need to figure out the specific ghost she's looking for."

"We know that. It's a minecart full of gold coins."

"The minecart is an object connected to the ghost. Think about Drummond's hat. If Drummond was not a ghost, if he had moved on, the hat would be gone, too. It only exists because he is connected to it personally, emotionally, and he is here."

"Are you saying we need the ghost of R. J. Reynolds?"

"I'm sure he's moved on, or we would've known about it by now. Besides, why would a bunch of gold coins mean anything to a guy rich enough to have a hundred minecarts like that? No, hon, what we need is somebody more directly connected. Like the guy who made a living pushing that minecart through the tunnels."

Feeling that surge of researching glee flood his system, Max sifted through his files until he found the breakdown of people interviewed over the years about the tunnels. Most of them reported knowing stories about the tunnels, being involved in maintaining them, or having studied their history. But there was one name that stuck out.

"Got him." Max re-read his notes like they might escape if he didn't keep an eye on them. "There was a man interviewed on the local news station. Oscar Dubicki. He was a gunman hired on as security to protect the gold. Now, the interview was from 2011, and back then he was in his 90s. Whenever he died, if he became a ghost, then he'd have a connection to that gold, right?"

"Possibly. Where is he buried? We can go find the gravesite and —"

"Holy crap." Max stared at his computer screen until Sandra nudged his knee. "I was searching for his obituary, but there isn't one. Not registered on the graveyard database, either."

"Was he cremated?"

He looked right at his wife and shook his head. "He's alive."

Chapter 29

BEFORE THEY LEFT FOR OSCAR DUBICKI'S HOUSE, Sandra made sure to call out for Drummond. When the ghost appeared, she explained what they had found and where they were headed. Max asked how the underground search had been going.

"Not good," Drummond said, his frustration slipping through his wall of manly stoicism. "Pauline and I have explored a lot of tunnels but no luck so far."

"Can't you start at the section where the ghost wards are and work back from there?"

"Gee whiz, why didn't I think of that? Look, partner, we tried following the warded area like a river, but the witches that made those wards made them extra strong. Rub near them a little and it hurts like hell. Get too close and it'll bash you several blocks away. The longer you're around them, your brain gets muddled. And going underground is like taking a submarine through mud. You can't see anything but the dirt in front of you. We've probably gone over or under tunnels without even realizing it. When we do find a tunnel, we try to stay inside its walls to see where it goes. A lot of them go nowhere. They end in a rubble pile or a brick wall. Others are part of a maze of tunnels." Forcing a grin, he added, "Don't worry, though. Pauline's working hard at it, and so am I. We won't give up."

Sandra said, "We know you won't."

"I'll keep an ear open for you. That Dubicki fella gives any trouble, you call me."

Twenty minutes later, Max parked in front of a stretch of rowhomes. Though a poorer area of the city, the locals kept the street nice with what little they had. There was pride in the planters with flowers or the clean swept sidewalks. Even the other cars, though not expensive, looked properly maintained. Kids played outside — something Max had not seen in a long time — and music thumped from a nearby window. An enticing aroma drifted on the air as they approached one rowhouse, and Max had a twinge of guilt ringing the bell, if it meant interrupting that meal.

A short, big-boned man answered. He had a crewcut of gray stubble, round cheeks, and a tight face in a constant state of squint. Max noted the cane at the man's side, and the heavy layers of shirts as well as a hooded sweatshirt.

"What do you want?" the man said, blurring the words in as few syllables as possible.

Max launched into his trusty cover story of working for a magazine that sought to write an article about Mr. Dubicki. Sandra was the assistant, and if they could take just a moment of his time —

"Not interested."

But as Dubicki closed the door, Sandra put out her hand. "Please, sir, wait."

He paused, and she appeared to be looking beyond him.

"This isn't some puff piece. We're investigating certain matters because there's a family in trouble."

"Family?"

"A daughter."

"Yeah?"

Max inched behind Sandra and spotted the small photo on the table in the entranceway. It showed Oscar Dubicki proudly beaming as he stood next to a lovely woman in a graduation gown. Overhead, a banner read: Class of '52.

Sandra said, "There is a dangerous group of people who have targeted this family's daughter, and we're trying to help."

"By writing an article about me?"

"Not exactly. This has to do with the time you spent at R. J. Reynolds."

Dubicki stood in the doorway, his narrow eyes gazing across the street. At length, he huffed and stepped back. "Come."

Sandra led the way into a narrow and sparse home. Stairs met the front door, and a tweed sofa lined the wall of a long room that ended with a kitchen. A recliner had been angled next to the sofa, and both faced a bulky television set that desperately sought retirement. It labored to produce a pale image of a football game. Wherever that delicious meal had been prepared, it wasn't here. This place smelled of cigarettes. An old bachelor's pad in beige.

Dubicki toddled to the recliner, set his cane against the wall, and plopped down. On the far side of the recliner, he had a folding table set up with an overflowing ashtray. A greasy burger bag lay crumpled on the floor underneath. He reached under his leg, pulled out a remote and shut off the television.

With an open hand, he indicated the sofa. Max and Sandra sat, though Max wondered if he'd have to throw out his clothes when they got home.

"Got no food to offer," Dubicki said.

Sandra said, "That's okay."

"My Jenny died thirty years ago. She always had food to offer."

"It's really not a problem. We're not big on formality."

Max said, "But we are big on the truth. That's why we need your help."

Dubicki puckered his lips as the rest his face wrinkled. "Funny, since you said you needed me 'cause some girl's family got in trouble."

With a placating calmness, Sandra said, "My husband means that —"

"Now you're his wife?"

"And his assistant. I can be both."

Grunting as he leaned over to grab his cane, he said, "You should leave."

Sandra stood, but Max remained seated. He looked around the house and shook his head. "Thirty years since your wife passed?" He pointed to a photo atop the television. "I guess that's the two of you. Looks like an anniversary party. Big one." He stretched his neck forward, making a production of checking out the picture. "Does that say fiftieth? Wow. That's impressive." With a slight tug, he brought Sandra back on the sofa. "Fifty years together. Then thirty more since she died. That's eighty. Plus however many years went between those events, maybe ten. Plus maybe twenty before you got married. Mr. Dubicki, you are looking incredible for a man of, at least, a hundred and ten years old."

The man threw out a dark scowl but made no attempt to deny the math. "You're hardly the first to notice that I look young for my age. My daughter use to say I was …" He rolled up his recliner and stared at Max as if spotting an imposter. Then: "Are you that fella from the TV? You are, aren't you? Um, Porter, right? Talked about ghosts and magic."

"A few years ago, yeah. I haven't done any spots since."

He looked at Sandra. "You say you're his wife?"

Sandra nodded. "Also, his business partner. Together we run The Porter Agency. We help people with paranormal problems."

Pushing back in his chair, Dubicki drummed his fingers on the armrest. "There is no article, then."

"No, sir," Max said. "We find that's an easier way to talk with people when we're not sure how they feel about the paranormal."

"Is there even a girl in trouble?"

"Absolutely. That is truly why we're here."

Dropping his head back, Dubicki glanced at the stairs. "I don't see how my story can help some girl, but then, I never seen how any of this was possible, and I've lived it. Yeah, I'll tell you about it. I suppose I should. But I got to ask you to promise me something."

"What do you need?" Sandra said.

"Promise that after I tell you everything, maybe you'll help me, too. I don't know what I did wrong in my life to deserve this, just tried to survive, and I was young, but if you can, please help me."

"With what?" Max asked.

"Ain't it obvious? I've been cursed."

Chapter 30

DUBICKI FOLDED HIS HANDS across his prominent belly. "What I'm about to tell you is going to sound like a lot of bull. You'll probably think I'm crazy."

"I assure you," Sandra said, "we are no strangers to hearing bizarre stories."

"I suppose not, but the fact that I am a hundred and thirty-five years old isn't even the strangest part."

Max said, "We've met older."

Dubicki wrinkled his forehead, making his eyes look even smaller. "Well don't that beat all. You want a medal?"

"Sorry. I didn't mean to insult you."

"My papa taught me to keep my mouth shut when I was getting what I wanted. You want my help, and I'm trying to give it." The recliner squeaked and groaned as he shifted his body. Pointing behind Sandra, he said, "Give me that."

Sandra grabbed a blue blanket that had been draped over the sofa. Dubicki spread the blanket over his legs and tucked in the sides. When he finished, he laid back and laced his hands once more. Max burrowed the impulse to speak, but the more Dubicki stalled, the more Max tensed.

Dubicki cleared his throat, rubbed his nose, and checked his blanket yet again. Finally, he said, "I was born on August 5th, 1890."

Unable to stop his mouth, Max said, "Sir, with all respect, a girl's life is in danger. We need to know how to reach the tunnel where you protected the Reynolds' gold, and we need to know who coveted that gold enough that they would still covet it after they died."

Sandra rested a cautioning hand on Max's knee. "Forgive my

husband. We're anxious and concerned for this girl."

"I understand that," Dubicki said. "None of this is easy for me to talk about. I've not talked about it almost ever. Except one time with my wife, and I think she came close to having me committed. I know you two deal with these insane things, but I don't know how insane. I want you to believe me."

"We will."

"Maybe not. I find it hard to believe my own thoughts sometimes." He looked to the far end of the room where corner shelving harbored several small figurines and four journals of different colors. "Get me the yellow one. I wrote it down once. Perhaps that'll be quicker since time is an issue for you two."

Max jumped so fast he stubbed his toe on the foot of the couch. Wincing, but trying not to show more of the pain, he grabbed the journal and returned to Sandra's side.

"Thank you," she said. "I'm sure this will make a big difference."

Max headed for the door.

"No, no." Dubicki waved his hands. "You can't leave with that. That's my life you're holding. You want to read that, sit back down, and read it here. I can wait."

Taking gentle steps, Max returned to the sofa. Between his throbbing toe and the urgency pressing upon his shoulders, he failed at offering a pleasant face. Sandra tugged the journal away from his clenched hands. She opened it. Though Max wanted to glower at how Dubicki's actions worsened the threat against Sister Moon, he did not want to waste the time. He did manage a few perturbed huffs, though.

A nudge from Sandra re-focused him. He looked at the yellowed pages of the yellow journal. The handwriting looked cramped and controlled at some points, flowing and vigorous at others. To Max, it suggested a man working hard to relate an ugliness he may have hid from himself. To Max, it suggested the truth.

Together with his wife, he read:

This feels weird. I've never tried writing down anything

but Dr. Lessing said it would help. Only reason I ever went to her was because Jenny insisted. She said my nightmares were more frequent now and the delusions were getting worse. She don't like hearing about my childhood or the curse or any of it. Can't really blame her. I sound nutty, and I don't like talking about it much. Except when I drink, I guess. That's when I first told her the truth. Everything I'm going to write down in this here book. Dr. Lessing says it'll be a relief for my mind, but I think Dr. Lessing wants some kind of evidence to have me locked up in a psych ward, if it comes to that. I said that last night, and that started a big fight with Jenny. Only way I could get her to calm down was to agree to write this, so I went out and bought this journal, and here I am.

I was born on August 5th, 1890. My parents, John Lee and Elizabeth Anne, were good people. Hard people, but then we all were back then. People are soft today. Not their fault. Life is soft. That's not quite right. We've gotten good at making life soft for us. Phones and computers and pizza delivery and thread counts on our sheets. But it all can go away. It's not real. Underneath it is Life, and she's a cold, hard bitch.

My folks never made things worse for me. They could've. Lots of parents did. But Mama said that life is hard enough. If I do wrong, it'll punish me plenty. She was righter than she'd ever know.

I'll skip ahead to when I was seventeen. This ain't no autobiography, and if I'm honest, and that's the point of this writing anyway, nothing much happened up until then. I was a kid and I did kid things. I worked on the farm, too — Papa had a small place growing strawberries. When I was little, I'd do little chores, and as I grew, so did my responsibilities. No different than any other kid.

But in 1907, I was a teen and wanting to leave the farm and go do something exciting. About the most exciting thing I could think of was working for Reynolds Tobacco. It'd be like working for a king, I thought.

Getting hired was easy. They always needed young muscle for any number of jobs. I bounced around as they wanted me. Some days, they'd throw me in a warehouse hauling crates, loading trucks, that kind of thing. Another day, I might be out in the fields dealing with hanging leaves to dry or I might even be in the factory using some of the machinery to roll cigarettes and stuff. I liked it. Each day was different, and I especially liked getting paid. I never got paid working on the family farm.

Over the next year, I worked hard, and I made sure to never be late, never slack off, always do a good job. Just like I'd been taught. But I'm not perfect.

One problem I got I think is a thing Dr. Lessing will have a party with. I like to be liked. I didn't know that back then, but in the years since and as I'm writing this now, I see it clearly. I guess that's part of the point of this journal. And I've learned that about myself. That I need other people to like me. At least, that was how I was back then. I didn't need to be the most popular, but I certainly enjoyed having people admire me.

As it turned out, one of the lunch pastimes was target practice. Some of the guys would set up empty bottles or tin cans outside and take shots with an old rifle. Not a good weapon, all beat up and the aim was off, but I grew up using secondhand rifles. We'd hunt down and get rid of anything that tried to ruin our crops. In other words, what I'm saying here is that I'm a damn good shot. When

I asked if I could have a go at their targets, they laughed, but when I finished shooting, nobody was laughing. They looked at me with a little bit of awe and plenty of admiration. I liked that.

Next day at lunch, there was a bigger crowd. They wanted to see "the kid" shoot ten for ten. I could do that. At least nine for ten. Day after that, even bigger crowd.

Eventually, that crowd got so big that those in charge took notice. When they showed up, and everybody dispersed back to work, I thought I was done for. They would fire me and I would have to go home with my tail between my legs, and Mama would cry and Papa would be forced to put me back to work and I would be forever on that farm. But I was wrong. They didn't fire me. Instead, I got me a promotion.

They told me that Mr. Reynolds had a bunch of tunnels underneath the city. These were for transporting sensitive things like payroll from the bank and these gold coins. The tunnels went everywhere to the different warehouses and factories that needed the cash and such. I'm sure there were many other uses for those tunnels that I know nothing about. But because I could shoot so well, they put me on the security detail. Me and another fella, Chester, stood guard at one of the tunnel entrances. Anybody showed up, they had to go through us, prove who they were, and that they belonged there. Anybody tried to make a break for it, tried to get that gold, tried to get that payroll, tried anything, I had been given permission to shoot them down.

I suppose they only intended for me to shoot in the leg because nobody wanted to deal with a murder charge. But that was fine. I'm good enough of a shot to handle that.

Though it wasn't the most exciting job, it sure beat getting dirty and sweaty dealing with the tobacco. I got a uniform and a rifle and a badge. I also got respect.

Did that for a year. Then in 1909 I got promoted again. This time I was running security for the cart of gold coins and payroll. The coins were only distributed on special occasions, but payroll was regular. First time I ever saw that minecart full of cash my jaw almost hit the floor. I had never seen so much cash. But I suppose it's the same with people who work in the banks. After a while, it stops being money and is just paper that I'm trusted to watch over. I certainly couldn't take it. So, who cares what it is?

Here's where things in my life took a big ol' turn. There are books I've read that say we have lots of these special points in life when if we had made other decisions, then our lives would turn out drastically different. Some for the better. Some worse. Those special points are different than any other decision. The others don't matter. The special points are the crucial ones.

If that's true, then I cannot think of there being a more critical decision in my life than when I became friends with the man who pushed that cart every day. Gene Temple.

Gene was a young guy like me. A fiercely loyal man. The kind of guy that you want at your side in a bar fight or when you're facing down somebody who done you wrong. He had street smarts. Good ones. If he had been born in New York City and had been an Italian, he'd probably be running one of the mafioso families. But those critical points never came to him. Instead, he ended up becoming a good friend with me. A close friend.

Come Christmas time in 1910, we were sharing a little apartment. We had a few beers each and had enjoyed the day off from work. Nobody worked the tunnels on

Christmas.

I don't know how we got on the subject, maybe I had fallen into a bit of the blues. Even now, looking back, I can't tell whether he had guided the conversation to that point or whether I had done it inadvertently. When I thought about it in the past, I dismissed the problem. What does it matter how I ended up there? But the point of this journal is to explore these things, I suppose, and considering what would happen after, and despite how much I don't want to think it, I have to conclude that Gene had planned it all. He brought us to that special point because he wanted to talk about what ended up happening.

And here it is. That point in my life story when everything I understood to be reality went wrong.

However he done it, Gene got me thinking about death that night. We lived a hard life, but I never wanted to die. I never wanted it to end. There was always the will to survive and the hope for a better day. By that point in my life, I'd been on a few dates, knew a few girls, but never knew them in a biblical sense. I certainly didn't want to die without experiencing that.

Gene asks me what if we could live on a real long, long time. Longer than anybody ever lived before. What about that?

I could tell the way he spoke that it was a serious question, but I'd never been one for hypotheticals. They seemed kind of useless to me. I said as much, worried I might offend him but not wanting to lie. Then he tells me that this wasn't no hypothetical. He says his sister dabbles in that occult stuff like Harry Houdini and if we could skim enough gold, she says she can cast a special spell. It would slow down our aging. Plus, and he made a big deal out of this point, we'd get to keep the gold. His sister wanted some of it, of course, but you can't expect to get this kind of service for free. Gene promised we would skim so much that we could quit our jobs and be set for life. No matter how long that life turned out to be.

If somebody besides me is reading this, and you better hope I'm dead or you better run far because nobody should be reading this, but if you are, there's no way I can prove the kind of man I am, but I didn't like the idea of stealing from Mr. Reynolds, and I doubted the seriousness of all this magic. Yet I couldn't let go of this plan. If we just took one or two gold coins each time, it would add up quick. Maybe we could set ourselves up even if we couldn't extend our lives.

I didn't come to the decision lightly. I wrestled with it for weeks. Gene had the brains to stand back. Let me mull it over. Let me come to my own conclusions. If I brought up a question or wanted to talk about some detail, he was there, happy to paint the rosiest picture ever. But otherwise, he did not push.

His patience won me over. Even if I didn't realize it at the time.

I suppose he didn't have much choice but to wait for me to come around. Only way he could skim gold coins without getting caught was having the security guard being in on it with him. That's another reason I think he steered that original conversation. He needed me in a way I didn't realize at the time.

I've always wondered if our friendship had been fabricated for this very purpose. Or maybe we became friends and that led Gene to realizing the opportunity our friendship presented. I hope for the latter, but I'm not unwilling to accept the possibility of the former.

I suppose by now it don't matter. He's long dead and I'm long in the tooth. Longer than a man should be. In the end, I agreed to his plan and went through with each step and that's what I did.

For the next five years, we skimmed gold coins.

Then, in 1915, three days shy of my birthday, Gene and his sister cleared our apartment floor so she could perform her little bit of magic.

The journal ended there. Max turned the next several pages to make sure. They were blank. He looked over at Dubicki, but the man stared straight ahead with glazed eyes.

Sandra said, "Can you tell us the rest?"

Dubicki pointed to the other journals. "The blue one. No, wait. The green one."

Max retrieved the green journal, and they read on:

I had never been so terrified. It wasn't just watching magic come to life in front of me, it was understanding what it meant. I've lived long enough now to become better read, to understand things that I did not then. But even as a young man, I grasped that the world had just proven to me it was far more than I ever thought possible. I had witnessed magic, not a party trick but the real thing. And if magic like that was real, then what else might be real?

It was a question I would ask myself many times over the next century. From that moment in 1915 straight through to 2000, and even now, far past the fears of the Y2K bug and all that went with it, it still seems too much to accept. I have lived through two turns of the century. Incredible.

In that time, I have lived many lives. I've had a few wives and some kids, but I outlived them all. That was one of the troubling trade-offs of such a long life. Anybody I knew as a young man, even as a middle-aged man, anyone I knew would die before me. Sometimes it was old age for them. Sometimes there were accidents and illnesses. It felt as if death took their lives from me as punishment.

Watching my children pass was the worst. Not only due to the great heaviness any parent feels outliving their children, but even more, I felt the alarm as they grew older and reality dawned upon them. Each one came to understand that I was not natural. That I would go on living as they aged past me. Not one of my kids ever broached the topic with me. But in their eyes, I could see the questions, the realizations, the horror.

Gene and I got together at least once a year, and those were often the highlights of my existence. Originally, we did these meetings to melt down some of the gold so that we would have the money we needed to continue. Later, after we both had suffered the losses of those we loved, we would meet because we had nobody else. Even when we had wives and families, we were alone. Only the other understood anything about who we were, what we had done, and where we came from.

You would think that would strengthen our friendship into something no friends had ever experienced. Only it didn't work out that way. It pushed us apart. Those joyful annual reunions became a dreaded unearthing of the past. A reminder of how we had harmed ourselves.

I think when Gene lost his sister to cancer, he really hit rock bottom. Throughout the 1980s and 90s, he started talking that we were cursed, that this magic had been a witch's curse, that his sister had been a witch, that we were doomed to be slaves of demons. Around that same time, he was in a car accident that put him in the hospital.

It had been a long time since either of us had to deal with a medical issue. Those were dangerous. Not only to our health, but doctors and hospitals meant paperwork and files.

Gene played up being addled, and I smooth-talked him out of there. But I also saw in him a desire to stay, a wish that the car wreck had been worse. We weren't immortal, after all. Just altered to live much longer and age much slower.

I tried many times to talk sense into him. I tried to convince him that we could use some of that gold to start a foundation, do some good in the world with it. Perhaps that would make our transgression with the natural world balance out.

He wouldn't hear none of it. In the end, in the year 2000, he couldn't take anymore.

We met like usual to melt down some gold. But this time, he handed his share to me. We always met in different places, and this particular time he had insisted on meeting out near the farm that had once belonged to my family. I had given up ownership in a divorce and my ex-wife had sold it since then. The land changed several hands after that, and now it had been clear-cut and subdivided. Soon it would be a housing development.

But we were there in the middle of the night standing in this open field filled with wooden stakes marking out where homes would be erected, and Gene handed me that gold. Before I could refuse the offer or question his motives or even say some form of thank you, he pulled out a revolver and blasted open his skull.

Since that moment, my life has spiraled away. I have not enjoyed the last twenty-five years, and I doubt I will enjoy any of the future. I am alone. My body is finally old, and I dare not try to meet somebody for companionship. No matter what happens, I will outlive them. I cannot endure watching another loved one die. Worse than that, I refuse to curse another with my friendship or love.

As much as it hurts to watch those I care about pass away, it is worse when some of them, like my children, have moments of clarity where they see what I truly am. They understand how unnatural I am. That I am a monster. I can bear that no longer.

I am cursed.

As Sandra closed the journal, Max digested everything he had read. Gene Temple. That was the man who had coveted the gold coins, the man who had pushed that minecart, and the ghost they needed to find.

"The tunnels," Max said. "In your journal, you said that your first security job was guarding one of the entrances to the tunnels. Does that one still exist? Can we use it to get in?"

Dubicki nodded. "I'll tell you exactly where it is. I promise. But you've got to help me."

Sandra said, "You want us to break the curse."

Dubicki nodded again, lowering his head. "I can't do what Gene did. I thought about it many times, but for me, that ain't right. No matter what I've endured, it just ain't right."

"But if I break the curse —"

"Then it's out of my hands. There's one gold coin left. Fully intact. Is that going to be enough?"

"I don't know yet. But we'll try our best."

Chapter 31

FOR SEVERAL MINUTES, Max and Dubicki watched Sandra, each man plagued with his own mixed emotions. Max knew that she weighed the limited information available to determine how she would go about breaking this curse against the limited time they had to get it done. Dubicki, however, opened his eyes as wide as they dared. He barely contained his silence. Eagerness, anticipation, hope — they radiated off him. Max worried the old man might have a heart attack if Sandra took much longer.

When she placed her hand flat on her lap, Max knew she had decided to help. Not that he expected any other outcome. More, he didn't know if they would be able to help right away or if an appointment for another day, one less pressured with the imminent death of a woman and rise of a witch, would be the answer. Before she spoke, however, Max read the truth on her face and mentally prepared — they would break that curse immediately.

"We can help," she said.

Dubicki lightened in his recliner. "You can? You will?"

"My husband and I need to go the car. Anything specific you can remember about this curse will be important. I mean specifics about how it was cast. I know that was a long time ago, but do your best."

"I-I'll try."

Together, Max and Sandra stepped outside. The late-evening air cooled as the sky darkened. Sandra called out for Drummond, and the ghost appeared seconds later.

"We got a name," Max said. "Gene Temple."

Sandra said, "We're also about to get information on how to access the tunnels."

"Great job," Drummond said, touching the brim of his hat and nodding. "You two make a good team. Maybe you should do something about that."

With a grin, Sandra continued, "This curse should be easy to counteract because I don't think it's a curse at all. It's really a spell meant for good. Most people don't think of living longer to be a bad thing. If we did, we'd never have invented doctors or medicine."

Max said, "Most people don't think they'll live nearly a century-and-a-half."

"We've seen enough people like this to know it's not a good thing. Not unless you can be young, too."

"That's exactly it." Drummond clicked his tongue. "That's what Sister Sadie's really after. It's been bothering me why she wants this specific gold. There's plenty of ghost gold out there. Go to a few Civil War battlefields. There were horrible people who'd scavenge the dead bodies after a battle, and I got no doubts that there were gold teeth or family watches or a beloved's necklace that went missing. Lot of ghost soldiers would be haunting those fields looking for their gold. You ask me, it'd be much easier to get that gold then go spelunking into the bowels of the city. But if she's after youth ..."

Sandra said, "Or at least to prolong the youth of the body she's in. She wants more than the money, she wants the magic connected to that gold."

Max said, "She can do that? Redirect magic off the ghost of an object?"

"She thinks she can. If she's right, she could probably improve on the spell, too. Keep her current body for hundreds of years."

"Then we better get working fast."

Drummond clapped his hands once. "This is good. You two go break that curse or spell or whatever it is."

"You're leaving? Dubicki's going to tell us how to get into the tunnels. You can stop combing the underground."

"Pauline is still out there. I'll escort her back to the Other, make sure she's set okay."

"What's that mean?"

With an impatient sigh, Drummond said, "The Other isn't immune to people's stupidity. Ghosts will break up into different groups. A lot gravitate toward those who died in the same time period or the same area. Sometimes it's based on being interested in the same subject. That kind of thing. But it can get insular. They often exclude those who look different."

"I take it not having a head qualifies as different."

"Plenty of ghosts bear the injuries they died from, but the truly gruesome are shunned. Not that different from the corporeal world. I think a lot of us don't want to be reminded how dead we are."

Sandra said, "Then go help her get back to the Other safely. Max and I can handle this."

"I'll return soon as possible."

Max said, "Can hardly wait."

Though he looked like he might engage in a witty back-and-forth, Drummond opted to wink at Sandra before disappearing. Max gave her a quick kiss, and they went back inside.

Dubicki had reached the top stair to the second floor. Wheezing, he slowly turned to look down. Max's heart skipped as he imagined the old man losing his balance and tumbling to the bottom. Though Dubicki had never given the details, he made it clear that the curse had not made him immortal. Merely aged him slower. A flight of stairs would still kill him. Especially at his age.

"If you don't mind," Dubicki said between huffs, "you can do your work up here. Door on the right is where I've got the coin."

They followed him upstairs. Three doors formed half a hexagon at the tiny landing. The door straight ahead led to a cramped bathroom. The door on the left was closed. On the right, they found a bedroom barely large enough for an unused treadmill and a rolltop desk. Thick, maroon carpeting deadened some of the sounds of their movement.

"Over here." Dubicki pointed to one wall where he had the gold coin mounted and framed.

Max paused at the coin. About the size of a quarter, it had the dull coloring of real solid gold. The letters *RJR* had been stamped on the visible side. Even behind glass, the coin pulsed an energy that could not only be felt, but Max swore he could taste it in the air — a metallic flavor like a penny.

"Honey?" Sandra said.

He turned back as she gestured to the floor. With her help, they moved the treadmill as far back as the walls would allow. The rolltop desk was then lifted onto the treadmill.

Making a pained expression, she said, "We'll need to rip up the carpeting so I can draw a clear casting circle."

"That's fine," Dubicki said. "Whatever you want." From his back pocket, he pulled out the blue journal. "I thought you might need this, too. It's got everything I could remember that Gene's sister did and said that night. I wrote it down back when my memory was better. Didn't know it would come in handy, but I'm glad now I did it."

Flipping through the pages, she said, "Thank you."

Over the next twenty minutes, Max sliced a large square out of the carpet using a dull box cutter and plenty of elbow grease. He then cleared debris from the flooring underneath while Sandra read the journal. When he finished, he flopped back against the wall, sweating and panting. Sandra rushed to her knees, pulled a piece of chalk from her purse, and drew the main part of the casting circle she intended to use. At length, she asked Max to go to the car and bring back two red candles and one blue candle as well as a collecting bowl.

Max hustled down the stairs and out of the house. From the trunk, he sifted through the box of candles and made a mental note to replenish their dwindling supply. He had to push aside two other boxes to get to the one with bowls. And he paused.

He could not recall it happening, yet the trunk of this car had transformed into something akin to the cluttered collections in a witch's house. But his home did not look like that. In fact, one reason among many that he felt at ease with Sandra's exploration of witchcraft was the un-witchy behavior she displayed. If the kitchen and bathroom and living room had been mazes of detritus brought in from every flea market and garage sale, he would have been worried. Yet now he wondered if he had been blind. Maybe Sandra didn't even realize she had started the chaotic collecting. Maybe she would be every bit as surprised to see this. And why was his brain noticing now? This wasn't even the first time he had opened the trunk this week.

A shiver ran across his back. He stopped. Held still. He listened. If a ghost attacked, he would feel it. If a witch attacked, he might hear it.

Nothing.

With a careful motion, he turned his body and scanned the dark street.

Nothing.

Closing his eyes, he tried to use his other senses more intensely. He had seen Sandra do it on rare occasions and wondered if it might work for him, too.

An unpleasant scent crossed his way. Stale and sour. His first thought — it was the smell of Dubicki. Max knew seventy-year-old men who smelled worse. At over a hundred, Max couldn't be surprised that the man had a strong aroma.

Except they had sat in Dubicki's house while reading his journals, and no stench drove Max out. Didn't notice a thing. Besides, this odor was less desperate and more final. Max's brain clicked on that idea. This was a different sort of death smell than he had ever encountered before, but it was certainly a scent of death.

If asked later, he would never be able to explain why he spoke, but he did. Without thinking, he opened his mouth and whispered, "Mom?"

No answer came. None that he heard, anyway. But the scent grew stronger before drifting away completely.

He grabbed the candles and bowl and returned to the house. When he handed over the requested items, Sandra gave a questioning look.

"Let's get this done," he said.

She let it go. For now. He knew she would. Just like he knew that at some point soon, she would ask for an explanation, and he would tell her everything. A part of him dreaded the conversation that might follow. One where he would have to do more than address his own sorrow over his mother, but also deal with the question — would she ever leave him in peace or would he forever feel her presence pressing down?

After drawing the final symbols, Sandra formed a triangle with the three candles and placed the bowl in the center between them. "I think we're ready."

Max glanced up from the work. Dubicki stood in the far corner, his side pressed against the treadmill arm. He looked simultaneously hopeful and terrified.

"You okay?" Max asked.

Dubicki shivered out a nod. "I think so. I haven't seen anything like this since that one night. You sure this'll be safe?"

"We're dealing with magic. Nothing's for sure. If you don't want to do this, that's your choice. Either way, though, we've got to have the location of that tunnel entrance."

The old man hesitated long enough for Max to think they might not have to go any further. But then he nudged his hand in Sandra's direction.

"Go on," he said.

"Okay." Sandra knelt at the edge of the circle. "We begin."

Chapter 32

NO STRANGER TO WATCHING A WITCH CAST A SPELL, Max held still so as not to disturb Sandra but at the ready should she require anything. Dubicki shrank further from the circle. He had asked for this, yet like many people, he danced away from what he sought.

Max's mother had been like that. Never satisfied. Always seeking some goal that would make everything right, yet when she reached that goal, it failed. Not because it didn't fulfill its promise — whatever that had been — but because his mother lived for the search. She feared what would happen if she accepted her goal as being completed. He couldn't fault her for that. Her world had taught her to think that way. It had a good side, too. It made some people ambitious to the point of greatness.

But looking at Dubicki's anxious fingers tapping the handle of his cane, Max wondered if those outliers only proved the horror most people endured by never admitting that they had reached the finish line. In Dubicki's case, however, he had good reason for his trepidation. He knew firsthand the perils of magic and its treacherous, unintended consequences.

Sandra whispered several phrases in one of her many witch languages before lighting each candle. The red ones first. Putting out her hand, she said, "The coin, please."

Max walked to the wall with the framed coin. As he looked over the mounting to remove it, Dubicki approached. He placed a shaky hand on Max's arm.

"Please, step aside. This is my curse. It should be me that does this."

Max moved back. Dubicki leaned harder on his cane as he

looked upon that coin. His eyes glistened. He must have been traveling back to those days when he skimmed the gold coins from the minecart, when he dreamed of living forever. With a resigned bob of his head, he lifted his cane and held it like a baseball bat. No practice swings. Just one firm whip around and the cane smashed through the glass framing. Dubicki paused to take in his work. Then he shuffled back to his shadowed spot by the treadmill.

Not wanting to make Sandra wait longer, Max carefully slipped his hand between the teeth of the jagged glass and plucked out the gold coin. He placed it gently on Sandra's palm. With a graceful motion, she rested it in the bowl warming amongst the candles.

Max expected a build — most spells started slow and rose into action. Instead, her eyes rolled up, leaving only the whites. The candle flames flashed bright. The house lights flickered. The hair on Max's arms raised, and a foul taste coated his tongue — like olives gone bad.

Reaching out with a gasp, Sandra said, "I need your energy."

Max inched closer, kneeling on the opposite side of the circle. At the instant he touched her skin, the buzz of electricity jostled through his body. Not painful, not even unpleasant, but noticeable. They held hands over the candles and bowl.

"Concentrate on the coin," she said.

Max did as instructed. While Sandra chanted, he put all his attention onto that coin. He noticed the imperfections, the nicks and bumps, the slight asymmetric shape, the way the RJR stamp had lost some of its sharp edges from years of use.

Those letters warbled in his vision. He assumed the heat from the candles had caused the illusion. But it happened again. Worse, this time. The letters slipped off the coin like writing on a slice of ice cream cake melting in the summer sun. While the coin itself held firm, the letters rolled around the bowl, gaining speed with each revolution.

Max wanted to ask Sandra if he was supposed to be hallucinating, but as with any spell, breaking her focus could cause serious damage to everybody in the room. Better to ride this out and ask questions later.

With a sharp cut of motion, the letters stood still — vertical but still. Max noticed a pulsing rhythm as if those letters tapped on the bowl. Soon it matched his heartbeat. Strong, steady, but threatening to slam into unbridled panic.

The world around him blurred and blended. Not the coin, though, or the dancing letters. And not the bowl, either. The rest, however, spun together like different colored paints spinning in a pail.

The kaleidoscopic display tried to pull Max's attention. It occurred on the periphery of the bowl and in the corners of his eyes like a visual song worming into him. He fought back — frowning as he bowed closer to the bowl. He would not be distracted. He could not allow that. Sandra counted on him.

He heard her voice but not her words. Not only because she spoke in a language he would never be allowed to learn, but because sound itself had warped. As if somebody had messed with the balance of bass and treble, her tones raised and lowered, thickened and thinned until all he heard were discordant notes played by an insane musician.

As these thoughts roiled within him, the letters from the coin continued to stand at military attention. Yet the moment he doubled his effort to focus, they behaved like actors enjoying the spotlight. He swore the *J* curtsied while the two *R*s skated circles around the coin. It would have been amusing if not for the seriousness of the situation.

Damn.

His job had been to focus on the coin. These letters had been as much a distraction as the swirls of color acting like Van Gough painted them while having an aneurism.

Shifting his eyes to watch the coin and only the coin, the letters blinked back into place on its surface. The acid trip surrounding him vanished. Sounds returned to making sense.

Sandra let go of his hands. "It's done."

He looked up from the coin. Perspiration trickled into the corner of his mouth. His muscles ached as if he had been lifting weights for the last hour.

Sandra stroked his cheek. "You did a good job."

"But I lost focus," he said.

"You kept enough."

A thump from the back pulled them away from each other. Oscar Dubicki had slumped to his knees. He white-knuckled his cane, acting as if he might pull up to standing again.

Max hurried over to the man. Dubicki's scrunched features paled. Age spots bubbled up on the backs of his hands. His hair turned white and pieces fell to the floor.

With his jaw quivering from effort, Dubicki raised his head toward Sandra. "Thank you."

The words came out slow and strained. Mere whispers. He flopped over, and had Max not caught the man, Dubicki's head would have slammed against the bottom corner of the treadmill.

"With the curse broken," Sandra said, "his years are catching up with him."

Max cradled the old man. "You're going to be okay."

"No." The word creaked out, and Dubicki lightened as if his bodied atrophied, his muscles escaping with his speech. "I'm dying."

Gazing over the man, Max saw his pudgy face turn gaunt. Those squinty eyes enlarged. Dubicki shivered as his skin thinned and chilled.

"You've lived this long," Max said. "You can hold on."

But Dubicki rolled his head from side to side. "I am done. Finally."

Burying the flashing images of his mother, Max gave Dubicki a slight shake. "You can't die yet. You haven't done your part. We freed you from that spell, and you've got to tell us where the entrance to the tunnel is."

Dubicki opened and closed his mouth like a fish struggling out of the water.

"What? Say something. A young woman is going to die. They'll cut off her head. Help us."

"Jenny?" Dubicki watched Max. "Jenny!" His face brightened.

"Sure," Max said. "I'm Jenny. I've been waiting for you."

"I'm almost there."

"But not yet. You can't come to me unless you help those people you promised to help."

"I'm so sorry, my love. I tried to live a good life."

Max's mother creeped into his mind. Again, he shoved those thoughts away. Forcing a smile, he said, "Tell them where you guarded the tunnel. Save that girl. Then you'll be allowed in, and we can be together for eternity."

Dubicki no longer appeared to see Max or Jenny or anybody.

"C'mon." Max shook the man harder. "We did our part."

A soft, whisp of air drifted out Dubicki's lungs, and the man died.

Max's mouth hung open. He gave Dubicki a shake. "No. You can't die." To Sandra: "He can't die. He didn't tell us where to go."

"It'll be okay," she said.

"How is it going to be okay? We're never going to get to those tunnels in time. Not a chance. Sister Moon is going to die. Sister Sadie is going to —"

"Honey, trust me."

Max swallowed his next words, his wife's confidence quelling his rising worry. Despite the physical drain of breaking Dubicki's spell, Sandra pushed off her knees and brushed down her clothes. She turned away from Max and faced the door.

"Mr. Dubicki? It's me, Sandra. Remember?"

Max wanted to smack his forehead. Of course. Though he saw nothing, he had no trouble picturing Oscar Dubicki's ghost floating in that doorway. He would look lost, unsure of what had happened, perhaps not realizing he was a ghost.

Whatever Dubicki said, Sandra chuckled. "That's right," she said. "It won't take long now. You get to see your Jenny and any other family members you want to — your kids, your ex-wives —" A pause. A laugh. "Then you don't have to see your ex-wives. It's up to you. But first, you need to tell me where to find the entrance to the tunnels."

Sandra held still and listened. Her right hand jittered at her side. No, not at her side — Max realized she was beckoning for something to write with. He opened his phone to the notes app and placed it in her hand.

Never breaking eye contact with the ghost, Sandra tapped away. "You're sure?" A pause. Then: "Thank you, Mr. Dubicki. You may have helped save a life. Yes, yes. I said I would. All you have to do is let go. Don't hold onto your old life and this old world. In your heart, in your bones, in everything that you were and are, show the universe that you are ready for whatever comes next. Do that, and an opening will appear with a bright light. Enter that and you will move on." Another pause. "I don't know. But I've spoken with a few ghosts that have come back, and they say it's wonderful. Good luck."

A moment later, she shielded her eyes. Max continued to see nothing different, but when she turned to him, she smiled.

"I know *exactly* where to go."

NOT EXACTLY. According to Dubicki's ghost, the one entrance he knew could be found under a road off the streets of Old Salem. Apparently, it looked like a culvert that let water run into a creek, but instead of a short pipe beneath the road, it became a tunnel leading deeper. Much deeper. The ghost did not provide the specific street, though. He claimed not to know, that he always accessed the location from elsewhere in the tunnels.

"But that meant he got in the tunnel some other way," Max said as he drove them toward Old Salem.

Sandra said, "I only have the information he gave me."

Without any other recourse, they meandered Old Salem for hours. While Max guided the car along the centuries-old roads, Sandra watched the homes pass by. She consulted maps of the area on her phone, searching for likely candidates to inspect further. Whenever the opportunity presented itself, they parked and walked along the side of the road, taking interest in wooded sections, scanning for creeks or any running water. As the night grew later, Max took care to avoid patrol cars cruising the streets. No good would come from trying to explain to the cops what they were doing.

As strange and tedious as the search had become, part of Max felt greater tension merely by being back in Old Salem. He had not returned since their first case.

Back then, everything was new. The idea of ghosts and witches and magic battled with what he had thought the real world was, leaving him in a constant state of apprehension. Watching Sandra talk to the numerous ghosts that populated Old Salem would have been memory enough. But as they drove by Single Brothers House, he recalled sneaking through that 18th-century structure, hiding in the basement, fearing for their lives, unsure if man or magical creature sought to harm them. It had been terrifying in a way that no longer plagued him. It had been the threat of the unknown.

All these years later, he knew exactly the kind of thing he faced. He understood witches and ghosts and the evils of mankind. It was the known that terrified him now.

After passing the giant teapot which marked the northern end of Old Salem, Max continued over several blocks and pulled into a gas station. He filled the tank while stretching under the stark late-night station lighting. Midnight neared. They were failing.

Sandra walked up behind him and placed her hands on his shoulders. She squeezed tight, digging her thumbs into the back of his neck. "We still have more than three hours."

He didn't bother to ask how she knew what he was thinking. No witchy ways, only years of marriage. "We had her," he said. "We had saved her. And now she's lost. If she dies, it's our fault."

"Don't think like that. We're going to stop that from happening."

"But if we fail again —"

"Then the only one responsible for her death will be Sister Sadie. You know that in your heart, so don't start creating trauma for yourself that doesn't exist."

Appearing in front of the car, Drummond tilted his head back and tipped his hat. "Sorry I missed you telling Max that he's an idiot, but please continue."

"You know you're not half as charming as you think you are."

"Doll, the world couldn't handle it if I was as charming as I think I am."

Max said, "What took you so long?"

"Pauline asked me to check on her coven, and I thought I might get them to agree not to curse you. Either with some good reasoning or a hefty threat. But when I got there, I found a *For Sale* sign posted in the yard. Flew through the house and it had been emptied. No ghosts around, but it feels like something bad happened there."

"More causalities of the witch war," Sandra said.

"That's two entire covens in two days. Things are escalating."

"On the brighter side, we've got something positive going our way." Max explained all that had happened with Dubicki.

The old ghost snapped his fingers and pointed at Max. "You should've called for me. I'm a better detective than you think. Give me a moment. I'll be right back." He disappeared.

Max finished up with the car. To Sandra: "What was that about?"

She had no answer. But by the time they paid for the gas and settled in for another fruitless search through Old Salem, Drummond reappeared in the back seat.

"I found it."

"What?" Max turned completely around, his knee banging the center console. "How?"

"You had me spending hours searching underground for these tunnels. I've become familiar with the bits and pieces of it. Some of it anyway. I had a suspicion, and I wanted to check on it."

"You knew about this entrance before and waited? Why have we wasted all this time when we could've been in there saving that girl?"

"I'll take your attitude as a measure of your desire to save Sister Moon and not an ill-advised criticism of your partner. Start driving and I'll explain." Drummond waited until Max turned around and got the car moving. "First off, I didn't know about this entrance. I didn't say I did. What I said was that I've become familiar with a lot of these tunnels due to the inordinate amount of time I spent searching through them. When you told me what Dubicki had said, I put two and two together. I used my good ol' detective brain to make a few inferences. The facts suggested one of three possible locations. That's where I went to check. Make a left up here and then your first right. Park the car, and I'll take you to the place you described. Is that okay with you?"

Max sunk a little in his seat.

"Before you ask, I know this is the right place, and it's not because of your brilliant retelling of what Dubicki said. It's because I can feel it."

Sandra said, "It's warded?"

"Heavily. Painfully. Pauline and I missed it because we avoided it. Thought it was more tunnel. But now, that makes it easier to find."

Tucked around the corner of a side road, Max immediately grasped why they had failed to locate the place. Between the trees and the lay of the land, people passing through would never think anything of importance could be found right beneath them. But by carefully climbing down the steep incline, Max and Sandra reached the body of a creek imperceptible from above. Especially so late at night.

Drummond lowered through the air, settling twenty feet away. "Until that ward is broken, I'm not getting any closer."

Made of brick, the entranceway formed a rounded arch not even six feet high. Corrugated metal lined the inner part of the tunnel stretching into the dark, and concrete appeared to act as a barrier between the metal and brick. Both probably had been added sometime in the last fifty years to shore up the strength of the road above. Water meandered out into the creek. One of the bricks close to the keystone position had a date engraved into it — 1880.

Peering into the tunnel with his phone, Max noticed they were far from the first people to have discovered this hidden gem. Graffiti tags could be seen on the walls as well as spray-painted markers from utilities workers.

Sandra said, "Hon, I need the light on me."

Max turned back to find his wife had chosen a wide, flat rock to use. She had a piece of chalk in hand. He splashed over and held his phone overhead, its flashlight washing the stone in stark clarity.

Lowering to her knees, Sandra began a new casting circle. "This shouldn't take long."

While she worked, Max thought about the number of spells she had cast in the last two days. If she felt anything like him, she was exhausted, sleep-deprived, and worried. That word — *worried* — Max was tired of it. He worried for Sister Moon's life, he worried at all the spells Sandra had cast, he worried that Sister

Sadie might achieve her goals. He thought that if he could get a full night's sleep or maybe a full day's break, then perhaps he could banish this never-ending cycle of dread. But that rest wouldn't come until the dawn. Maybe not even then.

Sandra lit a candle before giving Max a push on the leg. "Go over to Drummond. I need space for this."

Cutting the light off, he pocketed his phone. As he trudged across the soft trickling creek, he watched Drummond floating in circles. Apparently, his ghost partner shared the burden of worry.

"You'd think we would be used to this by now," Drummond said, keeping his voice low so as not to disturb Sandra.

"If each time was the same, we probably would. But these witches keep changing their playbook."

"Not very courteous of them."

"Downright rude."

A blast of smoke and water shot upward forming a foaming pillar. Sandra toppled back, her feet springing over, the momentum sliding her through the muddy bottom of the creek. The pillar crashed down, splashing mini-waves in all directions. Max leaped over the rocks and fallen branches to reach his wife.

"Well," she said, taking his arm to get up, "that wasn't graceful."

Pushing mud from her cheek yet smearing it, Max asked, "What happened?"

"I discovered the hard way that there's a second ghost ward."

Drummond bent closer. "Two wards? Isn't that a bit overkill."

"Not if the second one is reversed."

"Trying to keep a ghost *in* the tunnels?"

Steering Sandra to a dry edge of the creek, Max said, "It's got to be Gene Temple and his minecart. Sister Sadie trapped him in there while she went searching for the heads she needed."

"That's what I think, too," Sandra said.

"Then we're screwed. If she still needed to call the ghost, lure him in with the minecart, something like that, we might have had a chance, but she's all set."

"No, hon, it's a good thing. If that spell fails, she won't get the gold, she won't get the power, and most important, she won't elongate her life. She's going to want to have the best opportunity for success, and that means her casting must be able to call upon the full strength of energy around her."

"Yeah?"

Drummond snickered. "Those same wards that are keeping me out are blocking that kind of energy."

"Bingo," Sandra said. "When the time comes, she's going to drop both wards."

That was enough for Max. He took Sandra's hand and stormed toward the archway. "We've wasted time and your power to break a ward we don't need to break."

"Hey," Drummond said, hovering in place. "I still can't get in there."

"You don't have to. Not yet. Be ready, though. If we don't get out with Sister Moon before the three o'clock witching hour, those wards will come down. We'll need you, then, for certain."

"I don't like that plan."

Max didn't offer an apology or an alternative. He rushed forward, pulled out his phone for the flashlight, and headed into the tunnels.

Chapter 34

FIRST CAME THE GRAFFITI. Then the sparse remnants of a squatter. But further in, the tunnel grew tighter, darker, less traveled. Max and Sandra moved through the brick and concrete passage, avoiding the center stream of runoff whenever possible. Echoes of their breathing bounced ahead and behind.

In mere minutes, they had crossed into another existence. The world they knew — Winston-Salem, open air, Lexington BBQ, cars, and people — had morphed into a dark tube closing upon them, weighing heavily above, smelling of rot, and always making noises that had no clear origin. Even the gentle roll of water blurred into a menacing plink that promised other passages in the dark, passages from which Max imagined strange albino creatures observed them. Or worse, hunted.

He gave his head a solid shake. Letting his mind loose with his nerves served no good. It only worked up anxiety and paranoia.

They stopped at a four-way junction. Max turned his flashlight upward to reflect as much light as possible in the boxy area. One path had collapsed, forming a wall of rubble. Of the two unknown paths remaining, Max found no discernible difference.

"We messed up," Sandra said.

"We'll try one tunnel. If it goes nowhere, we come back and try the other." He checked the time on his phone. "We've got a couple hours to go."

"Not that. We don't have a map, and we haven't planned for making one. This can't be the only junction we'll hit. I think it's going to be too easy to get lost down here."

She was right. Until this junction, they had no choice in

direction. The tunnel went where the tunnel went.

Max used his flashlight on the walls. No more graffiti. Kids looking to tag a tunnel had no interest venturing so far into the bowels of the city. They wanted to paint where others might see their work.

"You have chalk," he said. "We'll mark the right side of the tunnel we came from. That way when we leave, we can see the correct path to take."

Sandra dug out a thick piece of white chalk and drew a large X to the right of the tunnel leading to the exit. "Okay. Which way do you want to go?"

Gesturing to the northern tunnel, he said, "How about this one?"

"Any particular reason?"

"It doesn't smell as bad."

"Good enough. Lead on."

In this way, they navigated through the tunnels, leaving a white chalk X wherever they needed. They often hit dead ends, either caused by collapse or walled off with cinderblocks, and were forced to double back. Over time, however, Max had the sense of moving in a direction closer towards the center of the city. Then again, buried in the dark with no windows or sky or buildings for orientation, his *sense* was more hope than fact.

He had tried pulling up his maps app to see where the GPS placed him, but no luck. Either the satellites couldn't reach him underground, the cell tower signal couldn't, or the heavy-duty spells interfered too much.

"Shh," Sandra snapped, though Max had not said a word.

Looking ahead, the amber glimmer of firelight spread across the walls where the tunnel cornered left. Muffled tones bounced along the stone — voices. Despite being alone in the tunnel, Max and Sandra crouched as they pressed to the side. With quiet steps, taking care to avoid splashing the draining waters, they worked toward the end of the tunnel and the amber light.

When Max could finally peek around the corner, he discovered a wide room held up with thick pillars connected by arches like an ancient wine cellar. It only lacked the casks. Several sconced torches added to the cloistered, medieval atmosphere, and moss grew wherever water ran down a pillar or wall. Nature's graffiti.

This must have been a central point of convergence for the tunnels because Max noted several minecart tracks crossing the visible areas. No carts around, but a stack of wood crates had been parked near one track. Untouched, abandoned spiderwebs formed thin veils between the crates and the floor.

Several feet away, Sister Sadie's healthy, young body commanded with an authoritative poise. Sister Gold backed her up as well as two other witches new to Max. They looked like a punk band — ripped jeans, stained shirts, and an indignant attitude.

To no surprise, a large casting circle had been drawn before them. Twenty green candles ran the edge of the circle. In the center, Sister Moon sat on her knees, her hands bound behind her, her ankles chained. To her right, the skull of Peter Ney had been placed upon a crystal stand. To her left, the head of Pauline Georgia-Ringo Lennon. The steady glow of the candles created sharp shadows on the witches' faces and strange shapes upon the ceiling.

Sandra pushed forward, brushing by Max as she slipped behind a pillar further in. He followed up behind, gaining a clear view of the situation. Sister Moon still lived. That much was good. But the rest held the potential for a great tragedy.

Max poked his head to the side of his pillar, hoping to catch Sister Moon's attention. If she knew the Porters were in play, perhaps she could say or do something to create an opening. But she kept her head bowed and her eyes closed. Her body swayed.

"Tonight," Sister Sadie said, tilting her head so that her voice reflected heavily off the ceiling, "the foundations of our coven will be built. Tonight, we will be more than witches in search of a home. We will become a family."

Sister Gold guided the other witches to the circle, placing each one in front of a specific green candle — one witch at five o'clock; one witch at two o'clock. Max did not see how the positions were determined, but they were clearly chosen with care. She even moved one witch after her green candle sputtered, taking her to the eleven o'clock position.

"Sister Carrie and Sister Page are ready," she said as she returned to Sister Sadie's side.

"The ancient spells are full of great power, but they are like an unbroken stallion galloping through an open plain. If we are to use this power, we will have to capture and tame it. We must be prepared for the challenges we will face. It is because of this that we turn to the blood." Sister Sadie held a wooden bowl over her head. "Blood is the life. Blood is the strength."

With their heads bowed, the other three witches repeated — *Blood is the life. Blood is the strength.*

Max looked to Sandra, but she had already dropped to the floor with her chalk. Whatever spell she worked at creating, it would take time to cast. He checked on Sister Sadie and her witches. While their spell was much further along, experience had taught him that such a big spell would require an even longer time to cast.

Usually.

There were always exceptions.

Placing her hand in the center of her circle, Sandra whispered a few mysterious phrases. She stood, checked her work, and then scurried toward the next pillar further from Max. She also did something he had never seen before. She drew a chalk line as she went — coming directly off the casting circle she had finished and connecting it to the next casting circle she began when she reached the pillar.

He threw a questioning brow her way. Instead of answering, she snuck back towards him. Once close enough to put her mouth to his ear, she said, "They're linked circles. If it works, they'll kick off like a string of firecrackers."

"You didn't need to stop to tell me that."

"I'm not. I'm still learning how to do this. I've never seen it before. Only read about it. But I don't think I'll have enough time to draw it all. I need you to do what you do best."

"Research? Now?"

"I meant what you do best in these situations — stall." A peck on the cheek and she returned to her unfinished casting circle.

Max peered at Sister Sadie's group again. The wooden bowl had been handed over to Sister Page — a woman with weathered skin and touches of gray starting in her auburn hair. She looked as warm and cozy as a cookie-baking grandmother. But from her robes, she produced a ceremonial knife.

Without any plan other than to do as Sandra asked, Max stepped out from behind the pillar and strode toward these witches as if stumbling upon friends at a restaurant. "Will you look at that? I go for an evening constitutional and find you wonderful ladies gathered together like old friends. Didn't think I'd meet anybody down here. What brings you to this neighborhood?"

Sister Page whipped her free hand toward Max and red blazes of energy followed. When they hit, Max had a distinct sensation of falling even as he lifted off the ground. He crashed into a stone pillar, sparkles dazzling his vision, and thumped onto the floor. As his brain tried to reset from shaking against his skull, he made a mental note — Sister Page was a stronger witch than he had realized. She had kept that spell rolling in her head, prepared to attack, while simultaneously performing her part in Sister Sadie's complex witchcraft.

Sister Page pointed her knife at Max. She managed three long strides before Sister Gold said, "No. His life belongs to Sister Sadie."

Still heated from her brief violence, Sister Page whipped back. "Then take it."

The witches looked at Sister Sadie. She gave a single, slow nod and gestured for everybody to return to their places at the casting circle. Sister Page scowled, and Max couldn't decide whether her disgust was for him in general or for the fact that she had been leashed from hurting him further. Hoping nobody minded, he remained on the floor, his head throbbing a thrash metal rhythm.

While the others resumed their positions, Sister Page remained halfway to gutting Max. "This is the man who has hurt so many witches."

"I am aware."

"Then let me kill him. It'll take seconds, and we can continue the spell uninterrupted."

Sister Sadie snatched a hungry glance at Max like a starved prisoner being served the steak dinner they had dreamed about. But her commanding voice stayed focused on Sister Page. "You speak like you think you should be in charge, like your words should have authority. You are nothing."

"I've just knocked one of your rivals out of his head. I am offering him out of deference to you. Do not waste this."

As the tensions between these witches grew, Max scanned the pillars and the area around Sister Moon. Her head sagged forward, and drool trickled off her mouth. Drugged? Maybe. More likely, the coven cast a spell over her with the same result. Max hoped she enjoyed a pleasant trip. Better than the distress running through his system.

He continued searching the area. If he could find something to distract these witches or create leverage in his favor. But all he had managed to do was stall with his presence, and it sounded like he had become a bargaining chip.

Then again, Sister Sadie spit on the floor. "You are so arrogant. You think you can dictate what I will do tonight or any night? You are less of a witch than I thought. I will take Max Porter, and we will cast my spell, and when we have finished, if you have not done your best and been your most loyal, your standing in this coven will be in question."

"How can you doubt my loyalty? I've served you Max Porter on a plate."

"After tonight, the witches of this state will hand power over magic to me. After that, it'll only take a few months and I'll run the entire South. But I cannot do this, our coven cannot accomplish this, if I have to worry that any of my witches will take action without permission." Sister Sadie licked her index finger and pointed at Sister Page. "Do we need to discuss this further?"

Max had no clue what kind of curse a spit-soaked index finger could create, but Sister Page clearly did. She lost all color. Her chin quaked.

"I'm sorry, ma'am." Sister Page scurried back to her spot.

Max did not know how much longer they had. Sister Sadie watched her witches obediently return to the circle before she sauntered into place. Why hadn't Sandra burst in already with a spell flying bright and bold?

His gut churned as he looked from pillar to pillar. But he caught a shadow dashing between the shadows. Okay, then. Max turned his attention back to the coven. His wife was out there working on her spells, and he would do his best to give her all the time he could.

Chapter 35

P RESSING HIS BACK AGAINST THE PILLAR TO HELP STAND, Max dug for the first line of thought he could muster, and he started talking. "You're being dumb about this."

Sister Gold said, "Nobody wants to hear from you."

But Sister Sadie's lips curled as if finally getting to savor the first bites of that long-awaited steak. "No, no. Don't stop him from begging."

No point in debating the idea of *begging*. Max went on, "You have rivals. Serious ones with real power. Madame Ti, the witches of Haven House, and probably more I've yet to meet. You also have rivals that are not a huge threat now but could easily become a problem. Like the Brotherhood."

"They will all bow to me soon enough."

"Casting this spell and then killing me, or torturing me and then killing me, or whatever you have planned for me and then killing me, well, you're doing the work for the other covens. They want you to take me off their hands. Not only would you get rid of me — I've stopped plenty of them from hurting the world — but they'll also get rid of you at the same time."

That caused Sister Sadie's glee to falter. "Me?"

"You are connected to the murder of a witch in a brutal fashion, the robbing of a grave with historical significance, the burning down of a house, and the slaughter of the women that lived there. Any one of these things would put you on the police's radar. All of them? I don't see how you won't have the entire Winston-Salem PD looking for you."

She paused to process the idea before a hideous smile broke through her lips. "If the police want to arrest me for all of those crimes, then why should I worry of one more?"

"Maybe you've missed out on some current events. Detective Jorge Osorio is now a member of The Porter Agency. Murdering me, the friend of a police detective — that's not going to end well for you. That's the kind of thing that leads to *accidental* death of a suspect."

"This is ridiculous," Sister Page said.

Her bloodlust matched her fury. If allowed, Max guessed she would have happily spent hours skinning him before watching him bleed out. But as much as Sister Page wanted to destroy him, she feared Sister Sadie more. So far, Sister Sadie's desire for vengeance overrode her desire to see Max dead by any hand.

Small blessings.

Max pushed further. "I'm sure the idea of the police doesn't matter that much. You probably have a dozen spells to protect you from being noticed. I mean, these aren't the first witch murders you've committed." He noticed an uncertain glance between Sister Gold and Sister Carrie. "What about the other covens, though?"

"We have no fear of them," Sister Carrie said, her voice meeker than her posture.

"That's good. Because if you succeed with this spell and you manage to dodge the police, then the top covens will realize you're a serious contender. What happens then? Those covens will band together against you."

"Covens don't work together," Sister Gold said, perhaps emboldened by Sister Carrie.

"It is unusual, but I've seen it before. I mean if Sister Sadie's boasting is half-true, you are going to be the number one danger to them. Every coven wants to win this war, but most of them know they aren't strong enough. They're more concerned with who they'll be serving under, and I guarantee not one of them wants to serve a crazy, body-snatching witch coven like yours. Yeah, I'm pretty sure they'll find a way to work with each other. They might hold their noses while doing it, but they'll do it."

Sister Sadie tossed a gray powder to rain upon Sister Moon. "You should stop talking. The only reason you live is so that I can savor your death."

Max put up his hands. "I'll be quiet. I promise." He mimed zipping his lips. Then: "Before I stop, though, you may want to consider that —"

"Shut him up," Sister Sadie said.

"Finally." Sister Page flashed a toothy grin.

"Without killing him."

Though her grin quivered into a frustrated scowl, she continued forward with her knife leading the way. Unless one of the spells she had prepared and recited repeatedly was a silencing spell, Max didn't think she would be casting him into being quiet. He didn't see any duct tape, either. All he saw was that knife. The closer she came, the more he pictured her forcing open his mouth and cutting out his tongue.

"That isn't necessary," he said, backing into the pillar behind him. "Really. I promise I'll keep quiet."

"You will now."

An enormous boom filled the tunnel like a forest tree plowing into the earth. The witches exchanged concerned looks before turning to Sister Sadie with the unspoken question — *was that supposed to happen?* Max, however, didn't need Sister Sadie's reaction. He already knew the answer.

Chapter 36

THE LONG HISS OF A SNAKE came from the darkness behind Sister Sadie. A lightning flash briefly brightened the shadows to the right. The crackling of firecrackers followed by a burning odor pulled attention to the left.

Sister Sadie demanded her coven to move to the circle. Sister Page tried to hide her worry and gave Max a final gaze of regret before hurrying to her position.

"If we had a full coven here," Sister Sadie said, even as another boom reverberated through the floor, "we would hold hands around this circle, but we will still achieve our goal for we our powerful witches. Stretch your hands out as if holding your sisters." Another flash. Sister Sadie glowered at the shadows.

Not knowing how much longer Sandra needed or if this was the limit of her spell casting today, Max tried to distract the coven once more. Raising his voice over the crackle and the next boom, he said, "Somebody doesn't like what you're doing. Better to stop now."

"Ignore him," Sister Sadie bellowed.

The next series of booms, flashes, and crackles arrived faster, and their pace continued to increase. Max chastised himself — of course Sandra's spell would be more than noise and lights. If she had wanted to flash blinding light, she could have done that already. But they were up against Sister Sadie. This was something bigger. Something that required more time and energy. Max gulped — something more daring, more perilous.

The hair on his arms lifted. The frizzy hair on Sister Carrie lifted, too.

"Chant with me." Sister Sadie's eyes widened as she lowered her chin to focus on Sister Moon. "Chant with me and we will achieve the impossible."

They never got the first word out.

A woman appeared directly behind Sister Sadie, floating a foot overhead, hands open and full of threat. A gray mist curled around her like flowing robes in a breeze. Her hair lengthened into the dark, streaks of white and gold pulsing through from her scalp to the unseen ends. And her eyes — sunken deep into her skull yet sparkling bright as if miniature suns burned within her.

"Leave this place," the woman said, her voice a chorus of voices speaking in different rhythms.

Sister Carrie broke. "What is that?" she cried as she stumbled back.

"Hold still," Sister Sadie said, harsh enough to choke the frightened woman into silence. "That is a witch I have faced before."

Max did not want to believe it, but he knew long before Sister Sadie confirmed it. This fierce and terrifying witch was his wife.

In her multi-voice, Sandra said, "Leave the man. Leave the sacrifice. And run."

Sister Carrie tripped on the mining track, stumbled into some crates, reoriented herself, and tore off into the tunnels. The other witches held, perhaps mesmerized as much as horrified. Except for Sister Sadie.

She turned to face Sandra. "You will not defeat us. You cannot. I'm too strong."

"We stopped you before. We'll stop you again. Leave our husband. Leave and we will spare you tonight."

We? Max didn't like the sound of that.

Sister Sadie motioned the other two witches closer so they could physically join hands. In seconds, the three chanted the same phrase and glared at Sandra. Though his wife did no more than hover, Max suspected she too chanted some disturbing phrase of a witch language. It was a race, and he could do no more than be a spectator.

Unless he attacked them. He could rush ahead and tackle one of them. Break their concentration, break their spell, and Sandra could take it from there. Sister Page wouldn't hesitate to try slitting his throat, though, and he didn't want to ruin whatever Sandra had planned. Yet he couldn't sit back and do nothing.

"Crap," he muttered as he sprinted toward the sisters.

The logical break point was the center. That meant tackling Sister Sadie. *Double crap*. He lowered and put out his arms.

But the flashing light turned bright and steady. The booms and crackles ceased. The coven witches jerked their heads up. But not in the exalt of a spell. They hadn't the time to cast a new spell, and prepared spells wouldn't work together — at least, Max had never seen such a thing. No, the same thing that had halted his assault now stopped these witches for the moment. They gazed at Sandra, waiting to see what happened next.

The moment held. But only for a fleeting breath.

Sandra's eyes flickered. Her flowing misty gown sputtered. She wobbled in the air. As her brow furrowed, she dropped, banging against the hard floor.

Sister Page laughed. "How is it that anybody fears the Porters?" She slid closer and stuck out her clawed hand.

"No!" Max dashed forward.

His scream startled the witches. They turned their heads, and Sandra lifted her exhausted body off the ground. When she thrust out her hand, Max could not believe she still had strength to cast another spell — to have held another spell. He was right. She didn't cast anything but a stone.

With the accuracy of a pro-baseball pitcher, she beaned Sister Page in the back of the head. The stone wasn't large, just the first thing she could grab, but it struck hard enough to cause a shout and send the witch to her knees. Max finished the tackle he had planned, slamming his shoulder into Sister Sadie's torso and crashing her down.

Recouping from her shock, Sister Page shot out her hand and shouted a blood-thirsty roar. Max raised an arm over his face, though it would do no good to stop the blast. He braced for the hit. And nothing. Sister Page's roar became a puzzled grumble.

He paused, lowered his arm, and stared with the same confusion that Sandra and the other witches shared. Together, they all appeared to draw the same conclusion — Max and

Sandra had disrupted them to such a degree that the coven had momentarily ceased the internal chanting that kept their prepared spells ready. They had no fast spells available.

"Bastards," Sister Sadie screamed as she threw a fist into Max's ribs.

The brawl that ensued lacked the strength of blue-collar men after a late night drinking, lacked the skill of experienced fighters facing off in the ring, lacked the grace of high-level martial artists locked in combat. The witches made up for their deficiencies with sheer rage.

Max, however, had some training and plenty of experience. As Sister Sadie followed her initial attack with a flurry of small punches, he evaded a few and blocked more. When the opening arrived, he pushed her away, slapping her cheek as a parting point — *don't mess with me this way.* But her infuriated face reddened as she rushed him again. He didn't need to remember training. Muscle memory reacted for him. He pivoted off the angle of her attack and brought up his knee. She ran right into it. A loud groan and her lungs gave up what air they held as she went to the floor again.

He turned to see Sister Page straddling Sandra, hauling off wide-arcing punch after wide-arcing punch. Before he could react, Sandra kicked out. Max cheered inside as his wife connected with Sister Page's stomach. The witch doubled-over, and Sandra jumped to her feet.

She noticed Max. He smiled at her, but she leaped by him, throwing her fists at Sister Sadie. Max had been so enthralled watching his wife, he forgot about the coven leader. She had found her way back to standing and would have dug her sharp claws into his neck. But Sandra popped the witch in the nose, causing blood to flow.

Before Max could say a word, Sister Gold entered the fray. She slapped his face and kicked his shins. He ignored the sting on his cheek and the bite in his leg and threw an elbow into her side.

One of the other witches sprang onto Max's back, locking an arm around his throat while beating him with the other arm. He spun around, leaning forward in an attempt to keep his airway clear. As he knocked over candles whisking by, he spotted Sister Sadie pulling at Sandra's hair.

If these women weren't trying to kill him, the whole thing would be funny — witches fighting without magic.

A burst of flames splashed across the ceiling. The fighting stopped in an instant. Breathing hard as Sister Page slipped off his back, Max looked for the source. She wasn't hard to find.

At the head of the casting circle, a new witch stood. She wore a black robe and watched them with a haughty frown. While her right hand had been held out with the palm up — a clear sign that she had cast the fiery spell — her left clasped Sister Carrie by the neck and forced the young witch to her knees.

"Who are you?" Sister Sadie said, trying to sound tough but out of breath and disheveled.

"Maggie McVeil."

"Never heard of you."

"You will. I'm with the Coven of Ti."

Chapter 37

MAGGIE HAD AN ANGULAR FACE, the kind hardened by years of work and difficult experience. She stood bold and resilient, an aura of authority surrounding her like the fear of a schoolmaster. Max had no doubt that her claim to be part of Madame Ti's coven would prove true. All of Madame Ti's witches held this same superior attitude.

Sister Sadie took two strides forward, but Maggie shook her head. "Back. Stay."

"We are not dogs."

"I'll decide what you are. On your knees. All of you."

Though Sister Sadie did not move at first, she must have recalled that she had spent her prepared spells. Max and Sandra clutched their hands together, watching as the slow realization of her situation came over Sister Sadie. She huffed and lowered to her knees. Her other witches reluctantly joined her. Sandra tugged Max's arm until he followed suit.

Once everybody had obeyed, Maggie released her hold on Sister Carrie and nudged the witch with her foot. Sister Carrie scampered on hands and knees to join the ranks of her coven.

"Leave us," Sister Sadie said, hissing as she spoke. "We've done nothing to you."

With clarity and control, Maggie said, "You've caught the eye of Madame Ti. That's enough. She doesn't like you, by the way."

When Sister Sadie did not respond, Max had to keep his jaw from hitting the floor. He had never seen her act contrite. Yet a nudge from Sandra and a nod of her chin brought Max's attention to the details.

Though on her knees, Sister Sadie leaned forward into a slight bow. Her eyes were closed, and her hands reached back as if trying to cup her ankles. Meek. Yet her mouth — her lips moved gentle and slow. Imperceptible unless one looked carefully.

Max understood exactly what Sandra had spotted — *Sister Sadie worked on a spell.*

Perhaps Sister Gold had noticed this too because the witch lifted her head and said, "Madame Ti thinks too much of herself and her coven."

"Careful," Maggie said as if daring a greater altercation. "The Coven of Ti will soon run everything. You should make sure you're on our good side. Now, Madame Ti has ordered me down here to see that this spell is stopped."

"You are not in charge. We have every right to cast any spell we want."

"This spell is more than a danger to you. Witchcraft of this kind is too unpredictable."

"We know the risks we take. If we get hurt —"

"Nobody cares about you. But when you fail, the danger of exposing witches to a fearful world is too great. And that, after all, is the point of having any leadership amongst the witch community, isn't it? The point of having power over magic is to make sure that we don't expose ourselves to those in the world not ready to see. This spell you're attempting threatens us. Though, Sister Sadie has failed as a witch on so many occasions that it boggles the mind to think anybody would follow her."

"You won't be so smug when we make history with our spell."

"You will cease now. The Coven of Ti will not sanction this."

"You continue to talk like you're in charge. You're nothing but a lackey."

Sister Gold held her hands open at her sides as if ready to strike. An empty threat, but Max did not know if Maggie understood. After all, there were a lot of people in the room to pay attention to. It depended on how long Maggie had been watching them fight.

"We are the leaders of magic. Madame Ti is the ruler of magic."

Sister Gold made a dramatic show of rolling her eyes toward

her fellow witches. "And they call us insane. Hate to break it to you, Maggie Mc-whatever, you are not the rulers of anything. This war is still going on, and between the two of us, Sister Sadie's the only one that's shown any real ability. Madame Ti's animal spells are the failures, but our leader is living proof of her power. She's in a new body. Can you do that?"

Maggie glanced at Sister Sadie. "She is already rotting away, but you sycophants cannot see it. In time, you will. In time, you'll smell the rot. Then her true insanity will return." Maggie's derisive sneer looked more menacing in the flickering shadows of torchlight. "How can you possibly expect to win this war when your coven mother can barely keep from falling apart?"

As long as these two continued to insult each other, Max figured they had a chance. To do what was the big question. There was no way to sneak over and free Sister Moon without being seen. She sat in the middle of everything. He glanced at Sandra. She held still, watching the proceedings with care but not attempting to cast a spell. Only Sister Sadie dared that.

Maggie gestured at him, pulling his attention back to the bickering witches. "You should not toy with the Porters. Many witches want vengeance against him and his wife."

"They have a ghost, too," Sister Gold said. "Or were you not aware?"

"I am quite aware of all that this man has and is." Maggie's eyes flamed until the young witch looked away. Then to Sister Sadie: "You want to claim him? You want to hurt him and destroy him? Madame Ti has given me the authority to allow it. You may. But take him and go. Return to these tunnels again, and you will face harsh consequences."

Sister Gold scooted close enough to bump Sister Sadie's shoulder. "You are the one who should leave. Your Madame Ti is clearly afraid of us."

"We fear nothing."

"You stand there and threaten but you do nothing. That's fear."

Max noticed Sister Page adjusted her hand so that it brushed against Sister Sadie. He raised a questioning eyebrow toward

Sandra.

She whispered, "That's not any spell. It's *the* spell. Be ready."

Struggling to hide his surprise, he looked again. Sure enough, he saw how the witches touched each other, how Sister Page had lowered her head and mumbled a phrase synchronous with Sister Sadie. For her part, Sister Gold continued to distract Maggie from the real situation.

"The Coven of Ti are cowards."

"Madame Ti offers mercy not from fear but because we understand the greater world. You only want power, but we want to protect all witches from the stake. Or do you like being burned alive?"

"Nobody does that anymore."

"If you continue to perform spells that murder people and defile graves, that might change."

"When Sister Sadie rules, there won't be a soul that dares think about burning us."

Maggie sighed. "I have tried to be reasonable, but you seem bent on stupidity. You disgust me."

"I'm so sorry." Sister Gold's sarcasm thickened with each syllable.

"One final chance. You and your followers leave this tunnel, forget about this spell, and there will be mercy."

"No." The air around Sister Sadie's fingers vibrated.

Max looked to Sandra. He hoped she could draw a casting circle, blind everyone, something. But no spell could come fast enough.

Maggie planted one foot behind her and wound up her shoulder, ready to throw. Fire glowed in her hand. But she had missed the real purpose of Sister Sadie's spell. No attack would be coming.

Sister Gold and Sister Page stood, their arms straight down, their heads lifted upward. Their hair puffed out with the energy charging around them.

Snatching a peek at Sister Moon who continued to sway in a drugged daze, Max itched to grab her. But Sandra put a hand on his arm.

"Not yet," she said. "Not until —"

With a sizzling sound and the scent of burning leaves, a green ring appeared in the ceiling. It burned outward and down like fire tracing the edges of a dome. As it neared the bottom, Sandra squeezed Max's arm tighter.

"The ghost wards are dropping."

Chapter 38

IF MAGGIE MCVEIL HAD ANY INTENTION of stopping the veohoxal spell once it had begun, her awe at the first major step in the casting prevented action. Max noticed her hesitancy because he felt the same. He should have jumped forward and destroyed the casting circle or tackled a witch. Instead, he marveled at the sheer power radiating throughout the room. Maggie's awe appeared to stun her. The might of her adversaries had shorted her willingness to act. He wondered if this would cow her into running off.

For Max, though, more than fear, more than awe, he stood his ground due to his wife's hand holding him. Through her clutching fingers, she reminded him that they need only wait. She had said it — the ghost wards had dropped.

Sister Moon lifted her wobbling head as if enlivened by a sound Max could not hear. But Sandra could. Sister Sadie could. They cocked their heads toward the silent echoes.

"This is over," Sandra said.

Maggie startled as if she had never noticed Sandra's presence until that moment. "What's going on? I don't see any gold. What did the spell do?"

With a disparaging snicker, Sister Sadie rose to her feet. "If you're the best Madame Ti could send, I've already won. The idea that you could stand up to me? You can't even understand a multi-part spell. You're nothing but a whining —"

Though Max could not hear the ghosts rushing through dirt, stone, brick, and tunnel, when they came close enough, he could clearly hear the one ghost that mattered — Drummond.

"This way everybody," Drummond said as he dashed through the wall and entered the pillared hall.

Max wanted to ask who was everybody when a surprised shriek burst from Maggie. She jumped sideways, clearly bumped by something cold and unseen. Sister Gold reacted the same to the flyby that hit her. But Sister Page attempted to punch the air. She received a strike in the back for her trouble.

"End the spell," Sandra said. "These ghosts won't stop until you do."

Sister Sadie cackled. "But this is what I want." She dodged to one side before swiveling around a ghost. "Sister Gold, resume your post."

Taking one icy hit after another, Sister Gold tangled with the air as she moved back to Sister Sadie's side. Several steps away, however, Drummond swooped in. Growling throughout, he slipped his arm around her waist, hauled her off the ground, and flipped her from the casting circle like a wrestler tossing an opponent out of the ring.

Free from touching her, the ghost rubbed his arm and looked at Max. "You going to keep standing there like a dunce or do you plan on helping?"

Maggie dashed in one direction only to gyrate away from another invisible strike. She shivered, changed direction but met another ghostly touch. They had her bouncing like a pinball.

"Sisters!" The gravelly anger snapping from Sister Sadie cut through their shocked cries as the ghosts continued their assaults.

"I'm here," Sister Page said, crossing into the casting circle. She trudged forward against a heavy, invisible wind. Every blast of cold smarted across her face, but she leaned into it, showing her grit step after step. Linking hands with Sister Sadie, she howled at the ghosts. "You can't beat us."

Sandra let go of Max, ushering him forward. "Get Sister Moon while you can."

Stumbling ahead, he glanced at his wife. She had started a new casting circle around herself. Turning toward Sister Moon, his legs stretched out, ready to rush onward, happy to be free to move. He would have to carry her — Sister Moon looked too far gone to walk out on her own — and he lowered his body, preparing to take on her weight. But as he reached to grab hold of her, Sister Page bashed into his side.

He tumbled over. The enraged witch straddled him, throwing punches with abandon. She snarled and spit. Even as he covered his head in defense, part of him recognized that Sister Sadie must have sent her. She never would have left Sister Sadie's side, otherwise.

"Stop it! Stop it! Stop it!" She belted out each word with another punch.

Max tried to get out from under her, tried to grab hold of her arms to halt her attack, but she had reached a frenzied state, flailing her arms as much as striking with control. Each time he attempted to clamp down on her wrist, she slipped away, only to resume the attack with the other hand.

Bucking his hips, he finally launched her sideways. He levered her off and scrambled to his feet. Sister Moon did not react to the aborted rescue nor the recovery and resumed attempt.

"Hold onto my shoulders, and I'll carry you out."

She did not move.

"Come on," he said, trying to get her help.

Sister Page blitzed after him, vaulting of the floor with her face raging red. She brandished her knife overhead, the blade waving in her seething hand. "Die!"

Max took on a fighting stance. He tightened his fists as she ran at him. But Maggie struck first, darting in from the flank. The two witches toppled to the floor, smashing two candles, and rolling into a pillar. Maggie got up first. As Sister Page attempted to stand, Maggie fought like a born brawler.

Not wanting to lose this sudden opening, Max jumped across the minecart tracks. He crouched in front of Sister Moon and looked over her chains. They had bound her hands and feet but never locked her to the floor. With that little grace upon him, Max knelt forward and lurched her over his shoulder. She draped on him like dead weight. Groaning, he pushed to his feet, keeping his knees bent and breathing hard.

"Put her down," Sister Page said, her legs planted wide. Nearby, Maggie teetered on her knees, dazed with blood dribbling down her forehead.

Heading toward Sandra and making slow progress, Max groaned out, "A little help."

Sister Page jerked as a ghost passed through her. Drummond appeared behind her and punched his fist into her head. She stiffened, her fingers spread at her sides, her eyes bugging open, before she collapsed.

A grunt and Max managed to swing his right leg forward. Another grunt and the left leg moved ahead. Grunt. Right. Grunt. Left. Short scream.

Scream?

Max looked up from his feet. Maggie had regained her senses and kicked Sandra in the ribs. Rather than follow through with more kicks or a grapple, Maggie focused on destroying the casting circle Sandra had worked on. She turned toward Max, appeared to weigh him as unimportant, and shifted back to the circle. Sandra launched at her, fists tight, sending punch after punch, not in blind fury but with controlled aim.

A flutter of pride danced through Max as he forced his legs to move onward.

Sandra cocked back her fist and let fly a fierce jab that caught Maggie on the jaw. Maggie's head pitched at an odd angle. Her legs weaved as she tried to remain standing. Down she went.

Drummond zipped by, returning Max to his task of walking Sister Moon to safety. The ghost flew between Sister Sadie and Sister Gold, his cold body whitening the skin on their held hands. When he flipped around for another pass, he stopped, his eyes locked along the track. "That's a problem."

"What?"

"He's here."

Max managed another couple steps as Sandra dropped to her casting circle to repair the damage and return to her spell. "Who?" he asked, finding it difficult to look around with a witch slumped over his shoulder.

Drummond pointed into the dark. "Gene Temple — the minecart man."

Chapter 39

ROLLING SISTER MOON OFF HIS BACK, Max leaned her against a pillar. Sweat stung his eyes and the abrasions on his body. But it was done. They had won most of the night. They only had to get out of these tunnels without further trouble from Sister Sadie. Not so easy, but Max could not deny the hope in his chest.

Yet Drummond looked worried.

"What?" Max asked the ghost. "Between you, me, Sandra, and all the ghosts you brought along, we'll keep Sister Moon out of that circle. No sacrifice means no spell. Not to mention those candles are scattered everywhere, and I can barely make out what she once had written on the floor. What's the problem?"

Sister Sadie held a confident stance. She grinned in triumph as if this had always been her plan. She gazed at Drummond and gave a little nod like a mentor waiting for her student to explain some hidden truth.

Drummond lowered his head and pursed his lips before turning his eye in the direction of Gene Temple. "We've forgotten what happened at the barn."

"The barn?" Max thought back to the year when they fought Sister Sadie at the barn of The Old Homeplace Vineyard. Sandra and Brenda had blasted her back into her withering body. "We beat her then, too."

"Barely. But even then, even when she was in her original body with her original insanity, that crazy lady showed a lot of power." He paused, but Sister Sadie made a guttural grunt, and he continued, "I think the spell she made here — the casting circle, the candles, everything but the heads — it's here to help, but not a requirement. Not for her. She's had a lot of time to get stronger, more focused." He angled his head at her. "That about right?"

The corner of her mouth lifted. "*The head of a cursed witch in decay.*"

Sister Gold hustled to retrieve Pauline Lennon's rotting head. "*The head of a cursed witch in decay.*" She plunged her knife into the top of the head.

Max turned to Sandra, but she put up a hand to stop him from saying a word. Instead, she shifted toward Drummond. "You have to stop Gene Temple. As long as he doesn't enter that circle, that spell won't work on him. At least, I hope so."

"It's a better shot than anything I've thought of. Unless you want to kill Sister Sadie?"

"We're not murderers."

"Just laying out the options." Drummond swept over several feet. Then: "Gene, you hearing me? You can stop pushing this old thing. It's time to move on."

The scattered green candles lit up. Even those on their sides and broken into pieces burned their wicks.

Sister Sadie gave a satisfied moan. Then: "*The head of a man who does not exist in dust and bone.*"

Hastening to bring Peter Ney's skull back into the remains of the casting circle, Sister Gold tipped her head in a short bow. She then smashed her knife down onto the skull, cracking it from the top. "*The head of a man who does not exist in dust and bone.*"

Drummond tried to push against the minecart. That's what Max thought it looked like. But no matter how the ghost dug into the air or turned to press with his back, he kept moving toward the casting circle.

"C'mon, Gene. Don't do this." To Max: "It's no use. He's not reacting to anything going on here. I think he's locked in looping this behavior. He can't hear me."

Producing a knife from the back of her belt, Sister Sadie said, "*The head of the newly reborn, fresh and full of lost life.*"

As Sister Gold moved, Max stepped in front of Sister Moon. "Not going to happen."

Sister Sadie repeated the phrase, only louder and drawing the words out. "*The head of the newly reborn, fresh and full of lost life.*"

Sister Gold froze. She appeared to digest this change in tone like swallowing a sharp tortilla chip and feeling it scrape down her throat. A hopeful glance at Max and Sister Moon, but then Sister Gold's body deflated. Her chin puckered as she sucked in her bottom lip. Letting out a shudder, she stiffened her spine to stand rigid and brave.

"The head of the newly reborn, fresh and full of lost life," she said, a slight waver in her throat. With an even, dreadful pace, she walked toward Sister Sadie.

"Don't do this," Max said.

Sister Gold did not stop. Max hopped closer in three strides and grabbed her arm. She whipped around, slashing down with her hands. He felt a sting followed by a deep burn. He was bleeding. In her right hand, she gripped her knife.

He wanted to rush forward, knock her out of the way, anything to ruin this spell, but his advantage had long since disappeared. Both women held knives. If he tried to disrupt them further, he would be stabbed to death.

Sister Gold watched Max with weary caution. Backing away from him, she angled her knife up to thrust. "Move towards this circle and I'll gut you."

She turned around, walked a few steps, and stopped in front of Sister Sadie. Max couldn't see her face, but from her posture, he guessed she looked at her coven leader with questioning eyes, begging eyes, asking if there was some other way. After all, she had cut Max Porter to make sure this spell succeeded. But Sister Sadie never responded. Not audibly, anyway. In some way, Sister Gold knew her plea had been rejected. She knew. She turned on her knees, facing toward Drummond and Gene Temple. Before Max could utter another useless word, Sister Sadie slit open the throat of the young, newly reborn witch.

Blood washed down Sister Gold's neck. She never cried.

For an instant, time stopped, and in that temporal hiccup, Max saw Sister Gold crumpling to the floor like a discarded tissue. Sister Sadie spread her arms wide as her body radiated heat like a broiling oven. Quivering with the power that built within, she called out a triumphant hoot that filled the cracks in the ceiling. Drummond pushed hard enough to hold Gene's cart from further progress, and Sandra finished out her spell. Wait. Max looked back at Drummond. The ghost appeared to be scooting to the side as if making room for another. Time returned to normal, but now Max had an idea. Great or otherwise, it was the only idea he had right then. It would have to do.

"Pauline," he called out, cupping his hands. "Step into the circle."

The shock on Drummond's face suggested Pauline felt the same. The ghost stuttered a few steps, but he reset his body and shoved against the area Max presumed to be Gene's minecart full of gold coins.

As confident as he could muster, Max said, "Enter the circle and you'll take the spell on. You'll be made whole — corporeal."

Drummond nodded to the space at his side. "I don't know. It's never happened to me, but yeah, I think you'll be able to touch her without pain."

The heat pulsing off Sister Sadie increased. Like a devout believer lost in rapture, she dropped to her knees, sinking into the blood pool of Sister Gold, arms still open wide, her mouth agape. "Come, Gene Temple, come to me."

Drummond's body scraped closer to the circle. Just how strong was Gene Temple? Max guessed *very*. After all, the man had pushed a heavy minecart filled with heavier gold for years.

The heck with this, Max thought as he moved toward the circle. One strong kick to knock over Sister Sadie, maybe a punch to the side of the head — break her concentration, break the spell. The repercussions might be high, but suffering burns, an explosion, or even death would be better than letting this witch attain control of magic.

"Stay back," Sandra hissed — a disturbing sound that forced Max to stop.

His wife stood with her arms down and open as if she wore chains locking her to the floor. Sweat drenched her hair into clumped strands. Her entire body vibrated like a tuning fork. Max saw the air around her match those vibrations the way a plucked note shivered the space around a string.

Blending anger and worry, Sister Sadie said, "No."

Max whirled back — feeling like a pinwheel — and saw Pauline Georgia-Ringo Lennon enter the casting circle. Smooth legs appeared first. Solid, firm, whole. The ghost slowly formed into the woman she had been. She wore a summer dress and had the youthful physique that made the dress light as a lovely breeze tickling the grass in a park. Not a hateful witch. Nor a crone bent on power. If anything, Max saw a woman with the same dreams and intentions for her witchcraft that Sandra held. Pauline wanted to do good.

But as her neck became a thing of substance, along with a gold pendant dangling around her thin chain, the transformation ceased. The top of her neck ended in jagged skin. She reached up to the empty space, felt around as if her head might appear suddenly, then her arms flopped down. Drummond had said that her ghost lacked a head, so there was no head to make whole.

"Find the light," Drummond blurted out. He floated upward, no longer needing to hold back the minecart. The spell was complete. Even Max could feel the magic easing in the room.

Max put a hand on Sister Moon's shoulder. "It's over. Her spell failed, and you'll live."

"This is no failure," Sister Sadie said, her voice deepening. "I have done it. I have brought a ghost back from the dead, made her complete. No witch before me has accomplished this spell. No witch will be able to stand against me now. I am the most powerful that has ever lived."

Wrong. The word assaulted Max's head but not in his voice. From the pained expressions on the other faces — including Drummond — they had heard it, too. Nothing more was spoken, but Max's intuition told him that Pauline had blasted the word.

Indeed, the former ghost charged at Sister Sadie. It looked like an amateur attempting to tackle her opponent but not lowering enough. From that angle, she could do no more than budge Sister Sadie an inch back. Sister Sadie must have recognized this, too, for she refused to evade the oncoming rush.

Or she may have been too wrapped up in her exalted state to notice.

That was her mistake.

Instead of a tackle, Pauline jabbed her hand under Sister Sadie's chin. She clutched the witch's neck, and with supernatural strength, she lifted her off the ground. Sister Sadie kicked out, gurgling and gasping.

Max and Drummond stared. Neither spoke. Max felt like a rubbernecker at a gruesome accident.

"We shall leave," Sandra said, each word coming from behind gritted teeth, sounding less like his wife and more like a storybook wizard.

But then Max saw that her body did not tremble with magic, it trembled *against* the magic. Whatever spell she had cast, she could barely contain it.

Drummond must have seen it, too. "Listen to her, partner. Grab Sister Moon and get out of here."

Nodding, Max lowered to Sister Moon. But Sandra screeched as a gust of magic released from her body. It burst out in all directions. Decades of dust puffed through the room.

As Pauline's body rocked from the energy flowing through her, she stumbled. Sandra's spell caused the floor to quake. A deep rumble of stone rolled throughout the tunnel.

Pauline dropped Sister Sadie's limp body. Though still alive, the witch wheezed each breath as she rubbed her throat. Max expected Pauline to finish the job with some final assault. Instead, she brought her hands to her chest and offered Drummond a grateful bow.

Another blast of energy exploded from Sandra's spell. The pillars nearest Sister Sadie's casting circle cracked. Rock ground against rock. Bricks added a higher pitch as they shattered.

Sister Sadie reached upward as if to stop the inevitable. But even if she had the strength, she lacked the time. A chunk of the ceiling fell out, smashing near the witch and creating a plume of dust and debris.

Drummond slid next to Pauline as she lowered to her knees, her neck dipping forward. "If what I think is going to happen to you happens, you'll see that light. Go for it. Don't look back. Just move on. It's time for you to rest."

Two more stone chunks plummeted to the floor. Sandra arched back with a hoarse inhalation. When the final shockwave of magic erupted from her, she screamed it out. Her cry continued long after the magic finished, but Max guessed he alone noticed. The ceiling above Sister Sadie broke into dozens of large pieces and thousands of pebbles. It rained over her — cutting, scraping, breaking, crushing.

It lasted seconds, but for Max, it couldn't end fast enough. The pain and torment this witch had caused — not only to him and those he loved but to countless others, many whom he would never meet — only paled in comparison to the number of people she intended to harm. While he had fought many witches over the years, most he considered to be good or, at least, average people that had been corrupted by touching the great power available through witchcraft. But this witch — if she had ever been a good person, she had been corrupted beyond redemption. Sister Sadie was dead. She was evil, and Max found no remorse in seeing her buried and broken.

Chapter 40

THE LAST OF THE RUBBLE FELL like remnants of hail plinking off the roof after a treacherous storm. Max coughed and rubbed the dirt from his eyes. He weaved over to Sandra, knelt down, and held her in his arms.

"Is she okay?" Drummond asked, drifting in closer.

"She's breathing." Max pressed her against his chest. Her skin felt cold, and he longed for his body warmth to be enough to sustain her.

Off to the side, Sister Moon sputtered as she thumped one foot, then the other, wobbling upright like a toddler. She took in her surroundings. "Sister Sadie?"

Drummond poked his chin in the dead witch's direction. "Under that pile of rocks."

"Good."

Somewhere within the walls or ceiling, wood whined like an old galleon in rough seas.

"What did you people do to this place?" Sister Moon said.

Though Max kept his focus on reviving his wife, he said, "Oh, you know, saved your life, defeated an evil witch. The usual."

Sandra's lips rippled into a smile. In a thin voice, she said, "We won?"

Tears fell down Max's cheeks as he gulped and kissed her. "Oh, yes. We won. You did it. It was all you."

"Hey," Drummond said. "We had our part to play, too."

Moving with more surety, Sister Moon inspected the rubble pile, taking particular interest in the broken hand poking out. "I'm sure each of you had something to do with your success. I don't really care." She gestured upward. "But I am concerned about those cracks in the ceiling."

Before Max could respond, a pillar in the back collapsed. It sandwiched in the middle, spewing rock out as an avalanche of dirt and stone poured in from above.

Drummond said, "Just a guess, partner, but I'm thinking you should get out of here."

Max pushed Sandra's wet hair away from her eyes. "Can you walk?"

She tried to sit up, but he could feel how weak she had become. Not waiting for an answer, he slipped an arm under her knees and another supporting her back. She clasped her fingers around his neck, and he lifted her. Much easier when the person did not lay unconscious across his back.

Carrying his wife toward the corner that returned into the tunnels, Max said, "Hurry up."

"Wait," Sandra said. "Don't forget Maggie. I knocked her out."

Though still unsteady, Sister Moon approached with a stronger gait. "Who's Maggie?"

"Witch of the Coven of Ti."

Drummond floated over the wreckage. "She's not here. Guess she snuck out when we weren't looking."

"Good for her," Max said. "How about we get out, too?"

Another pillar cracked like a gunshot, and the dust of its collapse billowed out of the dark. They hurried into the tunnels.

Pushing as fast as he dared but not wanting to trip in the dark, Max worked his way back to each junction. Every time, he had to stop and search for the chalk X that marked the correct path. This worked fine until he came to a junction with two Xs.

"How the heck did that happen?"

"You don't know which way to go?" Sister Moon said.

"I must've made a mistake. Gone down one of these and hit a dead end. When I came back, I accidentally mismarked it."

"Your genius is going to get us killed. Which one do we take?"

The clatter of falling stones mixed with the crumbling of ceiling stones preparing to fall. Max peered over his shoulder. He couldn't see the destruction, but the echoes came louder and faster. They were not that far ahead.

Sister Moon moved toward one tunnel. "I pick this one."

"You pick wrong, you're not going to have time to get back."

"It's better than standing here."

"Not when we have help."

She hesitated. "What help?"

"Drummond? You still around?"

The ghost appeared through the ceiling. "I wouldn't leave you. Just checking to see if there was a path toward one of the tunnels that had been more recently fixed up."

"And?"

"No dice."

Sister Moon clapped her hands as if disciplining a dog. "How about telling us which way to go? Can you do that?"

"I can and I will. But only for my partner. You, I'm not so sure about."

Another gunshot and crash from behind followed a flickering. From the zapping sound, Max guessed some old wiring had been severed. "I'm all for witty banter, but I can't hold Sandra forever. Which way do we go?"

"Follow me."

Drummond raced down the tunnel on the left, and the others followed. Nobody worried about getting their feet wet nor what kind of toxic sludge they might be wading through.

Perking up, Sandra said, "I might be able to walk."

"Save your strength." Max readjusted his grip. "I can still carry you for now."

Another junction. This time they cut straight across and onward. Max could feel the destruction behind them speeding up like a runaway train. With his muscles shaking, he tried to pick up his pace. Even tried to run. He couldn't — not with Sandra in his arms.

"Put me down," she said. He started to protest, so she kissed him. "Put me down, or we won't make it."

Bending at the knees, he set her on her feet. She kept one arm around his shoulder, and he placed an arm around her waist. Leaning into each other, they found enough support to walk faster.

Several feet ahead, Sister Moon considered them with a disappointed sigh. "Thanks for saving my life, but I'm not in the business of doing the same. Good luck."

She hurried off, the darkness swallowing her.

"I'll stop her," Drummond said.

"No." Sandra put her hand on the nearest wall. "We need you to guide us. We can barely see in here."

"But she shouldn't get away with —"

"Our job was to protect her from a spell. Her appreciation isn't required. Now, get us out of here."

The next series of collapses splashed into the water, causing ripples heavy enough that Max felt them against his calves. "We're out of time."

Hobbling like contestants in a three-legged race but lacking any of the fun, Max and Sandra pushed each other. Though Drummond's pale ghostly glow did not reflect on any surface, they could see him, and in the sections that were pitch black, that was the only light they could follow. The old detective also acted as cheerleader, throwing out an occasional *Keep going!* or *Don't give up!* Max wanted to yell back a hearty *Shut up!* but doing so expended too much energy.

When they entered the final junction, Max tripped on a hunk of metal hidden under the dirty water. Sandra tried to keep him upright, but he staggered ahead and flopped into the grime. Tremors of razor pain ripped up his leg. Sandra cried out as she fell a few feet ahead.

A series of crackling breaks from the back tunnel swelled into a vicious thunder. Max tried to stand but his knee shrieked. He rolled to the semi-dry concrete of the tunnel, panting and cringing. His muscles refused to hold him. Trying to sit up, he failed. So, he lay there, listening to the approaching doom in the darkness.

Sandra crawled next to him. Her sweat-soaked hair slapped against his shoulder, and he smelled the foul water drenching them both. Neither said a word, but he knew that she thought the same — they didn't have the strength to get out of the junction in time.

This was it. Max looked at his wife. She brushed his cheek with her thumb. She smiled, and a tear blurred his vision.

I don't want this to end, he thought as she pressed her lips against his. And while the crushing bricks and stones bellowed toward them, he kissed her harder. This was what mattered. This was life. Together. This was why watching the Sandwich Boys grow up and go out on their own hurt. This was why losing his mother hurt. They were part of what made life *life*. He was happy for the boys. He was happy for his mother's peace and freedom from pain. But it hurt.

Pulling back, he smiled at Sandra. "At least, we die together."

She clutched him. The ground shook. The water splashed. A stone knocked against his thigh. With the roar of destruction filling every space, Max couldn't hear his own thoughts. But he thought them anyway — *love, family, death* — he seemed to understand these larger ideas in a new light. Not something he could put into words, but rather an instinctive light. Perhaps an understanding encoded in his DNA to be revealed at the moment of death. Perhaps —

"Are you two going to hug in that slop all night?" Drummond said.

Max lifted his head. The echoes of the collapse had died, but nothing else had. Silence rolled back in like a tide. The tunnel that they had run through, that connected to the junction, had become a wall of rubble, but it had ceased its unrelenting attack.

"The walls are holding." Sandra's disbelief matched her weakened state.

Max grinned. Then laughed. "The walls are holding."

"Yeah, yeah," Drummond said. "Let's not poke Fate about it. Get out of these tunnels before she changes her mind."

Like two soldiers, bloodied and bruised, Max and Sandra limped from the tunnel supporting each other. The late-night quiet of Old Salem covered them with a fresh sensation of the normal world. Water trickled to the creek while leaves rustled in a gentle breeze. A frog sang out looking for a mate.

"You both lived." Sister Moon rested her back against a tree, sounding more surprised than anything.

"I told you they would."

Max glanced across the creek, searching for this new voice. A woman stood on the incline back to street level. The soft amber of light bleeding from nearby outlined her with dramatic flair, but he still recognized her. Maggie McVeil.

Floating next to Max with his fists up and his hat low, Drummond said, "You two were in cahoots the whole time?"

Sister Moon chuckled. To Maggie, she said, "The ghost thinks we're working together."

Maggie grinned. "Not tonight. But it doesn't have to stay that way. The Coven of Ti is still looking for members, and you've shown yourself to be quite powerful. I think Madame Ti would find you more than worthy of joining us."

Sitting on the wide rock Sandra had used earlier that night, Max said, "You're overplaying your hand. After everything that's happened, what makes you think she would want to —"

"I'll do it." Sister Moon hopped across the creek to reach Maggie.

Max's brow crinkled. "But the covens betrayed you. One even tried to take your head. Why would you trust another one? And Madame Ti, of all people."

To Sandra, she said, "Are you going to start a coven?"

"No," Sandra said. "Never."

"Well, I'm a witch, and Madame Ti is the strongest out there." Sister Moon shrugged. "What else am I going to do?"

Watching the two women stroll away, Max dropped backward, letting the cool earth comfort him. He wanted to sleep for a week. At least until the police told him to move or be charged with vagrancy.

Sandra settled next to him. "I didn't mean for my spell to cause all that damage. I was trying to knock Sister Sadie down, disrupt her spellcasting in some way."

"You certainly did that."

"Did I really kill her?"

He patted her knee. "She killed herself long ago."

"Max is right, doll." Drummond watched the tunnel opening as if he expected somebody to emerge. "The moment she started playing with the kind of witchcraft that smart witches deemed too dangerous, she took on that risk."

"That sounds nice and comforting, but my spell dropped the entire tunnel onto her head."

Max sat up. "You want the truth?"

"Always."

"Yeah, you killed her. But don't let another second go by with her death eating you up. You're not a crazed murderer. You are a witch in a witch war, and in war, people die. It's kind of the main thing about war."

"You saw me, though — what those spells did to me. I took risks that I shouldn't have. Linking spells, pushing myself. You saw what I became."

"And I see you now." He kissed the back of her hand. "I'm glad you're concerned. You know I've been worried ever since you started delving into witchcraft. But I trust your heart. It's what makes you different from people like Sister Moon or Madame Ti."

"You weren't scared for me?"

"I was terrified. If I wasn't concentrating on us surviving, I would have been angry, too. But you came back to me. You're my Sandra again. We can figure out the rest little by little. No need for guilt, though."

"Because this is war."

"Exactly."

"Hate to break this up," Drummond said, "but dead or alive, Sister Sadie is still in that tunnel. If she's alive, she might be coming out of here with vengeance on overdrive. If she's dead, then she might not move on, and we'll have to be dealing with an angry ghost soon enough. How about you two get some much-needed rest? I want you ready for anything."

Sandra stood and helped Max to his feet. Brushing off the dirt, she said, "Not the most uplifting speech, but yeah, let's go home."

Max's sore legs loathed the idea of hobbling the incline to the road, but the rest of him couldn't wait to reach home. He could wrap up his knee and climb into his bed. Digging deep, he found his last drip of stamina. Together, they limped for their car.

Chapter 41

MAX HEADED HOME IN A DAZE. Sandra's dead stare suggested the same. Each traffic light they drove under, each crack in the pavement they bounced over, every random noise they heard — drunken partiers singing on the sidewalk, an emergency vehicle's siren screaming from blocks away, the heightened silence of four in the morning — became a tether to reality, a lifeline that hauled Max and Sandra back into the boat of normalcy, bit by bit. It would take days, maybe weeks, for them to digest and accept all that had occurred that night, but by the time Max pulled into their driveway, they could breathe again without shuddering.

As they exited the car, Drummond appeared with his hands in his pockets and his hat tipped back. "Wanted to make sure you got home safely."

Sandra leaned against the car, the effort of getting out requiring a moment. "You ol' mother hen."

"I got a lot invested in you two. The Porter Agency is not allowed to fold, and that means that the both of you have to stay alive."

"You sure it's not my charming smile?"

"Doll, it's always your charming smile." He wiggled an elbow towards Max. "It certainly ain't his."

She giggled. With a grin of his own, Max relaxed at her sound. Perhaps that had been the intent of their ghost partner. A familiar ribbing to act as a final jolt to return them to a familiar world.

After having climbed back to the car and driven home, Max discovered his knee held firm. It hurt brutally, but it didn't collapse on him. As he unlocked the side door that led to the kitchen, he said to Drummond, "You're a good friend." He pushed the door open. Then: "Lousy at a ton of things, but a good friend."

Drummond chuckled. "You'll both be okay. Rest. We'll deal with tomorrow when it comes."

Following Max indoors, Sandra said, "What about Pauline? Did she move on?"

"She did. Wanted to make sure I thanked you on her behalf. So, consider yourselves thanked." Drummond slid through the walls and met them by the kitchen table. "I want to thank you, too. Helping Pauline meant a lot. It's a big part of why we do this, and it's easy to forget. Fighting witches is a by-product, not the point. We're here to help those in need — people *and* ghosts."

They exchanged another round of goodnights — throwing a few more playful jabs, too — and Drummond left for his own relaxation in the Other.

Stretching her arms overhead, Sandra said, "I'm taking a hot bath first. My bones are killing."

"Maybe go for a shower. I don't want you falling asleep and drowning in a bath."

"Honey, if I go under, I'll wake up. Inhaling water tends to do that."

"With the amount of magic you cast tonight, I don't think you should make assumptions."

She bounced his words around before nodding. "A shower will work. See you in bed."

Sandra headed down the short hall to their bedroom, and Max dropped into a kitchen chair. Every muscle in his body complained along with his pulse. He ached, yet the act of finally not moving turned these small agonies into pleasant relief.

When the shower started, Max considered undressing and joining his wife. The hot water would feel wonderful, and it never hurt to appreciate each other. He doubted either of them had the energy for more than a hug, but that simple act often helped recharge them both.

Closing his eyes, he rubbed his face. The shower idea, though enjoyable to imagine, required too much from his exhausted body. Besides, the kitchen chair hugged him enough for the night.

He forced his eyes open and noticed some dirty dishes next to the sink. They needed to go into the dishwasher. Seeing them, his mind promised that if he didn't get up and take care of them, he would fall asleep in this chair. He might sleep for hours and wake feeling stiff, bruised, and worse than he did at that moment.

"Okay." He groaned as he willed his body up and took care of those few dishes. That led to wiping down the counter which led to clearing off the kitchen table which led to cleaning the table. When he finished, he wondered what had gotten into him. He had never been fastidious, and this late at night with this much pain in his body, he shouldn't have cared at all. But after two days of chaos with little to no sleep, perhaps he needed some order in his life.

Sandra's shower continued. If she had taken a bath, he'd expect her to be in there for an hour, at least. Perhaps the heat of the shower soothed to the point of keeping her around for the same.

Bumping along the hall, he moved toward the master bedroom. But stopped.

He looked back.

That closed door to his mother's room watched him.

Not giving his brain a chance to alter course, he shambled the few steps it took to reach the door. The metal knob chilled his hand. The lock clicked, and he pushed the door open.

The room had not been touched since his mother's passing, and dust had accumulated like an unopened crypt. Everything as it had been the moment she left for the hospital. The comforter on her bed still wrinkled with one corner thrust aside for her to get out. The book on her nightstand still open and face down because she assumed she would be back later to enjoy it. The small water glass still next to her pillbox. The water had evaporated, and the rim revealed the imprint of her mouth where she had last sipped.

Motionless in the doorway, Max's chest burned. A hardness formed at his bruised ribs like a heavy chain wrapped around him. He stared at a mausoleum. Yet at the same time, he saw the room the way it had been when they first moved into the house.

Back then, it had belonged to the Sandwich Boys. There were two beds, parallel against the walls with a narrow aisle between. They shared the nightstand, and PB had a grade-school desk pressed into the corner so as not to block the closet door. Each boy decorated their half of the room as they saw fit. Their personalities shined through.

The two rooms — that of the Sandwich Boys and that of Max's mother — overlayed each other in his mind. No matter where he looked, he saw all the permutations of the rooms. Where PB's bed had been positioned under the window, and where his mother had her chair to look out the window. Where the boys shared a dresser and where his mother had a vanity.

He even saw a third room — J's room after PB had left and before Max's mother had moved in. A room of transition. Of emptying out and of refilling.

He entered these three rooms, moving with hesitant steps as if afraid to disturb any restless spirits. But there were none. The boys still lived, appeared to thrive, and had much living ahead of them. His mother — she had already moved on.

He could smell her, though. Both the pleasant — her floral perfume, a bit thick but not disagreeable — as well as a darker scent — the way her skin had soured. The way her medications had tainted her breath. A desiccated odor, weak and withered, thinning each day until soon there would be nothing left to smell.

Max lowered into his mother's chair. The room felt even smaller from there. He became acutely aware of the short distance to the doorway and the kitchen. He could hear every tiny noise in the house — the whine of wood, the flow in pipes, the bugs hitting the window. Glancing outside, observing the world at night like she had done during her many bouts of insomnia, he could feel life draining, ushered out on each breath.

Had she been sad? Sitting and watching. Counting the time left to her existence. Or did she think back on her life with joy and nostalgia? A bittersweet happiness that filled her mind with a lifetime of memories until she drifted off to sleep.

She had been so frightened in his arms at the hospital. But now he wondered if she had seen more. Perhaps she saw peace overlay that moment of fear.

He tried to picture her exact expression. If he could see that, he might be able to read the nuances that would let him know the answer.

At the nightstand on his left, he regarded the book. She mostly sat in this chair listening to audiobooks, but she had insisted on purchasing some physical books for bedtime. Maybe knowing what she had read would provide a clue to her thoughts. But when he lifted the battered hardcover — *The Thorn Birds* of all things — an envelope sat underneath. An envelope addressed to him.

He tensed as if discovering a rattlesnake under a rock. The long rectangle of paper did not hiss or strike out, but this danger he could not walk away from. Didn't even try.

He snatched the envelope, ran his finger along the side to tear it open, and pulled out several full pages. He swallowed down the lump rising through his chest.

And he read.

> *I never thought I'd write this, but my mother wrote a deathbed letter to me and a good mother must also do the things that are right even if they hurt.*
>
> *As I sit here, you and Sandra are off on one of your cases. I know I don't have much time left, a mother can tell these things, and if any of what you say is true about your job, then maybe I'll see you after I die. It would be nice. But don't be upset when you don't see me. The nonsense you peddle isn't real, and I know it. It's wishful thinking, good and hopeful thinking, but it isn't real. My death, on the other hand, is real. I can feel it, and while I don't know if every father feels this way, I guarantee every mother does. She knows when her time has come, and a*

good mother will try to prepare her children. She will have to hope that they listened to her enough to have learned their lessons well. I know you have. I don't worry about your welfare, because you've always been a good boy.

I do have one worry, though, and it's because of this that I decided to write this letter. I know you too well, and that's how come I worry. I want to reach out of this paper and shake some sense into you, give you a piece of my mind as my mother would say, but this is the best I can do. Please, listen to me. I know you will not let Aunt Jane go. If you haven't already found her, you will keep trying until you succeed.

I don't know if you remember, but when you were a child, you kept asking me to explain how the light went on and off in the refrigerator. No answer I gave would satisfy you. You must've been three or four. That's an age where you should have believed anything I said, yet you had to see for yourself. You came up with the idea of putting setting the timer on my camera and putting into the refrigerator to record what happened.

Your Aunt Jane is nothing but an adult version of that refrigerator. No matter what I say, you won't believe me until you find out for yourself. The problem is that the refrigerator was a mechanical device. Aunt Jane is a human being. She can lie.

Please be careful. When you eventually find her and speak with her, she will say awful things about me. She will say how wonderful a sister she was to your father and how I drove them apart. But you should know that she has always rewritten history to benefit herself. She's very good at it. She knows how to blend her lies with the right amount of truth to not only sound plausible, but make it difficult to separate the two.

I would love to go on for pages about how wonderful a son you've been, how much I love you, and I'd even give Sandra a few words to ease her mind. But this MS is painful. I can't write anymore tonight. If I have the strength, perhaps I'll add more another day. But I don't think I have many days left.

I love you, and even after I'm gone, I will always be,
your mother

Max held still, thinking about rereading the letter. But the words blurred. The paper shook.

There was no doubt anymore. Nobody who wrote a letter like this would have been so plagued by guilt or so angry for vengeance that they would have remained a ghost.

The fear in her eyes had been for him not herself. No matter what she had said, this letter provided the truth. She worried about his future, not hers.

He set the paper down and rose to his feet. His knees wobbled. A massive air swelled up from his lungs, and he gasped as he toppled forward. His arm caught the bed easing his throbbing knees to the floor. The sound that broke out of him shook from the pit of his stomach up through his chest and out his throat.

He wailed.

Tears flowed as he turned his back against the bed. Another cry. Then quiet. His mouth hung wide open, yet no sound came out. Not until his lungs forced him to inhale — and then allowed another wailing sob to rip out of him.

He never heard when Sandra came running in. He would have no memory of what she said. But as he convulsed, as his throat burned raw with his sorrow, she held him. She kissed his head. She let him grieve.

Thank you for joining me on another round with The Porter Agency. If you would, please leave a review wherever you purchased this book. It makes a huge difference. But, of course, you're reading this to get to the good stuff, and I won't keep you waiting. Here we go:

I'll start with the big one first. Yes, there really are tunnels underneath Winston-Salem. A lot of them. Not only that, but R. J. Reynolds did have special tunnels built, there really was a manmade lake in case of fire, and yes, there really was a minecart full of money. Usually, cash used for payroll. The question of the gold coins is a little murky. My description of the gold coins is entirely my creation. All the direct quotes regarding the tunnels are from real interviews with one exception. Oscar Dublicki is my invention (as is Gene Temple, but I never quoted him).

More about the tunnels, those underneath the Reynolds High School also exist. They were built as a shelter for life-threatening weather, bombs, and such.

Despite describing the tunnels in detail, this was one instance where I did not go in them myself. Most have been sealed off, and those you can access (if you can find them) are truly dangerous to enter. I relied on photographs and articles for the majority of description.

There is a video of some young men who found the entrance Max and Sandra used, and they explored quite a bit inside. But when Max and Sandra reach the first junction, my imagination took over from there. In the case of the arched room where Sister Sadie met her demise, I fabricated that completely.

In fact, it was hearing about those tunnels that fired my imagination so strongly, it pushed me to write this book sooner than I had scheduled. For those of you waiting for my dragon/horror series to start, this is the reason you're waiting a bit longer. I heard about the tunnels on the radio, and I couldn't let it go.

Beyond the tunnels, there were a few things worth bringing up here. With regards to Reynolds High School's long list of famous alumni — that's all true. I only mention a few note-worthy names in the book, but you can look it up and see that there are many, many people who stumbled through their teen years in those halls. Maybe a few even found the tunnels.

The story of Peter Ney, the ex-military Frenchman who served under Napoleon and may have faked his death, is true. His grave in a little town in North Carolina sits quietly as described, and if you want to, you could visit. The write-ups in old papers tell the story, and while there is debate about Ney's final words, he clearly made some kind of confession. Unfortunately, recent DNA tests finally put to rest this every-growing tall tale, debunking that the man buried in North Carolina and the man buried in France are the same. Why Peter Ney made himself out to be a man he was not we'll probably never know. But why should I let that ruin our fun? This is fiction, after all.

That's it for this time. Thank you for continuing to support this series. I hope you enjoyed it. And while you wait, please explore some of my other series. I write a lot, and if you've read this far, you probably enjoy the way I tell a story. So, dig in and find some other wonderful tales while I cook up the next Max Porter Paranormal Mystery.

About the Author

Stuart Jaffe is the madman behind the *Nathan K thrillers, The Max Porter Paranormal Mysteries,* the *Ridnight Mysteries,* the *Parallel Society* novels, *The Malja Chronicles, The Bluesman, Founders, Real Magic,* and much more. He trained in martial arts for over a decade until a knee injury ended that practice. Now, he plays lead guitar in a local blues band, *The Bootleggers,* and enjoys life on a small farm in rural North Carolina.